Outcast

Outcast

Lewis Ericson

www.urbanbooks.net

Urban Books, LLC
78 East Industry Court
Deer Park, NY 11729

ISBN 13: 978-1-60162-364-5
ISBN 10: 1-60162-364-X

First Trade Paperback Printing January 2013
Printed in the United States of America

10 9 8 7 6 5 4 3 2 1

This is a work of fiction. Any references or similarities to actual events, real people, living or dead, or to real locales are intended to give the novel a sense of reality. Any similarity in other names, characters, places, and incidents is entirely coincidental.

Distributed by Kensington Publishing Corp.
Submit Wholesale Orders to:
Kensington Publishing Corp.
C/O Penguin Group (USA) Inc.
Attention: Order Processing
405 Murray Hill Parkway
East Rutherford, NJ 07073-2316
Phone: 1-800-526-0275
Fax: 1-800-227-9604

Outcast

by

Lewis Ericson

This work is dedicated to my mother who inspires me in more ways than she could fathom.

I also dedicate this gift back to God, the Master Author.

Acknowledgments

This story would not be told in a manner befitting the subject matter if it had not been for the collaborative efforts of a group of extraordinary people who have given of themselves and shared their hearts and souls.

A very special Thank You to Mr. Pleas Butts, III

Mitchi, author of *Angel Blues*

Brad "Baruch" Stone, NREMT—Intermediate

Thanks to my screeners and sounding boards that keep me honest . . .

A.F. Scott

Angelia Crawl

Adriane Rivers

Dianne Hamilton

Grady Harp

Travis Lee

Kim Sims author of *Transcendent* and *Sensuously Seasoned*

Tim Dahl, thanks for your indulgence.

And finally a big THANK YOU to the editors and staff of Urban Books.

E-mail: lewiswriter@earthlink.net

It is much easier to recognize error than to find truth; for error lies on the surface and may be overcome; but truth lies in the depths.

—Johann Wolfgang von Goethe (1749–1832)

1

The crunch of teeth grinding against one another and the copper taste of his own blood made Tirrell Ellis as angry as an attacking lion. He drunkenly stumbled into a wall of antagonistic hands that pushed him back into the center of the melee. It didn't matter that his opponent was taller and outweighed him by almost fifty pounds; Tirrell had learned to fight with everything—anything at his disposal.

A jarring left uppercut to his chin sent Tirrell flailing to the floor. The roar of the crowd around him was deafening. Through the delirium of beer and tequila shots, he struggled to get up, pulling on the brass rails of the bar. Before he could collect himself he felt the sting of a steel blade slice into his forearm. Tirrell grabbed a bottle lying inches away from his fingertips, turned sharply, and lunged at his assailant. Swinging violently, he knocked the knife out of the man's hands and smashed the bottle against his skull. Tirrell repeatedly hit the man as he fell backward. Blood sprayed from his open gash like water. He pleaded for Tirrell to stop.

"Drop it and put your hands in the air! I said drop it, Ellis!" The commanding voice that exploded above the jeers brought a halt to the attack.

Tirrell dropped the shard that was left of the bottle and he sank slowly to his knees. As he raised his arms to surrender he was snatched by the scruff of his neck and his face was shoved into the floor. "Get off me, man," Tirrell yelled as a knee was jammed into the small of his back, pinning him down. He winced as his hands were twisted and locked into a pair of handcuffs; then he was yanked to his feet and dragged out of the bar into the humid night air.

It was just after five-thirty in the morning. The scorching orange-yellow-white glow of the languid summer sun boiled over the horizon early, unwilling to relinquish its grip over North Carolina, or the rest of the eastern half of the country.

Tirrell lay wide awake atop an unyielding metal bunk, restless and disgusted that he couldn't get comfortable enough to get a good night's sleep. He flexed his bandaged left bicep and grunted. Lifting his head slightly from the flat pancake of a pillow, he stared at another man sleeping in a bunk across from him. His bearish snoring indicated that he was not at odds with the conditions in any way.

Tirrell glanced at the cracked face of his wristwatch, threw his legs over the side of the bunk, and slowly stood up. He yawned and arched backward to stretch out the kinks in his taut six-foot-one-inch frame. The muffled sound of marching and cadence nearby piqued his interest. He glanced up toward the long rectangular window encased in the impenetrable cinder-block walls and hoisted himself up onto a small rusted metal sink to get a look. There was a certain curiosity as to whether or not the ceremony would have a different perspective with him locked away in this fortress.

"Man, you gon' get yourself into worse trouble if you don't get down from there."

Tirrell looked over his shoulder to see that his cellmate had awakened. The surly man scratched the whiskers of his unshaven chin and propped himself up on his elbows.

"Mind yo' damn business," Tirrell shot back. His eyes darted toward the small window in the steel door that stood between him and freedom, defying the guards to catch him in the act.

"A'ight, tough guy. Suit yourself." The man rolled off his bunk and shuffled across the concrete floor to relieve himself at the shared metal toilet next to the sink.

Tirrell focused his attention back outside, where the Honor Guard, accompanied by six privates, marched toward the flagpole in the center of the courtyard to commence their morning ritual.

"Detail. Attention!" barked the husky sergeant as the Stars and Stripes were raised upward into place.

The company of soldiers snapped and saluted as the familiar sound of reveille resonated throughout the campus. Military and non-military personnel alike stopped in homage of this time-honored tradition.

Tirrell ran his hand over his close-cropped fade and down his face, pondering for the umpteenth time why he'd ever signed on. It wasn't as if he took any of this seriously. He didn't want a career. He bought into the commercial hype and was just looking for a little adventure—maybe even garner some respect along the way. He'd grown weary of aimlessly running the streets of his hometown neighborhood, but what exactly was he hoping to prove by joining the Army? His chance to be all he could be, or at the very least more than he was, had taken a toll.

With a sense of misdirected pride, Tirrell ran his tongue over the cut on his bottom lip and glanced at the bruised knuckles on his hands, recalling the incident that landed him in this predicament. He heard the rattling of keys and jumped down from his perch just as the steel door swung open. He sucked in his cheeks and glowered at the MP, following his eyes as he surveyed the ten-by-ten space. Tirrell leaned against the wall and folded his arms across his chest with equal amounts of arrogance and insolence, taking a stance that was sure to provoke them.

The MP moved his hand slowly toward his holstered weapon as if to intimidate him. It didn't work.

The guard didn't say a word—he didn't have to. Tirrell knew what was coming. He retrieved his fatigue shirt from the foot of his bunk and slipped into it.

"Can I at least have a last cigarette?" He smirked.

The guard was not amused and grabbed him by his wounded arm, shoving him toward the door.

Tirrell scowled. "Man, damn. Watch it!"

Outside the cell they were joined by another MP and the two escorted Tirrell to his fate. Preparing himself for what lay ahead, he silently counted the steps from the cell to his sergeant's office.

First Sergeant Ken Horton did little to dispel the stereotype of the hard-edged career soldier. The barrel-chested man who stood a foot shorter than Tirrell was just as gruff inside as he was outside. Not one to mince words, and never very tactful when it came to dealing with the men in his charge, he sneered at Tirrell's salute and laid into him as soon as he entered his office.

"Ellis, what the hell is wrong with you? I got a phone call at two in the morning about your stupid ass gettin' into some more dumb shit."

The man was two shades darker than Tirrell's paper-sack brown complexion, but if he could have turned red from his acerbic attack he would have.

"Are you fuckin' retarded? I told you what would happen if you didn't keep a lid on that temper of yours, didn't I?"

"Yes, sir."

"Shut the fuck up! I can't save you this time, boy. I don't know what the captain is gonna do to your sorry ass! I can't believe you did all this over a piece of pussy!"

A knock at the door brought an abrupt end to the sergeant's tirade. A bespectacled, bookish-looking clerk stuck his head inside.

"Excuse me, Sergeant Horton."

"What is it?"

"Captain Walters is ready to see you, sir."

The man nodded and waved the clerk away. He looked at Tirrell and shook his head. "Ellis, I don't know what the hell you're thinkin'. Do you know that you can be kicked out on your ass for this or worse? Is that what you want? A dishonorable? Answer me, boy!"

"No, sir."

"Then what the hell did you enlist for if all you're gonna do is keep fuckin' up?"

Tirrell's hazel eyes shifted from the sergeant to the floor. "I don't know, sir."

The sergeant squared his shoulders. "I really hoped you were gonna be able to pull your head out of your ass. You could have been a halfway decent soldier, Ellis. Instead, you're a goddamn disgrace!"

Tirrell closed his eyes, demeaned by the dressing-down and disappointment he heard in his superior's voice.

"Let's go. We may as well get this over with."

Sergeant Horton stepped quickly into the company commander's office ahead of Tirrell, who was flanked by the two stoic MPs. They saluted the white-haired grandfatherly man seated behind a large oak desk as he raised his eyes above the rims of his glasses. He closed the thick official manila folder in his hands and laid it down in front of him. "Private Ellis." The man stood, rounded the massive desk, and removed his glasses.

Tirrell unflinchingly met his cool blue-eyed gaze. Working in the motor pool, he'd seen the captain a few times, but had no direct contact with him until now.

"You've been seeing Dr. Miles for anger management for the past few weeks. That arrangement apparently isn't working out very well for you."

"Yes, sir." Tirrell read the captain's puzzled look. "I mean no, sir. It doesn't seem to be."

"Some very serious charges have been leveled against you, obviously not the first time, but definitely the worst. How do you answer to them?"

Tirrell swallowed back the acid rising in his throat. "You got my file right there, sir."

"I can read, Private. But, I want to hear what you have to say. A man is lying in the infirmary with his head split open as the result of a common barroom brawl. Was it worth it? Was it worth almost killing a man and putting your career on the line?"

Tirrell shot his Sergeant a side-glance and then his gaze returned to the captain. "No, sir."

"You've been in trouble before. You've been warned."

"Is he going to die, sir?"

"No. And you can be thankful that he's not, otherwise, you'd be facing a murder charge."

Tirrell's jaws tightened and he sighed. "May I speak freely, sir?"

"By all means."

"I've been thinking. If it's all the same to you, I'd like to forgo any formalities and just plead guilty."

The man scratched his bushy brow; he appeared bewildered. "So, you're taking complete responsibility here?"

"Yes, sir. Just do whatever it is you feel you have to do."

"I've spoken to the judicial advocate in regard to your many offenses, and I have his recommendation as to how to best handle this situation, Private. I don't necessarily agree with it, but I have taken it under advisement."

Silence fell in the room. The captain moved to the window and stared out over the parade grounds. "Before I make my decision I'd like to know what happened in your own words."

Tirrell cleared his throat. "I was out at the Enlisted Men's Club with a couple of the guys from B Company."

"Privates Hutch and Caldwell."

"Yes, sir. We were just hangin' out, you know, havin' a good time."

"Drinking?"

"Yes, sir. We had a few beers." Tirrell neglected to add that they'd been smoking marijuana as well.

The captain turned and glared at him as if expecting him to admit to more, but no such confession was forthcoming. "Go on."

"Private Sims came out of nowhere, shoved me into the wall, and accused me of messin' around with his girl."

"Messing around with her?"

"He accused me of havin' sex with her, sir."

The captain nodded.

"He got all up in my face sayin' how he was gonna kick my ass. I laughed it off and tried to walk away, sir. That's when he grabbed me, spun me around, and punched me in the mouth. He had a knife. He cut me. I thought he was gonna kill me. I had to defend myself."

"With a beer bottle?"

"Yes, sir. I hit him with it."

"And you kept hitting him, didn't you, Private? Over and over and over until he was damn near unconscious?"

"Yes, sir. The next thing I knew the MPs were draggin' me out of there and tossed me in the stockade."

The captain pointed to Tirrell's arm. "You paid a little visit to the infirmary yourself, didn't you?"

"Yes, sir."

"Was Private Sims right? Were you having sex with his girl?"

"Yes, sir. But I wasn't the only one. I told him that, too. His girl . . . His girl is a whore, sir." Tirrell stifled a smirk.

The captain returned to his desk. He slid the glasses in his hand up on his face until they rested on the bridge of his nose, and leaned over and picked up the folder.

"Private Ellis, you've been charged with being drunk and disorderly on base, and aggravated assault. Looking at your history and the outcome of your actions in this matter, you could be facing a minimum of eighteen months to three years' confinement. You'd lose your rank and your pay. I've spoken with Dr. Miles; he believes that, given another chance and more therapy, you could learn more self-control. But, taking into account what I've seen in your file, I'm not inclined to believe it. I could perhaps swing this situation in your favor. You claim that this time it was an act of self-defense—perhaps that's true. Maybe you should get a chance to redeem yourself. Tell me, Private; what do you want to do? Should you be given another chance?"

Tirrell inhaled, filling his cheeks with air and blowing it out slowly. Here he stood desperately wanting to walk away from the regimented order he never really wanted to be part of. He'd always been rebellious, but acting out and doing time were two different things. The stockade was definitely not going to be the answer.

"Private Ellis?"

Tirrell glanced shamefully toward his sergeant and then turned back to the captain.

"Captain, I never thought of this whole Army thing as a career move."

"What did you think it was going to be? Club Med?"

"No, sir. I just wanted to do something different with my life. Give my life some meaning, but this isn't for me. This is somebody else's dream. Not mine. I think I'm done here, sir."

"Done?"

"You can lock me up. Take away my pay. But, in all honesty, I just want out, sir."

"Are you sure about that, Ellis?"

"I'm more sure about this than I was about signing up in the first place."

"I don't know why I'm surprised. Though, for what it's worth, I think you're making a mistake, son."

"With all due respect, sir, it's my mistake to make."

The captain leaned against his desk and shook his head. "All right." He nodded to the guards. "Take him back. Perhaps some time in the stockade will clear your head and give you the opportunity to reconsider what all of this could mean for your future. That's all."

The soldiers saluted and turned to leave.

"Sergeant Horton, I need you to stay. We need to talk," the captain said.

Back in his cell Tirrell found that his cellmate was no longer there. He sat down on the edge of his bunk and gingerly rubbed his hands together, contemplating his punishment. Would the price he'd pay be worth his unbridled aggression?

Twenty-nine days slithered by at a snail's pace. The stench of incarceration had almost been enough to derail Tirrell's resolve. Sit-ups and pushups occupied his time as he grappled with the likelihood of a prolonged sentence. On the thirtieth day his answer came, along with the documents that would earmark his disgrace.

"Let's go, Ellis," Sergeant Horton barked.

Tirrell closed the magazine he was skimming, rolled off the bunk, and laced up his boots. He didn't look up, but he could sense his superior's scorn and hear the disgust in his voice.

Tirrell was led back to the barracks to collect his belongings. The handful of soldiers present who were preoccupied polishing boots, playing a raucous game of dominoes, or writing letters to loved ones snapped to attention when the sergeant walked in.

"As you were," the sergeant allowed.

They relaxed and quietly watched Tirrell as he moved to his bunk and began stuffing his things into a duffel bag. One of his comrades who was with him the night of the fight hurried over to him.

"Are you okay, man?"

"Yeah, Hutch. It's all good," Tirrell responded without looking at the man.

"You sure you wanna do this?"

"Nothin' I can do about it now."

The last thing he did was remove a photo of his mother and father he had taped to the inside of his footlocker. He smiled sadly before putting it into his shirt pocket and turning to face his friend.

"You take care, Hutch. Keep your head down."

The man nodded. "You too, bruh."

Tirrell threw the duffel bag over his shoulder and walked toward the sergeant and the MP who were waiting near the door. As he stepped toward them he sneered at one of the other guys and flipped him the bird: his last "fuck you" to someone, other than the man he'd beaten up, who had given him the most grief.

Another MP, sitting behind the wheel of a Jeep, waited as he walked through the gate at the mouth of the base. No more words were exchanged between him and his sergeant. He was being banished. There was nothing more to say. Tirrell would never know that it was this same crotchety authoritarian who interceded and spoke to the injured private and appealed to the captain to change his mind in regard to the judgment he was within his right to impose.

Tirrell tossed his duffel bag into the back seat and hopped in. Before pulling off, he took one last look over the expanse of Fort Bragg, and relief washed over him for the first time since this all began. Whether it was the wrong decision or not, at least he wasn't going to spend any more time locked away, at least not here. That was enough—for now.

2

Peering out the window, Tirrell sat anxiously at the back of the Greyhound bus as it motored up the highway toward the Georgia state line. The dusty haze of heat that suffocated the countryside was almost visible; he was thankful for air conditioning. There were hardly any other passengers on the bus; for that he was grateful. He was equally relieved that they all stayed to themselves. For several minutes he considered getting off the bus when it stopped. He thought that perhaps it would be best to head for Charlotte, or Greensboro, or Raleigh-Durham and start over in a place where nobody knew him; somewhere no one had expectations. But, he'd been enough of a coward running away from the Army.

He could already hear the disenchantment in his grandmother's voice telling him how he demeaned his grandfather's memory and all that he stood for. He hadn't called her in over a month, and he still didn't feel ready to talk to her. At least the ride back home would give him enough time to devise an adequate cover story for his unexpected return to civilian life. Regret was slathered on his tongue like harsh-tasting medicine as he sat plotting the details and trying to make the words fit the crime. He was a man now and men had to take responsibility for their actions—cowardice or not.

He'd hoped that Noonie would understand. Maybe even in time she would forgive him. "Noonie" was the endearment his half-brother, Kevin, bestowed on their grandmother, which grew out of her inexplicable love of Moon Pies. As a boy, Tirrell jokingly called her "Moonie," but "Noonie" was the moniker that stuck. Despite his misgivings, he would be glad to be back in her house again, if she would have him. She was the only one in the family who ever cared enough to love him regardless of his shortcomings.

The twenty-two-year-old Ellis was a product of an affair between his Puerto Rican mother and an African American father. Tirrell's grandmother often reminded him of how much of his father, Curtis, was in him. There was a lot of his mother in him, too, especially his volatile temper. Tirrell missed them both more than he ever confided to anyone. They died when he was ten years old, after the car his father was driving skidded on a patch of black ice and careened off an embankment on their way back to Atlanta from Tennessee. Curtis Sr. and Betty Ellis took Tirrell in without hesitation; regardless, he never really felt that he was wanted or belonged.

Changes began to manifest in his behavior soon after. Initially, he was withdrawn and despondent, but once he settled into a new school and had to make new friends, he began to lash out. Tirrell was expelled from school three times for fighting and ended up repeating the fifth grade. That set the tone for what was to come.

"I'm just gonna love that devil right out of you," Betty would say. After many deserved whippings, she would pull the penitent child to her generous bosom as he cried tears of repentance. She loved him, knowing all too well that it would take more than a belt to his naked backside to cleanse him of the anger that festered within him.

Kevin didn't help matters. When he was sure no one was within earshot, he viciously reminded Tirrell that he was their father's bastard son. It didn't matter what Betty did to show him that he was as much an Ellis as either Kevin or his sister, Jacqui; he knew he was still an outsider.

Still unsure of what he would say to his grandmother, Tirrell reached into his duffel bag and pulled out an envelope that contained tangible proof of his dishonor: his DD-214 discharge and separation papers.

"Dishonorable discharge," he spat. "I'll be damned!"

For a half second he thought about ripping the papers up; instead he stuffed them back inside the envelope and shoved it in his bag. Extracting an iPod from one of its pockets, he plugged in the ear buds. The driving groove of Kanye West's "Stronger" began to soothe his anxiety. He laid his head back against the seat and closed his eyes and mouthed the words: "That that don't kill me can only make me stronger. I know I got to be right now 'cause I can't get no wronger."

By seven o'clock that evening, the bus pulled up outside the downtown terminal. The passengers nosily gathered their bags and filed off. Tirrell stepped onto the sidewalk and inhaled Atlanta. He turned and observed the varied faces inside the bus station: some greeting loved ones—others sending them off. But there was no one there to welcome him. He needed to keep the fact that he was back under wraps for a little while longer. He thought about calling one of his partners to pick him up, but instead decided that it was female attention that he needed.

As he started up the block to the MARTA transit station he was amused by the stir he caused. With his well-defined physique, mesmerizing hazel eyes (more brown than green), and deep dimples that showed when he smiled, it was easy to see why men and women alike tried to capture his notice.

This area of downtown was known for its questionable inhabitants. All sorts of interesting and unsavory characters loitered there, especially after dark. It seemed to be as much a point of departure as it was a haven for mischief. The homeless weren't the only obstacles in or around Forsyth Street. The vicinity was inundated with surreptitious exchanges of drugs and sex.

Tirrell felt a tug on the strap of his bag and sharply turned to see a scantily clad woman in an unflattering platinum wig.

"Hey, cuteness. You lookin' for a good time?"

Tirrell couldn't even offer the woman a smile. He shook her off and continued walking toward the MARTA station. He made it to the platform just before the train doors closed, jumped in, and found a seat.

A broad-shouldered dark-hued man with short, cropped, twisted locks sat across from him, motionless. He was dressed in a pair of oversized blue jeans that sagged at the waist and showed the top of his striped boxer shorts, and a wife-beater T-shirt that exposed excessive tattoos on his arms. The name CALVIN was etched around the side of his neck, and a distinguishing scar cut from his left ear and ended in the middle of his otherwise flawless skin near his mouth. Despite the mirrored sunglasses covering his eyes, Tirrell could feel them boring a hole through him. His bearing would have bullied most men, but not Tirrell.

"Dude, what the hell are you starin' at?"

The man stood and Tirrell stilled for a fight. The few people around them moved nervously in their seats as the announcement of the next stop filtered through the speaker. A couple of passengers advanced quickly to the door, keeping a watchful eye on the pair. As the train came to a stop and the doors sprang open, the man laughed and sauntered off. Tirrell rode on to the Kensington stop, got off the train, and connected with a bus that took him the rest of the way.

He bought a pack of cigarettes, gum, and a beer at a gas station on the corner across from the apartment complex where his girlfriend lived with her cousin. He hadn't seen her since she visited him in North Carolina eight months earlier and he couldn't wait to surprise her.

It was Thursday night and, for the most part, Tasha Parker was a creature of habit. That was one of the things he liked about her. Her predictability was also one of the things that frustrated him at times. Still, he was sure he would find her at home after a long day on her feet at the hair salon where she worked. She didn't go out much and when she did it was hardly ever during the week. As he thought about the possibility of sex and a good meal, he decided to pick up a bouquet of the half-wilted flowers that sat in a bucket of water near the cash register.

A short hike to the complex and he was at her door praying that her cousin wouldn't be home. He knocked and covered the peephole with his fingertip.

"Who is it?"

"It's the police," Tirrell shouted, trying to disguise his voice.

Tasha didn't respond.

"Open the door, ma'am."

"What do you want?"

"We have a warrant to search your apartment."

"You what? Um, I'm gonna need to see some ID."

Unable to maintain the pretense, he laughed. "Open the door, baby. It's me, Tirrell."

The lock clicked and the door flew open almost as soon as he announced his name. The cocoa-skinned five-foot-eight-inch female jumped into Tirrell's arms and kissed him.

"Oh my God," Tasha squealed. "What are you doin' here?"

"Ain't you glad to see me?"

"What do you think? I'm just surprised, that's all. What would you have done if I wasn't home?"

"I would've camped outside your door until you got here. That's how much I missed you, girl."

He held her at bay and examined her as if it were the first time they'd met. "Damn, look at you. You look good!"

"I've been working out." She blushed. "I've lost twelve pounds."

Tirrell smacked her rear. "You know you don't need to lose none of this here."

Tasha giggled.

Tirrell took a couple of steps into the apartment, dropped his duffel bag, and set the tangled mess of flowers on the coffee table. He laid her down on the sofa and rested his weight on top of her. The heat between them caused his nature and his temperature to rise simultaneously. In one movement, he pulled her tank top up over her head, exposing her plump, bare breasts, and discarded his T-shirt as well.

"What happened to your arm?" Tasha noted.

"It's nothin'. Don't worry about it."

"It looks like it hurts."

"I said don't worry about it."

He undid the button of her shorts and tried to pull them down.

"Baby . . . baby . . . wait," Tasha pleaded, pushing his hands away. "We can't do this out here."

"Why not?"

Tasha motioned toward the bedroom up a hallway past the eat-in kitchen. "Darnell's here."

Tirrell sat up as Tasha retrieved her tank top and slipped it back over her head.

"Yes, I'm here, honey. I pay half the rent. Why shouldn't I be?"

Tasha pulled her legs from around Tirrell's waist and stood up. Tirrell looked up to see her lanky six-foot-tall cousin, Darnell, traipsing up the hallway.

Darnell picked up Tirrell's T-shirt and took a whiff. "Ooooh, there ain't nothin' quite like the musky scent of a man to make a girl weak, baby!"

Annoyed, Tirrell reached out and snatched his shirt.

"Hey, Magnum, P.I. How's it hangin'?"

"Darnell," Tasha injected. "Aren't you on your way out?"

"I was," he chirped. "But we got company now, and I hate to be rude."

The flamboyant man lit a cigarette, took a seat facing them, and crossed his legs. "Damn, Tirrell. You have really filled out. Shit, you were cute before, but you fine as hell now. What's a girl gotta do to get some of that action?"

Revolted, Tirrell rolled his eyes. "Be a real girl for one damn thing."

Darnell ran his hand over his shock of dyed-blond hair, and stood back up. "Oh, okay. It's like that, huh?" He started back toward the door. "When y'all get through doin' whatever the hell y'all be doin' up in here just make sure I don't come home and find your nasty-ass used condoms in the trash. Keep your *dick*-tecting private, okay?"

"Darnell," Tasha snapped.

Tirrell shot Tasha a look.

"Ooops," Darnell teased. "Sorry, I guess that was s'pposed to be just between us girls. I'm just gonna get on out of here." With that, the man picked up his keys and backpack, and headed out the door.

Tirrell sat back on the sofa and squeezed his legs together. "Damn, what was with all the dick jokes?"

"You know Darnell. He was just bein' . . ."

"A sissy."

"C'mon, baby. It's not like that."

"Really? Then what's it like?"

"We'd had a little too much to drink one night and he was goin' on and on about his boyfriend, and I kinda let it slip out."

"Let what slip out?"

"We were talkin' about a man's size, and if gay sex is better than straight sex."

"You're kiddin' me, right?"

"Well, it ain't like he ain't never heard us through these thin walls before."

"That's because of all that noise you make." He threw his head back and mocked her. "Oh . . . Oh . . . Oh, shit, daddy. Right there. That's it. Oh, hell yeah."

Tasha slapped his head. "I do not sound like that."

"Yes, you do." Tirrell laughed and pulled her into his lap. "You know I love it when I make you scream, girl." He cupped her breasts and licked the nape of her neck.

Tasha trembled and caught her breath. "It's not that I'm not happy to see you, baby, but what are you doin' home?"

"I'm on leave."

"For how long?"

"A couple of months." Tirrell halted his seduction and reached to collect the loose flowers strewn on the table. "I bought these for you. I guess they got a little banged up on the way here."

Tasha took the nearly petal-less arrangement from his hands and smiled, rewarding the gesture with a long, deep, wet kiss.

After several seconds, Tirrell pulled away. "I'm hungry. What do you got to eat?"

"I made a salad earlier."

"Salad? I want some meat."

"Me too," she purred, stroking his escalating passion.

"Uh huh, I need to take a shower."

The corners of Tasha's mouth curled devilishly. "You can shower after."

She pulled her top over her head again and let her reddish brown mane fall loosely around her shoulders, and took his large, warm hands and placed them on her succulent breasts.

Tirrell squeezed gently, feeling his manhood strain against the denim of his jeans. He leaned over and his tongue flicked her protruding nipples as he continued to hold them firmly. His hands glided over her smooth brown body and he coaxed her out of her shorts as she lay back on the sofa. He slowly pulled at her laced panties and kissed and licked her stomach.

"Shit," she moaned.

"You sure you want this?"

"Hell yeah, boy."

Tirrell jumped up to make sure the dead bolt on the door was secured and then returned to the sofa. Sliding the panties down over Tasha's buttocks and thighs, he nestled his nose in her neatly trimmed bush and kissed her hidden mound.

Tasha gasped, letting him know he was headed in the right direction. Tirrell nimbly prodded her outer walls with his index finger, gently pulled her lips open, and playfully darted his tongue in and out.

He ravenously licked the fleshy part of her inner thighs, marking his territory. Reeling with delight, she pulled his head back up to her and they shared more kisses. He pulled up and untied the laces of his boots, kicked them off, and threw them across the living room floor, disrobed quickly, and returned to Tasha's waiting arms.

"It's been too long." She sighed.

Tirrell kissed his way down her body. "Damn, girl. You taste so good." He pushed her legs apart. She panted and pulled her fingers through her hair as he greedily fed his desires. Tears streamed down the sides of her face as he brought her to orgasm more than once, her quivering body writhing as her thighs clasped tightly to the sides of his head. He pulled away and reached for the condom he had in the back pocket of his jeans. Ripping open the packet, he deftly rolled it on and braced himself against the back of the sofa as he slowly and purposely entered her warm, wet hole.

"Damn," he cried, electricity shooting through his haunches. With each stroke, his breathing became more erratic. Tasha dug her fingernails into his butt cheeks and spurred him on. Changing positions, he took her around the waist and flipped over on his back, pulling her on top. He delighted in her piercing shrieks with each deep, piston-like thrust. She clamped down when his pace quickened. His distorted sex face and syncopated groans preceded a toe-curling climax.

His smooth chest rose and fell like a great mountain as he caught his breath and the aftershocks of orgasm lingered. Tasha leaned down to kiss him—his penis still in place. Her hair fell around her face and she pushed it back behind her ears.

"I love you so much," she whispered.

He opened his eyes, looked at her with solemn intensity, and pulled her back into a kiss. "I need to take a shower." He swatted her lightly on the rear and nudged her off. He stood up, pulled the condom off, and sauntered into the kitchen for a paper towel. He thought about Darnell's remark and chuckled as he tossed it in the trash anyway.

"You want some company?"

Tirrell looked at her. "In the shower? No, I'm good."

He gathered his clothes and duffel bag and headed to the familiar surroundings of her bedroom. Tossing his things near the foot of her bed he proceeded into the bathroom and turned on the water. He pulled the bandage off his arm and examined the wound before stepping into the tub. The gush of the pulsating jets washed what was left of his anxiety down the drain.

After his shower, he toweled off and went to find Tasha in Darnell's bathroom. He pulled his beer from the duffel bag; it wasn't as cold anymore but he popped it open and sucked it down. Lighting a cigarette, he sat down on Tasha's bed with the damp towel wrapped around his waist. He stared at the telephone, contemplating whether to call his grandmother. He opted to wait.

Tasha walked in as he stretched out across the bed. He looked up at her, smiled, and held his hand out, beckoning her. As she drew closer, he snatched her towel off and opened his to reveal that he was ready for more.

"All aboard."

"Yes, sir." Tasha saluted and climbed on top of him.

She rolled her moist clitoris slowly over his penis. They both moaned with anticipation. When she prepared to mount him, he stopped her.

"Baby, what's wrong?"

"No glove, no love, right?"

She moved. He got up and extracted another condom from his bag, then turned back to the bed.

"Why you lookin' at me like that? You wanna play safe, right?"

"Yes."

"A'ight, then." He opened the package with his teeth, noting her forlorn expression. "What, Tasha?"

"Nothing."

"Girl, I can't read your mind. You're gonna have to talk to me. What's goin' on?"

Tasha pulled the sheet up. Tirrell sat down beside her and caressed her cheek. "I know you are not poutin'. Do you wanna have sex without protection? If you do, it's okay by me. I'll pull out before . . . you know . . . Cross my heart."

Tasha kicked at him and he playfully fell on the floor, laughing.

"I crossed my heart." He stood up, bringing attention to his deflated member. "Now see what you did? Li'l T is goin' to sleep."

Tasha rested on her knees and took Tirrell's hand. "I know how to wake Li'l T back up."

"Nope, the candy store's closed."

"C'mon, baby. I'm sorry."

"I said no."

"Please."

"No, girl. Stop, now." He smacked her hand away. "Let's go get somethin' to eat. I'm starvin'." Tirrell slipped into a pair of clean boxers and pulled back into his jeans. "C'mon, now. Get a move on."

Tasha jumped off the bed and grabbed a pair of shorts and a pink cotton chemise from her bureau drawer.

"What? No bra. No panties?"

"Easy access for later." She laughed.

"Will a dinner jacket be required or not, madam?"

"What do you think?"

The two laughed together as they finished dressing and headed out the door. They found a KFC and ordered food to take back to the apartment. It was late but despite her new body consciousness she ate with him. She would pay for her indulgence at the gym later. For now she was simply going to enjoy the pleasure of her man.

"Shit, girl. That gym must be doin' you a world of good. You wore me out."

"Is that why you're breathin' so hard?"

"Hell, I'm tired. I've been up since five this mornin', took the Greyhound, and the MARTA to get over here and see you."

"I was just tryin' to show you my appreciation."

"Believe me, I appreciate it." Tirrell reached over to the nightstand and pulled a cigarette from the open pack.

"That's why your ass is breathin' so hard, right there."

He lay back and rested on the headboard, taking a drag. "What are you, the surgeon general?"

"I'll let that slide because you're so damn cute."

"Cute is for babies and puppies, girl. You heard what Darnell said, my ass is fine."

"Since when do you care what Darnell says?"

"When *she's* right, *she's* right."

Tasha laughed, snuggled up close, and laid her head on his shoulder. "Have you seen Miss Betty yet?"

"No. I told you I came straight here."

"She's gonna be so happy to see you. She was just talkin' about you Sunday."

"How do you know that?"

"I went to church with her and she invited me over to your brother's house for dinner after."

Tirrell blew smoke from his nostrils like an enraged bull, pushed her away, and sat up. "You've been hangin' around with my family?"

"Yeah, so. What's wrong with that?"

"Nothin'." He sighed heavily.

"Then why you actin' funky all of a sudden?"

"Nothin's wrong, a'ight. I told you, I'm just tired. I haven't had a lot of sleep the past few days."

Tasha took the cigarette from Tirrell's hand and put it out.

"What are you doin'?"

"If you're tired you need to sleep." She positioned herself behind him and massaged his shoulders.

He closed his eyes. "Mmmmm, that feels good."

"I thought we worked out all of your tension. I guess you still have a lot more."

"You have no idea."

After a satisfying rubdown, Tirrell lay back on the bed.

Tasha noted the far-off look in his eyes. "Are you mad at me?"

"For what?"

"I don't know. Seems like you got pissed when I brought up your grandmother."

"No. Don't worry about it. I just need some sleep, that's all."

Tirrell rested his head on her breasts and wrapped his arms around her waist. She lovingly caressed his head until he drifted off.

Tasha eased out of bed early the next morning as Tirrell snored. She grabbed her cell phone and slipped into the bathroom.

"Hey, it's Tasha," she said in a hushed, husky whisper. "Listen, I'm not gonna be able to do your hair today. Can I reschedule you for early tomorrow morning? No . . . I'm fine, just crampin' like crazy. You know how it is, that time of the month. Hey, I'll even knock twenty dollars off. Great, I'll see you in the morning. Is seven o'clock all right?"

Tasha followed that phone call with three others. Turning off the phone, she stepped back into the bedroom to check on Tirrell. Satisfied that he was still asleep, she slipped into her robe, and pulled the bedroom door closed. She could see by his bed that Darnell had not come home. He wouldn't have been able to get in anyway with the dead bolt on. She proceeded into the kitchen to make breakfast. She retrieved eggs, cheese, milk, and bacon from the refrigerator after starting a pot of coffee. Tirrell emerged from the bedroom just as the toast popped up from the toaster.

"Wow, look at you, all domestic and shit."

"Good morning."

"What time is it?"

"Almost nine."

Tirrell rubbed the sleep from his eyes and sat down at the dining room table. "Why you let me sleep so long?"

"'Cause you looked like you needed it."

"Don't you have to work today or somethin'?"

"I'm doin' all my clients tomorrow. Want some coffee?"

"Yeah. Sure."

Tasha poured them both a cup and served him a plate full of bacon, toast, and scrambled eggs with cheese. Tirrell practically inhaled the food right before her eyes.

"So, why did you really take off today?"

"I wanted to spend some time with you. Is that all right?"

"I'm goin' to see Noonie."

"Are you goin' down to the hotel?"

Tirrell put his fork down and leaned back. "Oh yeah, it is Friday, ain't it?"

"If you want to wait until she gets off work we could do somethin' together."

"Like what?"

"I don't know. We could find somethin' to get into."

Tirrell took Tasha's hand and pulled her over to his lap. "You wanna go back to bed?"

"I was thinkin' we could do somethin' that would require puttin' some clothes on. How about goin' down to Atlantic Station? Or we could go to a movie."

"I don't feel like sittin' in a theater for two hours. But we can go down to Atlantic Station if you want. And maybe we could stop by the Marriott on the way? I don't wanna wait. I wanna surprise Noonie."

"Okay. Sure."

Tasha finished her coffee and got up to do the dishes. After polishing off a second helping, Tirrell dropped his empty plate into the sink full of suds, wrapped his arms around her from behind, and kissed her neck.

"That was good, baby."

"I'm glad you liked it."

"You know what else I like." He squeezed her butt cheeks and proceeded into the bedroom to get dressed.

Tasha followed once she was done cleaning the kitchen.

While he waited for her, he booted up her computer to check his e-mail. He waded through the obligatory spam messages, and then responded to a few correspondences from a couple of his buddies from Fort Bragg, asking how he was and filling him in on what was happening in the short time since he'd gone, including their impending deployments. He leaned back in the chair and rubbed his hand over his face. "Damn."

Once they arrived at the downtown hotel, they pulled into the underground parking garage and walked into the service entrance. The basement bustled with energy. Housekeepers were running around with arms full of linen, and carts of toiletries, or pushing large tubs of dirty laundry toward big industrial washing machines. Tirrell caught the eye of a young girl who nearly tripped over her own feet looking at him.

"Can you tell me where I can find Betty Ellis?"

The lusty-eyed female smiled and pointed. "She down the hall. Take a left."

Tirrell nodded. "Thanks."

"'She down the hall,'" Tasha mocked.

"Jealous?" Tirrell teased.

"Hardly."

They continued up the hall and found his grandmother in her small office, seated at her desk, massaging her feet.

Betty Ellis was a stout, down-to-earth woman with a pleasingly plump brown face and eyes that sparkled when she laughed. She was kind and fiercely loyal, but if crossed, she wasn't one to hold her tongue. She'd been working as a housekeeper for twenty-nine years, and served as head of housekeeping for the last eight. Everybody respected her, and if they didn't they kept it to themselves. In her position, she was more like a mother to the thirty-member morning crew, juggling work schedules, refereeing petty disagreements, and keeping a keen eye on inventory.

When she spotted Tirrell at the door she slipped back into her shoes and stood up to greet him. "Oh, my Lord. Will you look a'here." She threw her arms open and pulled him into her.

His eyes misted in the comfort of her embrace.

"When did you get back?"

Tirrell checked his emotions. "Last night. I stayed at Tasha's."

Betty squeezed Tasha's hand. "How're you doin', sweetheart?"

"I'm fine, Miss Betty. How are you?"

"Hangin' on by a thread, girl. But God is good."

Betty turned back to Tirrell. "Baby, how long before you have to go back?"

"I'll be stickin' around for a while."

"How long is a while?"

"A couple of months. I got leave. Is it okay if I stay with you?"

"Is it okay?" Betty pulled him back into her. "Boy, I will beat your narrow behind if you even think about stayin' anywhere else. It is so good to have you home."

"It's good to be home, Noonie." Tirrell beamed, examining his grandmother. "You cut your hair. It looks good on you."

Betty delicately ran her hand over her tapered silver coif. "Tasha did it. I think it makes me look twenty years younger."

"Noonie, you ain't never gonna get old."

Betty smiled. "Tell that to my aching back and feet."

Guilt swept over Tirrell when he thought about the money that he would no longer be sending her from his military stipend. "I'm gonna take care of you, Noonie. I promise."

She caressed his cheek. "You are doin' too much already. You need to be savin' your money and not sendin' it to me. Besides, I can retire if I wanted. I'm just not ready."

The walkie-talkie on the desk buzzed. "Betty Ellis, you're wanted in the front office."

"I gotta get back," Betty said as she hustled to the desk and picked up the walkie-talkie. "Are you headed over to the house?"

"Not yet. Me and Tasha are gonna hang out for a while."

"Have you talked to your brother?"

"No. Other than you, Tasha is the only one who knows I'm here."

"You should call him."

Tirrell balked. "For what?"

"I'm sure he'd wanna see you."

He looked at his grandmother. She knew better.

"I don't want him to know I'm back yet. And I don't want you to tell him either."

"Well how about I have the family over for dinner on Sunday? You can surprise him at church."

"Church?"

"Tirrell Ellis, you can at least go to church with your ol' gran'mama."

He nodded. "Yeah, I guess that would be as good a place as any to drop the bomb on Kevin."

"Tasha, I want you to come too. You know it's about time for you to become a member. You've visited enough times."

"I wouldn't miss it."

Tirrell shot Tasha a side-glance.

Betty took Tirrell's hand. "Lord, it's so good to have my baby home."

Tirrell kissed his grandmother's cheek and she darted from the office and up the corridor.

His lie about being on leave wasn't going to hold up for long. Hopefully, by the time it unraveled, he'd have a job to help soften the blow.

"Tirrell, are you ready to go?"

"You know what, can we run by and see Marquis real fast? I need to holler at him for a minute."

"Why?"

"I just need to see him, a'ight?"

"Tirrell, I didn't mind bringin' you here, but I took the day off so we could spend time together, not to run you all over Atlanta."

"We are spendin' time together, ain't we?"

Tasha sucked her teeth and folded her arms across her chest. "You know what I'm talkin' about."

"I didn't ask you to take the day off, Tasha."

"You're right," Tasha scoffed. "What the hell was I thinkin'?"

She pushed past him and headed for the door. He grabbed her arm and spun her around and tried to kiss her. She pushed him away.

"Stop, Tirrell."

"Baby, I'm tryin' to say I'm sorry. Look, I just need to see Marquis for a couple of minutes, and then we can have the rest of the day together. I promise."

Tasha hesitated. "All right. Fine. Let's go."

Marquis Crawl practically grew up with Tirrell; his mother, Anne, lived across the street from the Ellises. The two were closer than brothers until Tirrell made the decision to sign up for the Army and Marquis, who had just been promoted to assistant manager of his father's automotive repair service, decided to stay behind.

The pudgy young man immediately recognized Tasha's Toyota as it pulled onto the lot of the service center where he worked. He was elated when he saw Tirrell step out of the passenger side.

"Yo, T!"

"Marquis, whudup, baby!"

The two embraced and bumped fists. Tasha half-heartedly waved and waited in the car.

"When did you get back, dude?"

"Yesterday. Marquis, look at you, boy. You ain't missed a meal, have you?"

The man smiled sheepishly. "Well, you know how it is. I ain't missed no tail either."

They laughed.

"I see you still kickin' it with Tasha."

Tirrell glanced over his shoulder and titled his head in recognition of her. He then turned back to his friend.

"What's goin' on, man?"

"Marquis, can we talk?"

"You know we can."

Tirrell pulled a cigarette from the pocket of his short-sleeved rayon-cotton shirt and took a few steps away from the car. Marquis followed.

"T, what's up with ya?"

"I'm out."

"Out of what?"

Tirrell leaned in and whispered, "The Army."

"What?"

"Yeah, some shit went down and I . . . I had to make a move."

Marquis scratched an itch in his cornrowed hair. "Serious?"

"Man, you can't tell nobody."

"You can count on me, T. What do you need? Money?"

"Naw, man. I got a few hundred dollars to hold me over."

"You need a place to crash? I'm stayin' with my pops right now, but he's got more than enough room if you wanna come there."

"Naw, I'm gonna hang out at Noonie's for a while until I figure some things out. I could use a job though. Is your pops hiring?"

Marquis wiped the sleeve of his uniform across his brow to sop up perspiration. "You wanna work here?"

"It can't be that bad. You work here, and your pops owns the place. Can you talk to him for me?"

"It would be cool for us to work together, but he ain't here today."

"When will he be in?"

"Not until Monday."

Tirrell took a last drag from his cigarette, thumped it to the ground, and squashed it. "Yeah, I guess it can wait 'til then."

"T, what happened . . . you know . . . with the Army thing?"

Tirrell peeped around the corner to see that Tasha was still waiting. Her eyes were covered by a pair of sunglasses, but even from a distance he surmised that she was irritated by being put on hold.

"We can talk about that later. I gotta go."

"What are you doin' tonight?"

"I'll probably be with Tasha."

"Well, I gotta work tomorrow. You wanna go down to the Compound tomorrow night?"

"That's what's up. I'll hit you back later."

Tirrell jumped back in the car. He reached over and stroked Tasha's cheek.

"So, what movie do you wanna go see?"

Tasha turned to him. "I thought you didn't wanna see a movie."

He leaned over and kissed her softly. "I'll do whatever you want to do, baby."

Tasha smiled, threw the car in drive, and took off.

Once inside the theater lobby, Tirrell headed to the restroom while Tasha went to the concession stand for refreshments. A good-looking man in line next to her winked and smiled. She blushed and stepped up to the counter. After paying for popcorn and sodas she stuffed her change into the pocket of her form-hugging jeans and turned to see that the man was still eyeing her. He made a move toward her.

"You need some help with all that?"

"Naw, she don't need your damn help!"

Both Tasha and the man turned to see Tirrell approach.

"My bad, dude."

Tirrell scoffed and picked up the sodas.

"What the hell was that?" he asked as they walked off.

"It was nothing."

"Did you know that punk?"

"No."

"Then why was he all over you?"

"Will you calm down? He was not all over me. He was just offering to give me a hand."

"He wanted to give you somethin' all right, but it wasn't his damn hand."

Tirrell bounded up the stairs of the auditorium to find seats. Tasha's whispered appeals for him to slow down were barely audible over the clamor of coming attractions flashing across the screen.

They settled in and Tirrell watched out of the corner of his eye to see if Tasha had any reaction to the man from the concession counter coming in shortly after them.

Tasha cut her eyes toward him. "What?"

Tirrell sneered and shoveled a handful of popcorn in his mouth. It wasn't as if he had a right to be jealous. He wondered why Tasha still tolerated him. She was smart and attractive. It was obvious that she could've had her pick of any man, and she picked him. She'd told him on more than one occasion that she loved him. He'd said the words once too when experiencing a particularly earth-shattering orgasm; he regretted those words as soon as they escaped his lips. He wasn't sure that he was capable of the love she wanted and knew that, in the almost three years since they first met, hope may have been the only reason she was still holding on.

3

It was easy for Tirrell to shake free of Tasha the next morning. She not only had her regular Saturday clients, but all those she rescheduled the day before. She would undoubtedly be busy long into the night. She dropped him off at the closest MARTA rail line on her way to the salon.

"Will I see you later?"

"I'll call you."

That was code for "don't count on it."

The train was running behind schedule, but when it pulled up to the platform it was empty. He rode to the Inman Park station and opted to walk the few blocks to his grandmother's house rather than catch the connecting bus.

As he approached, he noticed his grandmother's car parked in the drive on the side of the house. He used his key, and tried to tiptoe in just like he'd done as a teen after he'd run the street all night. Betty's seniority allowed her the luxury of weekends off. It was seven o'clock in the morning and she was already up eating a grapefruit and dry toast, drinking coffee, and poring over the *Atlanta Journal-Constitution*.

She peered over the metal rims of her glasses and chuckled. "I thought you were gonna be here when I got home from work last night."

"Mornin', Noonie."

"Good morning to you too. You want some breakfast, or did you eat at Tasha's?"

"You got any cereal?"

"I stopped by the store on my way home and got all your favorites."

Tirrell wrapped his arms around his grandmother, squeezed, and sucked her cheek. "You're the best!"

She pulled away laughing. "Go on now. Slobbering all over me."

Tirrell went to drop his duffel bag off in his old bedroom. Everything was as it had been—right down to his posters of Halle Berry, Ciara, and Beyoncé plastered on the walls.

With a few upgrades the structurally sound single-story three-bedroom brick-front house had been standing for forty years. The roof replacement and updated plumbing, and the new living room furniture and kitchen appliances had all been purchased courtesy of the insurance policy left by his grandfather, Curtis Sr., who passed away eight years earlier from prostate cancer.

Tirrell couldn't help smiling as he passed through the only real home he'd ever known. Like the house, Betty Ellis was a constant in his life, and that was reassuring.

Tirrell bounced into the kitchen like a little kid without a care in the world. He poured himself a large bowl of Cheerios and sat down facing his grandmother at the dining table. She'd polished off the grapefruit and was chewing on a chocolate Moon Pie. Tirrell laughed. Betty laid the newspaper down and looked at him.

"What's so funny?"

"You. How can you eat a Moon Pie right after you ate a grapefruit? That's just nasty."

"Hey, you eat what you want for breakfast, and I'll eat what I want."

"*Moonie.*"

She cut him a look. They laughed.

"Are you and Tasha gonna hang out again today?"

"Naw, she's gotta work."

"So, what are you gonna do all day?"

"Not much 'til Marquis gets off work. Then we'll probably do somethin'."

"When did you see Marquis?"

"Yesterday, after we left the hotel."

"You could go see Marquis, but you can't give your brother a call."

Tirrell opted not to raise an argument and kept eating.

"I wish you'd let me call Kevin and tell him you're home. Why wait?"

"You still cookin' tomorrow?"

"Yes."

"Then I'll see him then."

Betty huffed. Tirrell finished his cereal and got up from the table.

"You still goin' to church with me in the morning?"

"We'll see."

"Tirrell Ellis."

"Yeah, I guess I can, since you asked so nice."

"Boy, don't be smart."

"What you doin' today?"

"Anne and me are gonna go to the mall and then we're goin' to the grocery store. Do you need me to pick you up anything special?"

"No. I'm good."

The telephone mounted on the wall in the kitchen rang. Tirrell started to answer, but thought that it might be his estranged brother. He picked it up and handed it to Betty. She frowned before taking it.

"Hello . . . Oh hey, baby. How are you?"

"Is that Kevin?" Tirrell whispered anxiously.

Betty nodded. He put his index finger to his lips, silently begging her not to tell him that he was there. She shook her head, waved him off, and continued her conversation.

"No, I'm still here . . . . I'm goin' shoppin' with Anne. She's drivin'. I don't trust that old car of mine. Are you all comin' to church in the mornin'? No, I'm ridin' with Anne, but you can give me a lift home after." She looked at Tirrell and winked. "Tell Pat I'm cookin' so you all can just come right on over here after service. How's my great gran'baby? Does he still have a cold?"

Tirrell shook his head, not wanting to challenge her in regard to the forced reunion she'd planned. He peered out the side window in the dining room toward the parked Grand Am. He was certain he could fix whatever the problem was. As his grandmother conversed on the telephone, he made his way into the living room and scanned the framed family photographs arrayed on the walls and tables. There were pictures of Betty and Curtis Sr. over the course of their marriage, and to him she was still as beautiful at sixty-four as she had been at forty, or even younger. He examined pictures of his father with Kevin's mother, and others of the entire family. There were shots of Kevin with his wife and son, and even some of him. Tirrell smiled sadly when he spied his framed portrait in his Army dress prominently showcased on the credenza next to that of his grandfather in uniform from his service time in Vietnam. He sighed, taking into account that there wasn't one picture of his mother with him or his father. It was a glaring reminder that even though he carried the surname, his mother was the interloper who threatened to tear away the fabric of the family.

Betty disconnected from her call.

"What's wrong with the car?" he asked.

"Kevin said it sounded like something with the transmission," she responded, pushing away from the table. "He said I shouldn't waste any more money tryin' to fix it."

"So, why doesn't Mr. *Big Shot* lawyer buy you another one?"

Betty shot Tirrell a look.

"I'll take a look at it."

"Don't go to any trouble, baby. Today it's the transmission. Before that it was somethin' tickin' in some belt or chain or whatnot. Who knows what's next. I'll just ride MARTA, or catch a ride 'til I decide if I'm gonna invest in a new one."

"Where're the keys?"

"Tirrell, you don't have to—"

"I just wanna look at it."

"All right, go look on the bureau in my room."

"You got any old rags?"

Betty went into the kitchen and came back out with a few old towels she'd recently washed that were used for dusting. He took the towels, collected the keys, and stepped outside.

The check engine light came on as soon as he started it. He raised the hood to check all the fluid levels and hoses for leaks or corrosion. Whether he'd be able to do anything or not at that moment, he was glad that he had the skills to offer his grandmother the service. There would be a real sense of accomplishment if he could actually get the car running properly. He soon realized that it would take tools he didn't have at his disposal to fully analyze and diagnose the issues.

After Betty left with Marquis's mother he went into the kitchen and confiscated one of her favored Moon Pies to snack on. He called another of his associates, one he knew had a car. It didn't take much convincing for him to agree to swing by and pick Tirrell up.

Tirrell was bowled over when he looked out his window and saw a shiny black Escalade, riding on twenty-four-inch chrome wheels, pull up to the curb. The hard, pounding bass was so loud the windows on the house shook, and you could scarcely make out that someone was rapping beneath the beat. He spied his friend Bobby seated and grinning like the Cheshire cat behind the wheel. The medium-brown-skinned thirty-year-old man stood five foot nine, with a stocky, muscular build and clean-shaven head. Originally from New York, when he spoke you could still hear traces of the Bronx in his inflection.

Betty never cared for Bobby. She frequently warned Tirrell that he was a bad influence, and cautioned him to keep his distance. Tirrell dared not invite him into her house, and he knew that she wouldn't be happy to see him parked on the street disturbing the neighborhood. He grabbed his wallet, keys, and cell phone and rushed out to meet him.

"Damn, man," Tirrell said. "Last time I saw you, you was drivin' a hoopty."

"Last time I saw you, you was wearin' a uniform. What happened? Did they kick yo' ass out?"

Tirrell didn't comment. It would have been funnier if it weren't true. "What did you do, rob a bank?"

"No, are you crazy?"

Tirrell looked around, examining the electronics inside the cabin. "Shit, you ballin' out of control!"

"All in a day's work, my nigga. All in a day's work."

One blunt, three beers, and a half bottle of Patrón later, Tirrell and Bobby were pulling into Crawl's Service and Repair.

"Yo, Markie-Mark, let's go," Tirrell slurred.

Marquis came out of the garage accompanied by a couple of his coworkers. He was incensed by Tirrell's drunken display, and the earsplitting entrance of the Escalade. Marquis only stomached Bobby because of Tirrell. In recent months Bobby's rumored rise in the Atlanta drug trade had become more fact than fiction. Marquis did little to cover his disdain.

"Man, what the fuck are you doin' here? And why are you with this clown?"

"Clown!" Bobby shouted over the thump of the music. "Doughboy, you better watch who you callin' a clown."

"Will you turn that shit down," Marquis demanded.

Bobby reluctantly complied.

"Marquis, let's ride, man," Tirrell injected.

"T, it's only four o'clock," Marquis replied. "I don't get off 'til five-thirty. I thought you and me were gonna hang out tonight."

"Change of plans, big man," Bobby said. "We're *all* goin' to the Compound tonight."

"T, c'mon man," Marquis pleaded.

Tirrell rubbed the delirium from his eyes. "Why don't we just come back by your place later and pick you up on the way?"

Marquis shook his head. "Naw, man. Y'all go 'head. I'll catch up with you later, T."

"C'mon, Markie-Mark. Don't be like that, man."

"Man, fuck him," Bobby spat. "If he wanna stand there actin' like a li'l bitch, let him."

Bobby revved the engine and sped off.

Tirrell felt bad watching Marquis from the side-view mirror as the Escalade screamed off the lot and he disappeared in the distance. The look in his eyes conveyed that he was betrayed by Tirrell's cavalier attitude. Bobby wasn't making it any easier.

"Your li'l girlfriend seemed upset."

Tirrell sighed and lay back on the headrest, allowing the overpowering bass to drown out Bobby's scathing cynicism and his childhood friend's disapproval of his choice of running buddies.

One o'clock the next afternoon Tirrell awoke naked in a strange bed with an equally bare blonde sprawled across his chest.

"Damn," he spat under his breath, attempting to lift his head from the pillow. His eyes squinted against the sun beaming through the vertical blinds. His head felt as if it had been pounded into the pavement repeatedly. He could taste the sour breath in his mouth coating his tongue like peanut butter. He eased the weight of the woman's body up and slid from beneath her. Getting out of bed he stumbled over shoes, clothes, and empty bottles and stubbed his toe on the leg of an end table—Sleeping Beauty didn't stir.

"I gotta get outta here."

Dressing quickly, he tiptoed out of the room, carrying his Timberlands. He surveyed the room and remembered it was Bobby's place. There was the unmistakable odor of cannabis in the air, mingled with traces of sandalwood. Empty champagne flutes lay amid the residue of cocaine in the center of a glass table in front of a contemporary leather sofa. Loud snores could be heard coming from a room at the opposite end of the apartment. Curiosity led him to peer inside. He spied Bobby curled up between a brunette and a redhead, all fast asleep.

Tirrell glanced at his wristwatch and realized that the promise he'd made to attend Sunday service with his grandmother had been broken. He hoped he could make it back to the house before any of the rest of the family. He quietly headed for the exit and locked the door behind him.

Once outside, he established his bearings and found the MARTA station a block away from Bobby's apartment. En route he checked the missed calls on his cell phone: two from Betty—two from Tasha—and, unexpectedly, one from Marquis. There would be much contrition before the sun set.

While waiting on the platform, he pulled a cigarette from the top pocket of the multicolored striped shirt he wore over a wife-beater T-shirt. He patted at the pockets of his jeans for a light. He felt his wallet in the back pocket—something he hadn't checked before leaving Bobby's place. Removing a lighter from his pocket, he also found a small plastic pouch, full of the white powdered substance that had contributed to his partial memory lapse. His eyes darted around to see if anyone was watching, and he stuffed the sack back into his pocket and lit the cigarette.

He'd started smoking cigarettes in high school. Betty caught him once and demanded her husband's discipline. Curtis Sr. only applied a stern rebuke, which did nothing to deter the recalcitrant teen. Beer soon became Tirrell's libation of choice as he opted to liberate them frequently from his grandfather's stash. Other than the occasional joint, he'd also known people who snorted cocaine, but never imagined himself with a taste for that particular high. Clearly, his interests were changing; and so too was he.

4

MARTA services were slower on Sunday than any other day of the week. It took Tirrell over an hour to get back to Eastland Avenue. As he rounded the corner at the end of the block, he spotted his brother's silver Ford Explorer sitting in front of the house; Tasha's car was parked behind it. He wanted to run back in the direction of the train station, but figured that Betty had already divulged the fact that he was back. He would have to face his brother eventually; it may as well be right now.

The storm door creaked as he opened it. What would sneaking in accomplish? They were all seated around the dining table when he walked in. Exuberant chatter and the passing of serving bowls ceased as reproachful stares zeroed in on him. A lump formed in his throat. Who was going to fire the first shot? This moment felt like a very high-stakes chess game where the wrong move would render one's opponent defenseless and the king susceptible to capture.

"Uncle Tirrell," shouted a gleeful six-year-old with big brown eyes. The small boy jumped from his chair and ran to the door.

Tirrell swept his nephew in his arms and kissed him on the cheek. He seemed the only one, other than Betty, willing to accept him as a real part of the Ellis clan. His nephew's unconditional move put the rest of them in check.

"You may as well go wash your hands and come get somethin' to eat," Betty exclaimed.

Tirrell vacillated between relief and sadness as he put the boy down and scooted him back toward the table.

"So, this was your big surprise?" he heard Kevin snap as he stepped into the bathroom.

"Kevin, stop it. Be nice, now," Betty admonished.

Tirrell washed his hands and threw cold water on his face in an effort to awaken from the dream he felt trapped in. But, this was no dream. Reality was lurking on the other side of the door. They were all waiting to insist on answers that he didn't feel obligated or ready to give. He closed his eyes and leaned against the wall.

"Baby, are you all right in there?"

"Yes, ma'am. I'm okay."

"The food is gettin' cold."

"I'll be right out."

As the water ran he remembered the little something he had stuffed in his blue jeans pocket. He opened the medicine cabinet and found an unused razor blade, and knelt down on the floor next to the commode. He pulled a dollar bill and the small plastic pouch from his pocket. He tapped a small amount out onto the lowered lid of the toilet, separated it into two lines with the blade, and rolled up the bill. *If I'm going to get through this, I'm gonna need some help.*

Pressing his index finger to close his left nostril, he put the tip of the dollar bill into the right and bent over to snort one of the lines. With a deep inhale he ingested the powdery white substance, then repeated the process on the other side. He took a deep breath and threw his head back, waiting for the euphoric sensation he desperately needed. He stood and wiped the residue of cocaine from the toilet lid and licked his fingers. After stuffing the pouch back into his pocket he turned off the faucet, cleared his throat, and went to join the others.

"Hey, Pat. How's it goin'?" Tirrell said to his sister-in-law as he took the seat next to Tasha.

"Things are good." The woman smiled politely. "How've you been?"

"Couldn't be better."

Tirrell leaned over to kiss Tasha's cheek and she pulled away.

"Well, well," his brother Kevin began. "The prodigal son has returned."

Both Betty and Pat shot him simultaneous glowers.

Tirrell pretended not to notice and reached for the bowl of mashed potatoes in front of him. "Everything smells great, Noonie."

Betty smiled. "I made one of your favorite desserts, too."

"Peach cobbler or German chocolate cake?"

"Peach cobbler." She nodded with pride.

"That's what's up." He beamed, filling his plate with several slices of meatloaf, hearty scoops of green beans, and generous squares of hot, buttered cornbread.

Conversation stalled. Utensils clicked on plates, punctuating the silence. Pat busied herself assisting her son to get more food in his mouth than on the tablecloth around his plate.

Betty strained for something to say. "Reverend Eason really preached this morning. Didn't he, Pat?"

"Yes, ma'am, he sure did."

"What was the title of the sermon again?"

Tirrell shot his grandmother a side-glance and held back a simper. He knew the woman could tell you every sermon her pastor preached for at least the last three weeks.

Kevin put down his fork, picked up another piece of bread, and glared at Tirrell. "So, how long have you been home, *little brother?*"

Tirrell didn't look up from his plate. Kevin's tone dripped with contempt. If he could have called him a bastard at the table and not gotten popped in the mouth by their grandmother, he would have.

"I got in Thursday night."

Eight years and oceans of misunderstanding separated the brothers. Kevin was as tall as Tirrell and possessed the same distinct facial features as their father had. He had his mother's eyes, but his father's intense scowl; all the Ellis men had it. Stubbornness was another trait they shared. These qualities had served Kevin well on his college debate team, and continued to do so in his position working in the prosecutor's office of Fulton County. His demeanor was as certain as his confident gait. Kevin's skin tone was a shade darker than his brother's, and he wore his hair short and faded just as Tirrell did. Aesthetically, one of the only other differences in their appearances was that Kevin sported a neatly trimmed moustache and beard.

"So, you're on some kind of leave?"

"Yeah." Tirrell took a break from shoveling his food in his mouth to wash it down with the glass of ice-cold lemonade.

"How long will you be here?"

The interrogation was not completely unexpected.

Betty interceded. "Kevin, let him eat."

Kevin looked at his wife. She arched her brow and pursed her lips in agreement—he returned to his plate.

Tirrell leaned into Tasha, who'd barely looked at him the entire meal. "You look nice," he whispered.

Tasha rolled her eyes and threw her napkin on the table. "Excuse me." She jumped up and bolted for the door. Tirrell chased after her and stopped her on the porch.

"Let go of me, Tirrell!"

"Tasha, baby, come on. All I said was that you look nice."

"Where were you all night?"

"I . . . I was hangin' out with Marquis and some of the fellas."

"You're lyin'." Tasha glanced over her shoulder to ensure no one was watching. She lowered her voice. "Okay, if you were with Marquis where'd you go? What did y'all do?"

"We just hung out. Watched some TV. Drank a few beers, then we went out to the Compound."

"Is that all?"

"Yeah, it got late, so I just crashed at his place so I wouldn't wake Noonie up comin' in."

Tasha clenched her teeth. "Then, why you come in here stinkin' like you been with some other bitch?"

Tirrell sighed, threw his head back, and wiped his hand over his face. "Tasha, c'mon . . ."

"Don't *Tasha* me. You reek of cigarettes and nasty-ass perfume. I hope you had a good time."

"C'mon, it wasn't like that."

"Why you gotta lie, Tirrell?"

"You don't need to know what I'm doin' every hour of the day and night!"

"You were ready to jump all over some guy at the movies just 'cause he wanted to help me carry popcorn. And you come up in here after bein' out all night and you don't expect me to have somethin' to say about it. If we're supposed to be together I got a right—"

"Whoa, hold up . . . You ain't got a right to a damn thing. I'm a grown-ass man, not no little boy. You don't have to chase after me. Poppin' up over here all the time. Tryin' to get in good with my grandmother and goin' to church like you all holy. Ain't no ring on your finger, and even if it was you ain't got to keep tabs on me!"

Their collective anger governed their tones. The commotion brought Betty to the door. Tasha turned away to keep her from seeing the tears welling up in her eyes. Realizing he may have gone too far, Tirrell leaned against the railing with his head down.

"Y'all all right out here?"

"Yeah, Noonie. We're good."

"Tasha?"

"I'm fine, Miss Betty."

"We're gonna have cobbler soon. I got some vanilla ice cream to go with it. Y'all wanna come back inside?"

Tasha turned to face her. "I think I'm gonna pass on dessert. I need to go."

"Are you sure?"

She glanced over at Tirrell, who hadn't looked up. "Yeah, I just need to get my purse."

Betty cleared the doorway and Tasha went in to retrieve her purse and say good-bye to the others. She hugged Betty and thanked her for inviting her to dinner. She said nothing to Tirrell as she jumped in her car and sped off.

"Tirrell?"

"I'll be in soon, Noonie."

Betty hesitated before stepping back inside the house.

Tirrell's cell phone rang; it was Bobby. He would have to call him back. He slipped the phone back into the pocket of his jeans and removed the plastic pouch of cocaine.

Before he could go back into the house, Kevin came out. Tirrell rightfully assumed it wasn't his decision.

He quickly stuffed the pouch back inside his pocket. They stood staring out over the neighborhood with no particular focus, or interest in the residents who waved in recognition.

"What was that?" Kevin inquired.

"What?"

"What you just put in your pocket."

"Nothin' for you to worry about, Kev." Tirrell opened his arms and smiled a big, toothy grin. "You wanna give your li'l brother some love?"

Kevin gave him the once-over and snarled.

"C'mon, man. How long we gonna do this?" Tirrell grabbed and heartily embraced him.

Kevin's body tensed and jerked loose. "Man, you have lost your raggedy-ass mind. Don't you ever do that again."

"I was just showin' you how glad I was to be home."

"Yeah, I can smell your happiness, and everybody else can too."

Tirrell caught a whiff of himself and realized he should have tried to clean up better.

Kevin stared off in the distance. "You never said how long your leave was."

"Awhile."

"How long's awhile?"

"A month," Tirrell snapped. "Is that a'ight with you?"

"Your girl took off in a hurry. She didn't even finish eating."

"So?"

"So, I'm guessing that's not her scent all over you. You just don't have any class about yourself, do you? It's obvious that Tasha likes you, and you want to treat her like she's just another piece of ass. "

"Why is this your business exactly?"

"Look, I don't really care whether you two work it out. I do care about Noonie, and I thought you did too."

"I do."

"So, this is how you show it?" Kevin turned to face him. "Let me make something clear to you. However long you're going to be here, you need to make sure that whatever other business you got goin' on doesn't come back on Noonie."

"You make it sound like I'm gonna do somethin' to hurt her."

"Just make sure you don't."

"Or what?"

"I'm gon' be all over your ass."

"Should I be turned on or scared?"

Kevin grabbed Tirrell's arm and pushed him into one of the columns that supported the front of the house. Tirrell tried to squirm free, but Kevin's grip tightened.

"I'm tellin' you one more time. Don't bring your shit up in this house. The sooner your leave is over, the better for all of us, especially Noonie. She's not stupid, you know. Now, she went to a lot of trouble to prepare this dinner. The least you could do is come in and finish eating it."

"Daddy."

Kevin looked over his shoulder and saw his son peering through the storm door.

Tirrell yanked his arm away.

"Noonie said for me to come and get you."

"I'll be right there, Micah. Go on back inside."

The boy hesitated at the door before doing as he was told.

Kevin turned back to Tirrell. "I meant what I said, *bruh!* And you may wanna do yourself a favor and take a shower. You dumbass."

***

Kevin didn't have Tirrell's temper, but his presence and manner of speech could be as intimidating as both his father and grandfather. By the time Kevin had learned of Tirrell's existence he was just about to graduate from South Cobb High School. He'd overheard his mother, Gloria, and his father, Curtis, arguing about the "Latin whore" he'd been cheating with. That revelation tore at the heart of the relationship he'd enjoyed with his father, believing that he was his only son.

Before Kevin went off to college, he was already distancing himself from his father. He died while he was away and Kevin never forgave himself for not being there, and he couldn't bring himself to forgive his father for what he'd done to their family. Kevin heaped all of his unresolved rage on to Tirrell. It didn't help that Betty wasn't particularly impartial when it came to the unexpected new addition. "Tirrell needs me. He doesn't have anybody else," she'd say. When Kevin came back to visit for holidays it galled him to see Tirrell living in his grandparents' house—calling her "Noonie."

There wasn't a lot of conversation that passed between Kevin and Pat on the ride home. She filed through his music collection and found the John Legend CD that he liked and slid it into the player. Patricia Ellis had a no-nonsense way about her that Kevin was attracted to from the first time they met.

He shot her a side-glance and smiled. "You think that's gonna help?"

"It couldn't hurt."

He reached for her hand and kissed it, allowing the easy melodies to pacify him. Pulling into the driveway of their suburban Alpharetta home, Kevin inhaled and exhaled slowly as he lay back on the headrest before turning off the ignition.

He got out and pulled his sleeping son from the car seat in the back. Pat went ahead and unlocked the front door. Kevin proceeded on up the stairs to put Micah down for the night. The boy barely woke up while his father pulled off his church clothes and slipped him into his pajamas.

Pat stepped into the doorway of her son's room. "I can warm the cobbler up if you want some."

"No. I'm good."

"Okay, I'll put it in the refrigerator."

Kevin kissed his son good night. He went up the hall to the master bedroom, pulled off his clothes, and got ready for bed. Pat was half out of her dress when she came back up the stairs.

"Can you believe this shit?" Kevin seethed, climbing into bed. "If I had known all Noonie wanted was to spring Tirrell on us, I never would have agreed to go to dinner."

"C'mon, baby. I thought you were over all of that. Let it go."

"I am over it."

"You don't sound like it."

She stepped out of her dress and went to hang it in the walk-in closet before proceeding into the bathroom to shower. Kevin was half-heartedly watching the news when she returned.

She brushed her layered brunette locks back behind her ears and sat down on the bed to continue her nightly regimen, squeezing lotion into her hands and smoothing it on her long, silky legs. "You used to help me with this, remember?"

Kevin cozied up next to her. He pulled her legs onto his lap, filled his hands with lotion, and absently rubbed it in. "I caught him with something when I went out on the porch earlier."

"You're not gonna let this go, are you?"

He shook his head and sighed.

"Okay, what was it?"

"I don't know. It could have been a piece of paper—it could have been something else."

"Like what?"

"Knowing Tirrell, it was probably a bag of weed."

"Did you ask him about it?"

"If it was drugs, he wouldn't have owned up to it. I just don't want any shit when it comes to Noonie. I'll be glad when his ass goes back to North Carolina. Maybe he'll end up pulling a tour in Iraq or Afghanistan—anywhere but here."

"Stop. You don't mean that."

"He needs to grow up, baby."

"He has to find his own way, Kevin. You can't make him be what you want him to be."

"I want him to be gone."

"Kevin. You're not kids anymore. Like it or not, he is your brother."

The look in Kevin's eyes let her know that he was resolute. They turned off the lamps on their respective sides of the bed and Pat wrapped her arm around his hairy chest. She then offered her lips for his kiss.

"Good night."

"That's it," he sulked.

"I've got to get up early. You know all the overtime I've had to pull lately."

Pat turned her back to Kevin with her rear pressed into his crotch. He was too wound up to sleep. He kissed her shoulder and gently ran his hand up under her nightgown.

"What are you doing?" she whispered.

"What does it feel like?" he teased, thrusting his erection forward.

"Kevin, I gotta get up early."

"I'm up now."

His hand swept over her soft buttocks to the front of her thighs. His fingers made their way under the elastic of her panties and tugged at them until they found what they were searching for. Pat acquiesced, turned over, and opened her legs, allowing him better access. He pressed his mouth onto hers and pulled off his boxers. He then slid her panties off and kissed and sucked a trail down her neck, shoulders, and breasts.

"I can't be late for work," she panted.

"I'll write you a note."

He came up on his knees with the head of his penis aimed at its target. His hands gently caressed the supple flesh of her inner thighs as he worked his way downward. Pat gasped and arched her back upward; her nipples were prone for attention. After massaging her clitoris to rapture his nimble fingers glided up her stomach toward the mounds of flesh that eagerly awaited his touch. He didn't disappoint. His tongue lapped and his lips sucked each one with passion and fervor. Slowly working his hips he pressed into her and she opened up to receive him.

"Damn."

After a while he bucked and grunted until the muscles in his backside, thighs, and legs stiffened.

"Damn," he cried, jerking into orgasm.

He collapsed onto her, smothering her with kisses until they fell asleep in each other's arms.

Tirrell and his issues were no longer of paramount concern.

5

Tirrell's repeated attempts to call Tasha went unanswered. He thought about going to her apartment, but taking the train at this hour on a Sunday night was out of the question. Betty was already off to bed. He sat in solitude outside on the porch, smoking a cigarette, surrounded by the stars. It was a clear night. Weathermen clamored about the drought, and the grass in and around the neighborhood testified to that fact. He listened to Bobby's message about the "gift" he'd left in his pocket, and decided to call Marquis.

"Hello."

"Hey, boy, whudup?"

A long silence, as dry as the weather, followed.

"Marquis, you there?"

"Yeah, I'm here."

"Look, man. I was just callin' to set the record straight and apologize for yesterday."

"It's cool. I understand."

"It's just that I got bored sittin' at home and Bobby came by and we rode out. One thing led to another and, well, you know how it is."

"Yeah, I know how it is."

"I wasn't tryin' to dis you or nothin'. I really wanted all of us to hang. I'm sorry about comin' by your job and actin' a fool like that, too. I still hope you can talk to your pops about me workin' there."

Another pause.

"Marquis?"

"If you get the job he's not gonna want Bobby Williams hangin' out up there."

"He won't. If you get me on I'll keep Bobby away."

"Okay, I'll talk to him, but I can't make any promises."

"We still boys?"

"Yeah, we're good."

"That's what's up. I'll holla at you tomorrow, a'ight?"

Squashing his cigarette and ensuring it was completely out, Tirrell pulled the pouch from his pocket and looked over his shoulder to see if Betty might be peering out through the drapes at the window. He stuck his finger in the bag and licked off the excess.

"'I know I got to be right now . . . 'cause I can't get no wronger.'"

Tasha stared at the ringing phone and forced herself not to answer. She wasn't ready to hear another one of Tirrell's patented excuses for bad behavior—but she was weak. He possessed a magnetism that she found hard to resist no matter his faults. That incomprehensible pull that made her stay with him even though she felt she should have moved on long ago. Sometimes she could see this angry little boy inside the façade of the man she knew he tried to be—the one he could be if given the chance. She rationalized that his sometimes erratic behavior justified one of the most difficult decisions she ever had to make.

Thank God for her cousin, Darnell. If he hadn't been there she would have completely fallen apart. Despite Darnell's counsel, she wanted to forgive Tirrell. She wanted to love him. In many ways she felt she needed to. She'd convinced herself that they were good together, even in the face of contradiction. She sat as the phone continued to ring, recalling the first time she witnessed his anger. They'd only been dating a few weeks and had gone Rollerblading in the park. A man jogging by them inadvertently made a comment about her rear end and Tirrell went ballistic. She could hear Darnell's voice: "Cousin, you a damn fool. His dick can't be that good." But there was a side to Tirrell that he didn't show everybody. He could be disarmingly charming when he chose to be. At the time Tasha told herself that he was defending her honor—but it was more territorial than that.

Tirrell was a brash nineteen-year-old when they met; she was twenty-two. He was riding the MARTA train to visit a friend and she was on her way to work. She smiled. He winked and smiled back. He got off at her stop despite his previous destination. They shared coffee and conversation and soon forgot all about their other obligations.

"How old are you?"

"How old do I have to be to apply for the job?"

"What job?"

"As your man."

She laughed. His flirtation was corny and appealing at the same time, and it didn't take long before she discovered that he was a more-than-satisfying lover; but sex wasn't love.

In time, her heart and her desire began to overrule her logic. How many times had she swallowed her dignity and looked past his indiscretions? How much more was she willing to take?

6

Tirrell sat staring at the application as if it were the SATs. His answers could mean the difference between getting a job and remaining unemployed.

"Have you ever been convicted of a felony?"

No.

"Have you ever served in the military?"

He leaned back in the chair and tapped the pen on the table in front of him and contemplated how to answer. He decided to leave it blank.

Though he was a bit distant, Marquis did get him in to see his father, who promptly grilled him about everything from an oil change and engine block to rebuilding a transmission. After the interview, Tirrell reluctantly opened up to Mr. Crawl about what happened with the Army. The man was unpredictably supportive.

"I know how these things can happen," he said. "You don't have to worry, I won't say anything to your grandmother or Anne. As long as you do good work and keep yourself in check we can work it out. Can you start Wednesday morning?"

"Yes, sir."

"All right then." Mr. Crawl stood up and shook Tirrell's hand. "We open at seven. Don't be late."

"Thank you, Mr. Crawl. I'll be here. I swear I won't let you down."

After the interview, Tirrell found Marquis elbow deep inside the bowels of a Chevy Impala.

"So, how did it go?"

"I got the job."

"That's what's up, T."

"Yeah, your pops was real cool about the Army thing. Thanks for puttin' the word in, man."

"It's all good."

"You, uh, you wanna go grab some lunch? Wherever you want to go—on me?"

"Shoot," Marquis responded with a smile. "Free food. Hell yeah! Just give me a minute to clean up."

It wasn't an outrageous gesture, but if a seven dollar buffet was the olive branch it took to get him back on track with his best friend, Tirrell would have gladly bought Marquis's lunch for the next month. He could only hope, as he rode the train to see Tasha, making up with her would be as easy.

Tirrell glared stared through the window of the Head-2Toe salon. Each of the seven stations was brightly lit, stocked with all the products, towels, and curlers the operators worked with. Mirrors and posters displaying the latest in hairstyles and hair care were showcased on the walls. He spotted Tasha in the back finishing a client's hair. There were a few other people inside. At least if she made a scene there wouldn't be too many witnesses.

Darnell, who also worked there as a stylist, announced Tirrell's entrance.

"Well, look who's here. Magnum, P.I., everybody." He applauded.

"Jealous, Darnell?"

"You wish."

Tirrell grabbed his crotch. "You wouldn't know what to do with all this."

"Try me."

"I'll pass."

Tasha looked up and returned to her client. Tirrell made his way to the back of the shop.

"Baby, can I talk to you for a minute?"

She ignored him.

"Please?"

"I don't wanna talk to you right now, Tirrell. I'm workin'."

"Can you take a break or somethin'?"

"Go away, Tirrell." Tasha offered a mirror to the woman in her chair. The woman admired Tasha's work as Tirrell stood by impatiently.

"Girl, I love it. You know you can do some hair," the woman said enthusiastically.

Tasha removed the nylon cape from around her client's neck as the woman reached into her purse for money.

"I'll see you next week. Same time?"

"You know it."

Tasha reached for a broom to tidy up around her work station, continuing to ignore Tirrell, as the woman left the shop.

"Baby, c'mon," Tirrell pleaded. "Talk to me."

Tasha sighed and started toward the back room with Tirrell in tow.

"I've been tryin' to call you," he said.

"You didn't leave a message."

"I didn't want to talk to your voice mail. I wanted to talk to you. I needed to explain about what happened the other night."

"Look, Tirrell, I don't doubt that you can talk your way out of whatever did or didn't happen Saturday night. Hell, you're even smooth enough to come up with a plausible lie for why you came home stinkin' like the skanky ho you were with, but it doesn't matter. Maybe we should just cut our losses and call this whole thing off so you can be with whoever you want to be with."

"Tasha, I don't wanna be with nobody else. I wanna be with you."

"Why, Tirrell? Huh? You don't love me."

"You don't want me to say it just so you can hear it, do you?"

"No, dammit, not if you don't mean it. But, I wanna be in a relationship with a man who wants to be in a relationship with me."

Darnell pushed the door open and stuck his head inside. "Cousin, are you okay in here?"

"Yeah, I'm fine."

Darnell smirked and stared at Tirrell. "Don't make me whup yo' ass up in here. I may be gay, but I'm still a man!"

"Whatever," Tirrell spat.

"Look," Tasha injected. "That was my last client for the day. I think I'm just gonna take off early and head home."

Darnell cut his eyes toward Tirrell. "Do you need me to walk you to your car, cousin? You know it's all kinds of unscrupulous characters lurkin' around these days."

"I think I can handle him," Tasha responded.

Tirrell reached out and grabbed her hand. "Could you give me a ride?"

"Why don't you go home the same way you got here?"

"Tasha."

She shook her head. "Shit. All right, come on."

Tasha collected her purse and shut off the overhead light at her station. Whispers and muffled laughter trailed her and Tirrell out of the shop.

She clicked the remote to unlock the doors of the car and they got in. "They're laughing at me," she observed. "They're probably thinkin' what a fool I am."

"Who cares what other people think, Tasha?"

"I care. I gotta work here."

She started the car and pulled off the lot. "I'm tired of goin' back and forth with you, Tirrell."

He turned on the radio and scanned the stations until he came upon his favorite song playing. He glanced over at Tasha. He knew she was serious. Despite the music it was an uncomfortably quiet ride.

They pulled up outside Betty's house. Tasha shifted the gear into park, but didn't turn off the ignition.

Tirrell turned off the radio and glared out the passenger window. "I got kicked out of the Army," he said flatly. "I was discharged because I got in a fight and almost killed this dude."

He could see her reflection as she turned toward him. He pressed on. "It was some stupid crap between me and this other private. We both had a little too much to drink one night and shit got out of hand. Some things were said and one thing led to another. We fought and he ended up in the infirmary. I told Noonie that I was on leave because I couldn't let her know what really went down. I wouldn't be able to take the look of disappointment in her eyes."

For the most part the story was true. Tirrell saw no real benefit in telling Tasha about the girl he slept with. It would have only exacerbated the situation.

Tasha shut off the ignition. Tirrell faced straight ahead.

"You know it's hard for me to open up. I'm not good with sayin' I love you, you know that. My mom and Noonie are the only ones I could ever say it to and mean it."

"It's not the same thing, Tirrell."

He looked at Tasha. "I know it's not the same thing, but I still have a hard time sayin' it. I know I fucked up, but I don't wanna lose you. I know what you wanna hear, but I'm not ready. Give me some time to figure all this shit out. I know I'm askin' for a lot. If you can't . . . If you don't want to . . . I understand."

Tirrell's vulnerability was disarming—his eyes even managed to tear. She kissed him softly on the lips. He followed with a more passionate one.

"What are you going to do now?"

"Believe it or not, I got a job down at the garage with Marquis. It's not the Army, but it's somethin'."

"You're gonna have to tell Miss Betty soon."

"I know, but not yet."

"She's gonna get suspicious when it's time for you to go back. What are you gonna say then?"

Tirrell shook his head. "I don't know. Maybe by then I won't be so scared of the truth."

Tasha stroked his cheek. "Thank you for at least telling me."

"Do you wanna come in? There's some peach cobbler left from yesterday."

Tasha looked up toward the house. "I don't think I need anything to eat. I'm too big as it is."

"Stop doin' that. You're not fat. I wish you wouldn't put yourself down. There's nothin' wrong with you, girl." He leaned in and kissed her again. "C'mon, we'll be quiet so we don't wake Noonie up."

The pair got out of the car and headed hand in hand into the house. They found Betty reclined in her favorite leather chair perched in front of the television. The opening door startled her awake and the *TV Guide* slid off her lap to the floor.

"Well, look a'here," she said, clearing her throat. She readjusted her reading glasses and sat up.

"Noonie, I'm sorry," Tirrell said. "I didn't mean to wake you up."

"Don't worry about it, baby." Betty smiled at Tasha. "I guess everything is all right with you two."

"Yes, ma'am," Tasha responded.

"I invited Tasha in for some cobbler," Tirrell added.

"Oh, well let me go warm it up for you."

"You don't need to do that, Noonie," Tirrell insisted. "I can get it. You should go on to bed. We'll try not to make too much noise."

Betty yawned. "Well, all right. I guess I will. Y'all eat as much as you want, hear? There's a little bit of meatloaf left in there, too."

Tirrell kissed his grandmother on the forehead. "We'll manage. You get some sleep, okay?"

"Good night, baby."

Betty gave Tasha a hug and squeeze before retiring to her room. Tirrell turned off the television and he and Tasha went into the kitchen.

Tasha leaned against the counter, smiling, as she watched Tirrell fill two bowls with heaping spoonfuls of cobbler and pop them into the microwave. He turned and noted the expression on her face.

"What?"

She shook her head. "Just watching you. I can see how much you love your grandmother and I can see how much she loves you. I know if you told her what happened she'd understand."

Tirrell shook his head in disagreement. "I'm just not ready to deal with it."

The beeping microwave interrupted the emotions that started to well up inside him. He pulled a carton of vanilla ice cream from the freezer and topped the steaming delight with a scoop.

Sitting together quietly at the kitchen table, Tasha's eyes filled with the unspoken sentiments that kept her connected to this man who found it hard to commit, and at that moment she convinced herself, as she had so many times before, that it didn't matter. Maybe it wasn't love that held her, but guilt; after all, she was no saint either. She had her secrets too.

7

Endless oil changes, engine tune-ups, and tire rotations filled the lazy summer days. Tirrell explained that he wanted to keep busy while on leave, and what better way than picking up a few hours at Mr. Crawl's garage. He'd made good on his promise to fix Betty's car and get her mobile so that she wouldn't have to rely on public transportation to get her back and forth to work. That made him happy.

There was an easy camaraderie between Tirrell and his coworkers. Sometimes after lunch he, Marquis, and another of the men would sneak off for a few tokes of a joint before returning to work. This did not go without the notice of the rest of the staff, but was only done when Mr. Crawl was not on the premises. Marquis didn't like to indulge as much as Tirrell, but he was always more of a follower than a leader.

Marquis was one of the first to befriend the introverted ten-year-old when he came to live with his grandmother after his mother's death. That early friendship blossomed and translated to Southside High School, where Tirrell's good looks quickly elevated his status. Neither boy participated in organized sports; still, Tirrell had the adulation of his peers (mostly girls). Marquis enjoyed the perks that came along with hanging with someone who was considered one of the coolest kids in school.

"So, you tell Miss Betty yet?"

Tirrell looked up from the engine block he was working on. "No, not yet."

Marquis chuckled. "You still scared?"

Tirrell rolled his eyes.

"I'm kiddin'. You know my mama had to ask."

Tirrell glared at him.

"Don't worry. I didn't say nothin' to her. You know she can't hold water."

"Yeah, well you just make sure you keep that shit to yourself." Tirrell returned to his work.

"We hangin' tonight?"

"Naw, I told you I'm takin' Tasha out."

"Y'all been pretty tight since you got back. Things gettin' serious?"

"What? Like marriage or somethin'?"

"You know that's what she wants."

"She knows I ain't ready for all that. We're just goin' to Bone's for her birthday."

"Sooner or later you're gonna have to step up."

"Tasha ain't goin' nowhere. Not as long as I got a hold to that little man in the boat."

Tirrell held his fingers up in a V formation and snaked his tongue between them. He and Marquis bumped fists and laughed like mischievous school boys.

"Is that what you're wearing?" Darnell asked, leaning into the doorway of Tasha's bedroom.

"Yeah, what's wrong with it?"

"It's all right if you're goin' to somebody's funeral. I thought you bought the red dress."

"I liked the black one better."

"So, you buy your own outfit, then you got to go across town and chauffeur him around, too. Couldn't he have gotten his grandmother's car?"

"He said Miss Betty had to work tonight and he didn't want her to have to take the bus."

Darnell smirked, folded his arms, and sauntered into the room, examining Tasha as she admired herself in the full-length mirror mounted on the wall. She delicately ran her hand over the beadwork that adorned the plunging bodice accentuating her creamy brown skin. She pulled gently at the hem of the sleeveless micro-mini and ran her hand down her nylon-covered thighs.

"This dress is sexy."

"I guess it'll do," Darnell agreed, pumping up the sleeves of his oversized sweatshirt. "You want me to do your makeup?"

Tasha shot him a side-glance and laughed. "I already did my makeup."

Darnell squinted and leaned in. "I can't tell."

"It's fine. Besides, the last time you offered to do my face I ended up looking like a drag queen."

"It wasn't that bad."

Tasha cut her eyes.

"Okay, well maybe it was a little over the top." Darnell laughed. "What else is Magnum gettin' you besides indigestion?"

"Darnell."

"He's been here practically every night for the past two weeks, and you know I can hear you. It sounds like y'all makin' a porno up in here."

"No, we don't."

Darnell fell over onto her unmade bed and thrashed around. "Oh, Tirrell. Oh . . . Oh . . . Oh . . . it's so big."

Tasha grabbed a pillow and smacked him in the head with it. They laughed raucously.

"Stop it," Tasha squealed, trying to regain composure. "You're gonna make me mess up my makeup."

"What makeup?"

"I'm serious, Darnell. Stop."

Tasha turned back to the mirror and fussed with her updo.

Darnell rolled off the bed. "Okay, I'll stop."

"Thank you."

"Seriously, you look hot, cousin."

Tasha turned and stepped toward Darnell. She wrapped her arms around him and squeezed. "Thank you for the earrings."

"Don't thank me. Thank that tired queen I boosted them off of at the club last night."

"What?"

"Girl, I'm jokin'. Now, go on and get outta here before your toad turns into a frog."

Tirrell hurried out of the shower. He quickly dressed in a dark gray three-button suit that he'd left behind when he went off to basic training; it was a bit more fitted around the arms and thighs than it had been, but not too tight. He rubbed Egyptian musk oil in his hands, over his face, behind his ears, and down his neck as he crooned along with Jay-Z blaring from his CD player. Betty knocked at the door. He turned the music down.

"Come in."

She stepped into the room. "Well, look at you all handsome."

"Noonie, I thought you had to work late tonight."

"I got off a half hour ago. You headed out?"

"Me and Tasha are goin' to Bone's for her birthday."

"Her birthday? Lord, I forgot all about that. You smell nice." Betty adjusted the collar of Tirrell's open shirt. "You know, I wanna say somethin' to you. I know this ain't my business; I'm just gonna say it anyway. I like Tasha. I think she's a nice girl. But, I'm no fool. I was young once. I know how these things go."

"What things?"

"Hear me out. She may or may not be the girl you're gonna be with for the rest of your life. Just be careful. I don't wanna see either one of you get hurt."

"So, what brought all this on?"

"Like I said, I ain't no fool."

Tirrell smiled, acknowledging her insight, and kissed her cheek. "I got somethin' for you."

"For me?"

He took out his wallet and handed her $200.

"What's this for?"

"I got paid today."

"Tirrell."

"I'm not stayin' here for nothin'. And I'm not gonna leech off of you."

"Baby, you're not doin' that. I don't want your money. You need to take care of yourself."

"Please, Noonie. Let me do this." He embraced her and kissed her again. "After all, it's the least I could do for my best girl."

"I'm sure gonna miss you when you go back to North Carolina."

"Let's not talk about me leavin'. I just wanna enjoy bein' here while I can."

"But we've barely had time to talk between you workin' and my schedule, and all that time you spend at Tasha's."

Tirrell took his grandmother's hand. "I promise. We're gonna have some time together. Just you and me."

The look in Betty's eyes melted Tirrell's heart. He wanted to unburden himself, but this wasn't the time.

Subconsciously he'd stayed away to avoid saying anything at all—and then there was Kevin.

"I tell you what. I'm off tomorrow. Why don't we go somewhere and do somethin'?"

Betty cupped Tirrell's cheeks in her soft, warm hands and her eyes lit up. "I would really like that."

The doorbell rang and drew their attention toward the living room. Betty headed to the door and Tirrell lingered behind. He pulled a plastic pouch of cocaine from his pocket and snorted a quick line before shutting off the CD player and following her.

Betty greeted Tasha at the door with a hug. "Happy birthday, sweetheart."

"Thank you, Miss Betty."

"I'm sorry. I forgot. I'm gonna have to bake you a cake or somethin'."

"Red velvet?"

"Anything you want."

"The last time I took some of your cake home my cousin ate it before I could get to it."

"Now that's a mess. You tell your cousin that I said he better behave."

"I'll do that."

Tirrell came into the room, sniffing the residue of ecstasy. He grabbed Tasha and spun her around to show her off. She laughed.

Betty smiled. "I like that dress, Tasha. If I was twenty years younger and a hundred pounds lighter I might have to go out and find me one like it."

"Noonie, where would you go in a dress like this?"

"There are some things you don't know nothin' about, Tirrell Ellis. I used to have it goin' on. I still got a few tricks up my sleeve that I could dust off if I needed to."

They all got a laugh out of that.

"Y'all go on now." Betty waved to them as they darted out the door to the car. "Have a good time."

The upscale atmosphere of Bone's offered the perfect backdrop for Tasha's twenty-fifth. She ordered a Long Island Iced Tea and Tirrell ordered beer. Tasha glanced around excitedly, looking for the occasional local celebrity who was known to frequent the restaurant. She also anxiously waited for the gift from Tirrell that she dared not hope for.

"You look good, baby," he said.

"Thank you," she responded.

A female server approached the table. "Would you care for an appetizer?"

Tirrell glanced at the menu. "How about the shrimp cocktail?" He looked up at Tasha.

She nodded.

"Anything else to drink?"

"Not right now," Tasha said, sipping slowly.

"I'll have another beer," Tirrell requested.

The server turned away and Tirrell tried to catch a sly glimpse.

Tasha cleared her throat.

He adjusted himself. "She ain't got nothin' on you, baby."

Tasha didn't respond.

"I got somethin' for you." Tirrell reached into the pocket of his jacket.

Tasha held her breath. Her countenance almost fell when she saw the size of the box. She knew better than to expect it, but the box was too rectangular to be a ring. She forced a smile.

"Happy birthday." Tirrell leaned and kissed her softly.

Tasha picked up the box and slowly pulled at the silver-rose inlaid wrapping. "Did Miss Betty wrap this for you?"

"No. The saleslady at the mall did."

Tasha smiled as she opened the box to find the diamond tennis bracelet inside that she'd spied as they strolled through the mall together the previous week. It wasn't a ring, but she knew it was all his heart was disposed to give.

"I love it," she gushed.

They shared another kiss and he helped her snap the clasp around her wrist. She held out her hand to admire its sparkle as the candlelight danced and reflected from it. The server returned with his beer. He promptly sucked it down and excused himself to the restroom.

While Tasha sat gazing at the bracelet, a well-dressed man sidled up to the table.

"Hey, Tasha. What's happenin', baby?"

Tasha gasped when she looked up into his eyes. He flashed a wicked smile and without waiting for an invitation eased into Tirrell's seat. He took her hand and squeezed. She abruptly pulled away.

"Rickey, what are you doin' here?"

"I gotta eat, don't I?"

Tasha nervously looked around to see if Tirrell was headed back to the table.

The man eyed her as if she were an entree on the menu. "Damn, girl. You look good as hell."

"Rickey, you gotta go." She swallowed hard. "I . . . I'm here with somebody."

"Another man? Is that why I haven't heard from you? You know, I must've called and left you a half dozen messages, and I don't do that for most women. I looked for you around the gym, too. Are you purposely avoiding me?"

"No."

"You know you did something to me that nobody else has ever done."

"Please. That line is so tired."

"I'm serious. How can I prove it to you?"

The server returned with their appetizer and saw the man who sat next to Tasha. She arched her brow, noting that it wasn't Tirrell, and smirked. "Can I get you something from the bar?"

"No," Tasha blurted. "He's not staying."

"Would you like another Long Island?"

Tasha glared at the girl and she left the table.

The man took Tasha's hand again and continued. "So, who's this buster you're out with?"

"Rickey, I'm not kiddin'." Tasha snatched her hand away. "You have to go!"

The man scooped up one of the shrimp from the cocktail and popped it into his mouth. "Maybe I should just stick around and see who my competition is," he teased.

"Dammit, Rickey . . . we . . . I . . . ."

"Who the hell is this?"

Tasha jerked and turned to see Tirrell behind her. She closed her eyes and murmured, "Shit."

"Rickey Hicks," the man said as he stood and extended his hand to Tirrell for an introduction.

Tirrell ignored the man and turned to Tasha. "What the hell is goin' on?"

"Sorry, man. I didn't mean to interrupt—"

Tirrell turned sharply toward him and snapped, "I wasn't talkin' to you!"

"Fine. Tasha, baby, I'll call you later."

"Baby?" Tirrell sneered. "What the fuck do you mean you'll call her later?"

Tasha eased from her chair as Tirrell blocked the man from moving away from the table. She reached out to touch his arm. "Tirrell—"

"What do you mean you'll call her later?"

"Take it easy, dude," the man insisted. "I get it. It was just a one-time thing."

"A one-time . . . What the hell?"

In a fit of rage Tirrell grabbed the man by the collar and shoved him into a neighboring table. Drinks and plates of food flew up in the air as the couple seated jumped and ran for cover. Rickey Hicks stumbled to his feet as a male server rushed to his aid. Tasha tried to pull Tirrell away. He snatched his arm from her grasp.

"Get up, you son-of-a-bitch!"

Rickey stood, wiping bits of lettuce and pasta from his brow. Humiliated, he took a swing at Tirrell and hit him in the face. Tirrell's head snapped backward and he stepped back into the man, punching him in the stomach, causing him to double over and fall to his knees.

Chaos erupted. The restaurant manager hung up the phone after placing a call to the police and hurried to break up the fight. Tasha grabbed her purse and bolted for the door. Tirrell spun around and chased after her. The manager followed them out.

Once outside, Tasha handed her parking ticket to the valet and waited uneasily for her car.

Tirrell caught up to her. "You fucked him?"

"Get away from me, Tirrell."

The manager was dead on his heels. "Sir, you can't just leave like this."

Tirrell pushed the man away and grabbed Tasha just as the valet pulled up with her car. The manager took hold of Tirrell again, giving Tasha the opening she needed to jump in her car and speed off.

Tirrell knocked the man into some customers who were passing into the restaurant and took off running up the street.

8

It was after nine o'clock by the time Tirrell made it back to his grandmother's house. The repeated calls to Tasha rang directly to voice mail, which infuriated him all the more. He wanted answers.

Betty was asleep when he slipped into the house, found her car keys on the dining room table, and headed back out to Tasha's.

The security gate at her complex was down. He waited for someone to drive up and followed them in. The gate came down with a hard thud on the roof of the Grand Am—he kept going. Tasha's car was parked in front of her building. He parked on the other side of the lot and looked up to the second story and saw lights on in the apartment. He tried calling her again—voice mail. "Shit," he spat and pounded the steering wheel.

He jumped out of the car and started into the building as a car careened around the corner, the headlights blinded him.

It was Darnell. He'd rushed home after receiving Tasha's hysterical phone call. "What are you doin' here?" he yelled, pulling up alongside Tirrell.

"Mind your damn business, bitch!"

"Bitch? Tasha is my business, bitch!"

Tirrell stormed the building. Darnell threw his car into park and ran to block him before he could take to the stairs.

"You get the hell out of here right now before I call the police!"

The two stood and stared each other down. Sensing that Darnell wasn't relenting, Tirrell backed away. Darnell waited for Tirrell to get back into his car before continuing into the building to check on Tasha. As he turned the key in the lock, Tirrell snuck up behind him and pushed his way into the apartment. Tasha came running from her bedroom.

"Tasha, call the police," Darnell screamed.

"Tirrell, go home," Tasha demanded.

"Dammit, I'll call 'em myself."

Darnell reached for the phone. Tirrell yanked it from his hand and threw it against the wall.

"You crazy-ass bastard," Darnell spat. "See, Tasha, I knew you should have tossed this sorry muthafucka a long time ago."

Tasha intervened before the two could come to blows. "Get the hell out of here, Tirrell."

Tirrell pressed on. "Did you screw that guy at the restaurant or not?"

"Does it matter?"

"Hell yeah, it matters. You're the one always talkin' about how you love me all the time. What the hell, Tasha! I can't believe this."

"Why are you tryin' to act all innocent and wounded?" Tasha screamed. "It's a two-way street. You can have sex with whoever the hell you want to, but I can't."

Tirrell lunged at Tasha and grabbed her arms. Darnell attempted to jump between them and Tirrell elbowed him in the mouth.

"Get your hands off me, Tirrell. You don't own me. And you obviously don't wanna love me either!"

"Is that what this is about? 'Cause I can't tell you that I love you? I thought you understood. I thought we were makin' progress."

"What I finally understand is I deserve more. I've given up enough for you already. I'm not givin' up anything else."

"What the hell is that supposed to mean?"

Tasha jerked away and went to tend to Darnell.

"What do you mean you're not givin' up anything else?"

Darnell and Tasha exchanged looks.

"Time," Tasha insisted. "I thought I could wait, but I can't put up with your shit anymore. Just go home, Tirrell."

"So, how many other guys you been layin' up in here with behind my back?"

"You're such an asshole."

Tirrell started toward Tasha again and she ran to the kitchen and grabbed a frying pan from the stove.

"Get out of here. I mean it."

"I'll be damned," Tirrell spat, and left the apartment.

Darnell got up off the floor and secured the dead bolt on the door and then hurried to the window to make sure Tirrell was gone. Tasha sat shaking on the sofa, rocking back and forth, with her elbows on her knees and her face in her hands.

"I was gonna blurt it out." She sighed. "I almost told him, but I stopped myself."

Darnell picked up the discarded telephone and discovered the jack was broken. "Where's your cell phone?"

Tasha looked up. "In my purse. Why? What are you doin'?"

"I'm gonna call the police."

"No . . . don't. Just let it go."

Darnell snapped, "Are you shittin' me? After the way he busted up in here?"

Darnell looked at the pleading in Tasha's expression, rolled his eyes, and shook his head before proceeding into the kitchen. He took two glasses from the cupboard and filled them with ice and Jack Daniels.

"Here. Drink this."

"You didn't put any Coke in it."

"Honey, after what just went down you don't need no mixer. Drink it. Take it straight to the head."

Tasha put the glass to her lips and sipped slowly, grimacing at the taste.

Darnell noticed the glitter around her wrist. "Oooh, look at the bling."

"This is what he gave me."

"Who'd he steal it from?"

Tasha shot him a look and took another sip of her drink. The bitter taste waned.

"Not tellin' him was the right thing, cousin. No tellin' what that crazy bastard would've done. It wouldn't have helped anyway—especially now."

Tears streamed down Tasha's cheeks.

"If you tell me you love him I'm gonna take that fryin' pan and bust you in your damn head." He chuckled. "Ain't that much love in the world." Darnell wiped a trickle of blood from the corner of his mouth.

"Are you okay?"

"Yeah." He turned up his glass. "Tirrell never deserved you, cousin."

Tasha lifted her glass. "Helluva birthday."

Tasha knew that she needed to take a long hard look at herself, her lies, and the dishonesty that festered between them—deceit that she was as much a party to as he was. The truth was a knife that would cut both ways and she needed some redemption of her own.

***

Tirrell ended up in a bar not far from Tasha's complex. One after the other, he tossed back shots of tequila and chased them with beer.

"Yo, Bobby . . . it's Tirrell. I need some dust, man. I'm all out. Call me when you get this." Tirrell flipped his cell phone closed and slipped it into the inside pocket of his suit jacket. "Give me another one," he demanded of the bartender and slid his glass across the bar.

"I think you've had enough," the man shot back.

Tirrell looked up at the man's brawn and decided it best not to challenge him. "Fuck," he spat and lit another cigarette before climbing off the barstool. He steadied himself, but his inebriation was evident as he staggered to the exit.

The bartender called after him. "Hey, man, why don't you let me call you a cab?"

"I don't need a cab. I'm fine," Tirrell slurred and continued.

He fumbled with the car keys, dropping them a couple of times before unlocking the door and getting behind the wheel. He sat there for several minutes with the car running and the music blasting, and rolled down the windows. The sultry August air was stifling. He wrestled out of his jacket and tossed it on the seat next to him.

He flipped the cigarette to the pavement and peeled out of the parking lot. The car weaved between the lines on the street as he accelerated through a red light and merged on to the interstate. He didn't get far before the flash of sobering blue lights reflected off the car's back window. He glanced up into the rearview mirror. "Shit."

Waiting for an opening he eased off onto the shoulder. Already knowing what to expect, he reached for his wallet. A DeKalb County officer ambled up to the driver's-side window and a blinding burst of white light met Tirrell's gaze; he raised his hand against its harshness.

"License, registration, and proof of insurance," the officer barked.

Tirrell passed the officer his driver's license and leaned over to the glove compartment as he spied another patrol car approach.

"Don't shoot me. I'm just gettin' the registration," he said with his left hand raised in the air.

The officer shined his flashlight in the direction of the glove compartment, while another officer, who sidled up to the passenger side, flashed his light in a sweeping motion to examine the rest of the car.

The first officer looked at Tirrell's license and then shined the light back in his face. "North Carolina." He then read the registration. "Who's Betty Ellis?"

"My grandmother," Tirrell responded, looking away from the light.

"Does your grandmother know that you have her car?"

"Yeah, she knows."

"Have you been drinking tonight, sir?"

"I had a couple of beers."

"A couple of beers, huh?"

The officer then made a motion toward his holster, but didn't remove his weapon. "You want to step out of the car?"

Tirrell scoffed but remained compliant. A field sobriety test proved that he had more than just a few beers. He blew a .18 into the breathalyzer.

The second officer rounded the car and asked Tirrell to put his hands on the hood of the car as the first officer made a cursory inspection inside.

"C'mon, man," Tirrell implored while he was patted down. "I didn't do nothin'."

A few minutes later Tirrell found himself handcuffed and sitting in the back of a squad car, grateful that he at least didn't have cocaine in his possession.

While the second officer waited for the tow truck, the first officer radioed in the arrest.

"Ellis? There's an ADA down at the Fulton County Courthouse named Ellis. Kevin, I think it is. You any kin to him?"

Tirrell had a fleeting hope the association would curry favor with the officer. "He's my brother."

"No shit," the officer responded. "You older or younger than him?"

"Younger."

"I got a younger brother doin' time for armed robbery. Yours must be as proud of you as I am of mine, huh?"

Tirrell wanted to throw up and shut down the officer's cynicism, but then he'd just have to sit in it and he was already in enough mess.

9

"Hello . . . Tirrell . . . What?" Betty sluggishly sat up and threw her legs over the side of the bed, trying to focus. Her heart raced. She glanced at the clock on her bedside table—it was nearly four in the morning. She called Kevin immediately after ending the call with Tirrell.

Pat was startled awake by the ringing telephone. She poked Kevin and he barely budged, waving her away. She stretched across him to answer. Betty's fretful tone alarmed her more. She shoved Kevin and handed him the receiver.

Kevin barely opened his eyes. "Hello."

"Tirrell's been arrested."

He pulled himself up. "Noonie?"

"He just called. He was picked up by the DeKalb County police for driving drunk."

Kevin rubbed the sleep from his eyes and said nothing.

"Are you there, Kevin?"

"I'm here. What do you want me to do?"

"You have to go down there. You have to do somethin' to get him out."

"If he was stupid enough to drink and get caught driving maybe he should stay locked up."

"Kevin, that's your brother."

"He's not . . ." Kevin stopped before completing the protest that he knew Betty never wanted to hear him articulate.

"Kevin, you're an assistant DA. There ought to be somethin' you can do. Would you please go down there?"

He could hear the worry in his grandmother's voice, anguish that he'd come to expect when it came to her constantly coming to Tirrell's defense. It vexed him. Poor, misguided Tirrell.

"Kevin?"

"All right . . . all right. I'll see what I can do."

He hung up the telephone and sat with his legs drawn up to his bare chest, rubbing his face. Pat sat beside him with a look of consternation. She knew that there wasn't anything she could say that would help.

Seconds later he forced himself out of bed and lazily walked to the bathroom, pulling at his boxers. When he came back into the bedroom he was dressed in a pair of loose-fitting blue jeans and a button-down, cotton white shirt. He grabbed his sneakers and walked out of the room. As he drew closer to the landing at the top of the stairs he could hear Pat moving around in the kitchen.

She'd started a pot of coffee and looked up at him when he entered. He shook his head; his expression was all too readable. Tirrell was in trouble and it was up to her husband to fix it, no matter how much she knew he resented it. He was the eldest—the responsible one. He had an obligation.

He wrapped her in his arms and nuzzled her neck. "Thank you," he whispered.

She didn't have to ask why. She'd come to know him as well as anyone. All he needed was a little quiet understanding and support; that was her obligation.

After paying a visit to the nearest bail bondsman, Kevin arrived at the DeKalb Law Enforcement Center just after six in the morning. Tirrell was brought up from a holding cell while his paperwork was being signed off on. Buzzing releases and the clanking of steel doors echoed off the walls. Kevin walked up the corridor toward him, looking as if he could have pummeled him right then and there. Tirrell swallowed back shame and scratched the stubble on his face as he shifted nervously from side to side. Still reeling from the aftereffects of the alcohol in his system, he inhaled and exhaled slowly, preparing for the worst.

"He's all yours," the officer sneered.

Kevin shook his head and seethed. "Let's go."

Tirrell apprehensively followed Kevin out of the building to the parking lot. He rightly suspected that Kevin was in no mood to hear anything he had to say, and a half-assed apology wasn't going to cut it.

The anticipated verbal assault didn't come. Kevin just sat fuming behind the wheel of his Explorer. Tirrell didn't even dare breathe in his direction. Before pulling out of the parking lot of the DLEC, Kevin turned sharply toward Tirrell and clocked him in the eye. Tirrell's head smacked up against the passenger-side window.

"That's for all your shit!" Kevin barked.

Tirrell put his arm up to guard against another punch. His eyes watered as he delicately ran his fingers across what was sure to become one hell of a shiner.

"You feel better now?"

"Not by a long shot."

"You wanna hit me again?"

Kevin glared at him and kept driving. "Truthfully, I want to beat the hell out of you. I'm taking you back to Noonie's. Maybe you can come up with a viable explanation as to why you're such a colossal fuckup by the time we get there."

Tirrell lay back on the headrest, keeping a watchful eye on Kevin just in case his fist decided to fly his way again.

Betty was standing in the door waiting when they pulled up outside the house.

"Get out," Kevin demanded as he turned off the ignition.

Tirrell did as he was told. Kevin got out too. Betty threw open the door and held it for them. There it was; Tirrell could see the disappointment in her face. It made him feel just as bad as he did whenever he'd let her down before. The words "I'm sorry" dissolved further into triviality before they could even pass his lips.

"What happened, Tirrell?"

He couldn't look at her. He sank down on the sofa, propped his elbows on his knees, and planted his face in his hands. Moments of noisy silence passed before he whispered, "I messed up. Me and Tasha were at the restaurant and some dude she'd been messin' around with stepped to her and I lost it."

Kevin stood, leaning on the wall near the door with his hands in his pockets, eagerly waiting to hear the rest of Tirrell's justification.

Betty eased down in a wing-back chair facing him. "What does that mean? Did you do somethin' to her?"

"No. I didn't hurt her . . . physically anyway. I came home and you were asleep, so I took the car and went to her place. We got into it. I said some stuff I probably shouldn't have said, and then I went to this bar and had a few too many drinks."

Betty reached out and touched his face. "What happened to your eye?"

Tirrell glanced up at Kevin and turned away. "Got it from a fight."

"Oh, baby."

"See, that's the problem," Kevin interjected. "He's not a baby and you need to stop treating him like one."

Betty looked at Kevin. "What's gonna happen to him now?"

"He's got thirty days before he has to go to court. He could have his license suspended. If he gets into anything else between now and then he could go to jail."

She turned back to Tirrell. "How is this gonna affect you goin' back to Fort Bragg?"

Tirrell swallowed nervously. "I guess I'm gonna have to call my sergeant and tell him what happened."

Kevin scoffed and pushed away from the wall. "I'm going to go and see about getting your car out of impound."

"You're probably going to need me to go with you."

"No, Noonie. I'll take care of it."

"You won't be able to drive two cars, Kevin. If you wait a few minutes I can put some clothes on and go with you."

"Fine. I'll be outside."

"Why don't you wait in here where it's cool? I won't be long."

"I need to call Pat and tell her what's happened."

"Can't you call her from in here?"

Kevin cut his eyes at Tirrell. "No."

Betty got up and went over to where he was standing. "Kevin, thank you for what you did."

"We're family, right? We got to look out for each other."

The sentiment hung in the air like the heat of the arid summer day. Even as Kevin said the words Tirrell could hear the loathing.

"I'll get dressed and I'll be right out."

When Kevin left, Betty went back over to Tirrell and gently rested her hand on his shoulder. "Lord, have mercy, boy. What am I gonna do with you?"

10

After a long shower and barely two hours' sleep, Tirrell was up again. Betty hadn't returned; she was undoubtedly still with Kevin trying to clean up after him, again.

Tirrell needed to make himself useful and at the same time stay close to the house to avoid any more problems. The yard was in need of attention. He slipped into a pair of ratty blue jeans and a T-shirt and went to a small shed at the back of the house where he found a lawn mower; it would be a decent atonement.

Sweat drenched his shirt as the blaze of the afternoon sun beat down on him. He pulled it off and used it as a damp towel to wipe his brow. He began to have second thoughts about taking on this chore. He was dehydrated from the alcohol and the heat wasn't making the nausea he felt any better. He turned up a plastic gallon container of water to quench his thirst and decided to tough it out. His glistening biceps and pectorals inspired more than a number of looks from passersby who drove up and down the street, but all he could think about was Tasha.

Just as he finished the yard and started to return the mower to the shed, Betty drove up in her car with a back seat full of groceries. He ran to greet her and helped carry the bags inside the house.

"Look at you." She smiled.

"It was the least I could do," he responded.

"The yard looks really nice."

"I'm gonna pay you back the money you spent gettin' your car back, too."

"You don't need to do that, Tirrell."

"Yes, I do."

"Here. Your jacket was still in the car." She passed it to him.

His cell phone rang just as he finished unloading the groceries. It was Bobby. He stole away to his bedroom to take the call. Bobby told him that he had what he was looking for; Tirrell was relieved to hear it.

"I can't meet you right now. I'm doin' some stuff for my grandmother."

"How long will that take?"

"Why don't I call you tonight?"

"I was under the impression you wanted something now."

"I do. I just can't get away yet. My grandmother usually goes to bed around ten o'clock. I'll call you after that." He hung up the phone and grabbed a dry T-shirt before he went back into the kitchen, where Betty was munching on a Moon Pie.

"Was that Tasha on the phone?"

"Uh . . . yeah. I told her that I would call her later." An easy lie in a string of lies.

"Is she all right?"

"Uh . . . yeah."

"Are you all right?"

"I'm good, Noonie. Can I have one of those?" he asked, pointing at her treat.

"You sure can," she said. "Wash your hands first."

Tirrell started to the kitchen sink.

"Not in here," Betty chided. "You know better than that."

He went to the bathroom and cleaned up. He then came back to the kitchen and pulled a Moon Pie from the open box on the counter and gnawed on it like a half-starved urchin.

"Baby, why don't you let me fix you some lunch?"

"I got a better idea." He smiled. "Why don't I take you out to eat?"

"Why would you wanna go out with all this food in the house?"

"Because I want to treat you."

"Tirrell."

"C'mon, it'll be fun. Just the two of us like I promised."

She couldn't say no.

Tirrell took another shower and then he and Betty went for lunch at a restaurant that just happened to be close to the salon where Tasha worked. Betty smiled, knowing full well why he wanted to drive so far out of the way. He was disheartened not to see her car parked outside.

"At least she called you," Betty said. "So you know she wants to see you."

Tirrell absorbed the sting of his earlier lies and went on to enjoy all the salad, pasta, and breadsticks he could handle.

After they ate, Betty reached across the table and patted Tirrell's hand. "It's all gonna work out. You'll see."

"Noonie, I have to tell you somethin'—"

Their server interrupted. "Did you folks save room for dessert?"

"No, Lord," Betty chuckled. "I couldn't eat another thing."

Tirrell shook his head and agreed.

The server laid the bill on the table. "I'll take that whenever you're ready." He turned to leave.

"What did you want to tell me, baby?"

Tirrell sucked down the remainder of his soda and cleared his throat. "Nothin'. I just wanted to thank you."

On the way home Betty asked to stop by Kevin's to give him the money he'd given her earlier that she knew he wouldn't take back. Her transparency was obvious.

"Noonie," Micah screamed as he jumped off his bicycle and ran to her car when it pulled up in the driveway.

She got out of the car and swept him up in her arms. Pat came out of the house to welcome them.

"Hey, Miss Betty. C'mon in." Pat offered Tirrell a wry smile but didn't say anything to him.

"Uncle Tirrell, you wanna come and play my new video game?" Micah asked.

Tirrell looked at Pat, silently asking for permission. Pat looked at Betty and then nodded to him. He lifted the boy up on his shoulders and proceeded up to his room.

Pat and Betty settled in the living room.

"Can I get you something to drink, Miss Betty?"

"No, baby. We just came from eating lunch. I'm stuffed and I drank way too much sweet tea. I just wanted to come by and see Kevin."

"I'm not sure when he'll be back, but you're welcome to wait."

They both turned toward the direction of the stairs as Tirrell and Micah's cheering and laughter drew their attention.

"I wish he could laugh like that with his brother," Betty remarked sadly.

"Maybe you shouldn't push them, Miss Betty. Certain things just aren't meant to be."

"I can't believe that. Those boys are family."

"And they've never gotten along. After all this time they can't even stand to be in the same room for too long without bein' at each other's throats. Kevin and Tirrell are a lot like Cain and Abel, and you know what happened between the two of them."

Kevin crept into Tirrell's bedroom and rifled through his bureau drawers, unsure of what he was looking for, but certain there was something to be found. Weeks had passed with Tirrell comfortably settling back into all of their lives and the thought of him having to wait another thirty days to make a court appearance barely registered concern. In Kevin's estimation, something was amiss.

He found a duffel bag tucked away in the back of the closet and pulled it out. He emptied the contents on the floor (a pair of boots, a fatigue jacket, and a few camouflage T-shirts). He searched the pockets of the bag and found the envelope that contained evidence of Tirrell's subterfuge. Kevin sat back on his haunches and read the documents inside.

When Betty and Tirrell returned, Kevin was waiting for them. Betty was laughing at some joke that Micah's young mind found funny. Something that he apparently didn't understand was more adult than he could handle. They found Kevin sitting at the dining table. Tirrell instantly recognized what he was holding. He froze with trepidation and anger.

"What the hell?" Tirrell snapped.

"Noonie, I'll bet you'll never guess what this is." Kevin sounded very much like a satisfied child who'd just caught another in a lie.

Tirrell lurched toward him. "What were you doin' in my room?"

Kevin jumped up from his chair and danced around the table to keep the envelope away from him.

"What in the world is goin' on?" Betty demanded.

"This is the real reason your *baby* came home," Kevin spat.

"You son-of-a-bitch!"

"Tirrell!" Betty shrieked.

"He shouldn't have been in my room," Tirrell continued.

"Kevin?"

"He lied to us, Noonie. He's not on any kind of leave. His sorry ass was thrown out of the Army." Kevin tossed the papers on the table in front of her. "It's all right there."

Tirrell lunged at him, knocking him to the floor, and started wailing on him.

"Stop it," Betty screamed. "Stop it right now."

Unfazed, Kevin and Tirrell rolled around on the floor, exchanging punches and bumping into things. Betty ran into the kitchen and grabbed a broom. She rushed back into the room and beat them with it until they tired out and separated.

"I don't know what the hell is goin' on, but I'm not gonna have this disrespect in my house," she shouted. "I'm sick of both of you actin' like . . . like hooligans. Now get up and stop all this foolishness, do you hear me?"

It took a lot to make Betty Ellis angry, and rarely did she swear, but when she did, you knew you'd crossed the line.

Kevin pulled himself up off the floor, righted a chair, and eased down into it. Tirrell stood up and snatched his papers off the table.

Betty composed herself and put down the broom. "Tirrell, what is goin' on?"

"Tell her," Kevin barked.

"Hush, Kevin," Betty commanded.

Silence ticked away at Tirrell's resolve. "I got discharged."

"Tell her why."

"Kevin, I said hush."

Tirrell heaved, catching his breath. "I got a dishonorable. I got into a fight with this other private and he ended up in the infirmary."

"Oh, my Lord." Betty sighed.

"He came after me with a knife," Tirrell continued. "I had to protect myself. They gave me a choice between gettin' locked up or leavin' the Army altogether, so I left."

"See, Noonie? It's a pattern with him. He starts stuff and then takes the easy way out. They should have locked your ass up!"

Betty cut her eyes. "Kevin Ellis, I'm not gonna tell you again, hear?"

"I should've told you," Tirrell cried. "I was embarrassed 'cause I didn't wanna let you down again—that seems like all I ever do. All I wanted was for you to be proud of me."

"Yeah, gettin' a DUI and gettin' kicked out of the Army tends to inspire a whole lot of pride. Poor baby," Kevin sneered.

Betty rubbed her hands on her face and through her hair, taking a minute to absorb the extent of what she'd witnessed between the two brothers. She thought about what Pat said earlier in regard to Cain and Abel, and feared that she was right regarding the hostility that existed between them.

"You don't have to worry about me causin' you any more trouble," Tirrell said quietly. "I'll get my stuff and leave. I never should've come back in the first place."

Defeated, he went to his room and closed the door behind him.

Betty moved to the table and pulled out a chair next to Kevin. He couldn't look at her. He turned his eyes downward toward his hands. His fingers interlocked and his forearms rested on his thighs. Betty reached out and tilted his chin up to meet her gaze.

"Look at me. Look at me, Kevin. You're a grown man. I've asked you time and again to stop treatin' your brother like he's the enemy. I can't make you do it, you have to want to. And I guess that's my fault for pushin'. You're still angry with your father. In a lot of ways I can understand that. Are you angry with me too?"

Kevin's eyes welled up. He cleared his throat and batted back tears. "No. I'm not."

"Then why can't you let this go?"

"I don't know why. Every time I look at Tirrell . . . I can't stop hating him."

"Kevin."

"I'm sorry, but it's true. I hate him and I hate Daddy for what he did to us. I can't forgive him. I won't."

"Kevin, you have to, otherwise, this thing is gonna continue to eat at you until there's nothing left."

"Before he died I told him I hated him. We got in a huge fight that year before I went back to school, and I never got the chance to make it right."

Betty took Kevin in her arms. "Junior knew you loved him. You have to find a way to get some peace out of this and forgive yourself. Punishin' Tirrell won't make you feel any better, and it won't take your pain away."

Kevin dried his eyes and abruptly stood up. "I gotta go."

Betty reached out and took his hand. "He's your brother, and he's hurtin' too."

Kevin slowly eased his hand out of Betty's and hurried out the door. She closed her eyes and sighed heavily before getting up and starting to Tirrell's room. She could hear the clanking of hangers and the clash of drawers being opened and closed. She knocked.

He didn't answer.

"Tirrell, I wanna talk to you. Can I come in?"

The noise inside the room ceased. There was an extended pause before the door opened. She peered inside to see clothes strewn on the bed and half sticking out of his duffel bag. He continued pulling his things out of the closet.

"I don't want you to go," Betty said, easing into the room. "This is your home."

Tirrell stopped moving but he didn't turn to face her. Betty moved up behind him and gently rubbed his back.

"When I found out that your father had another child I was as shocked as anybody. I knew what he did affected Kevin and Jacqui. It wasn't fair to them and it wasn't fair to you. But, I fell in love with you from the minute I saw you. Head full of hair and fat little legs and cheeks. You were such a beautiful little boy. And despite a few bumps in the road, you're a fine young man. You're a handful, there's no denyin' that, full of piss and vinegar, but I never once stopped lovin' you. All I ever hoped for you and Kevin and Jacqui was for you all to get along. And I pray to God that I'm still here to see that happen one day."

Tirrell slowly turned, his hazel eyes stained red with tears and embarrassment. He embraced his long-suffering grandmother. Her touch, her love, these were his lifelines. He wanted to be a better person just because she believed he could be.

***

Later, after Betty had gone off to bed and he'd put his room back in order, Tirrell slipped outside and sat on the front stoop to have a smoke. His thoughts glazed over with all the many things that he wanted to say to his grandmother and what was left unsaid between him and Tasha. Perhaps, now that his disposition from the Army was out in the open, he could make a fresh go of it. He thought maybe he would start with church—he knew Betty would like that.

His cell phone rang as he squashed the butt of the cigarette under his heel and flicked it out into the street. It was Bobby. He wiped his hand over his mouth, recalling the sensation that the cocaine had given him. His pulse quickened. Should he respond to the growing desire, or should he steer clear of temptation? The decision was made for him when the ringing stopped—there was no voice mail. He quickly dismissed the notion of calling Bobby back, and got up and went into the house. This was a call better left unanswered.

11

To his surprise, Tirrell had awakened before his grandmother. He found a nice pair of dark blue slacks and a complementary shirt to wear and went on to the bathroom. When he stepped out of the shower he heard Betty in the kitchen. Steam gushed out when he opened the bathroom door and he could smell coffee brewing. With his towel wrapped around him, he walked into kitchen—the soles of his feet leaving damp prints on the hardwood floor.

"Good morning," he said enthusiastically, kissing her on the cheek.

"Good morning." Betty smiled and turned away from the oven. "What are you doin' up so early?"

"It's Sunday, ain't it? I thought I'd go to church with my best girl." Tirrell opened the cupboard and reached in for a Moon Pie. "I'm gonna go put my clothes on."

"Well, now. Ain't that somethin'." Betty couldn't keep from smiling. She didn't want to make too much of the gesture, but she was thrilled that he was making the effort.

Tirrell could hear her singing as he dressed. It made him happy that he could make her smile after he was sure he'd broken her heart the day before.

He could see the Crawl house from his bedroom window. He spotted Marquis's '95 Sedan de Ville De Ville and figured that he was escorting his mother, Anne, to church as well. With the exception of the requisite

Christmas, Mother's Day, and Easter services, Tirrell hadn't been to church much since his grandfather died. He chuckled when he thought about how he and Marquis used to cut up as kids. He mischievously looked forward to what the day might bring.

As Betty dressed, Tirrell went to the kitchen and filled up on sausage, biscuits, gravy, and scrambled eggs. Marquis didn't attend church regularly either, but as he ate Tirrell called him to ensure he would be there.

Decked out in a lavender two-piece skirt suit, Betty sat near the front of the sanctuary next to Anne Crawl. Pat and Micah sat a row behind them; Kevin was conspicuously absent. Tirrell and Marquis, thick as thieves, hung near the back. Throughout the opening of the service Marquis childishly taunted Tirrell about his night with Tasha. It didn't sit well with him, especially since the night ended with his arrest.

"Did she give you that black eye?" Marquis teased.

Now was not the time or place for Tirrell to share all the sordid details.

Marquis spied a young woman across the aisle who he'd been intimate with, and brazenly whispered his conquest to Tirrell. They laughed out loud. An older woman sitting in front of them turned around and shushed them. Tirrell pressed his lips together to squelch his amusement. When they were asked to stand for prayer, an usher navigated up the aisle to help latecomers find seats; Tasha was among them. Marquis poked Tirrell in the side and pointed. Tirrell's demeanor changed. He slapped Marquis's hand away. Whether she had seen him he couldn't say; she didn't acknowledge him.

The choir sang. The preacher preached, but Tirrell remained focused on Tasha. After the benediction he quickly excused himself from Marquis and pressed through the throng of parishioners to get to her. When she spotted him she looked away and tried to go toward another exit.

"Tasha," he yelled, pushing in the opposite direction of the flow of people. She had to have heard him.

"I smell trouble," Marquis said from behind him.

Tirrell turned and scowled.

Betty and Anne made their way over to let them know that since neither of them had prepared anything for dinner, this would be a good time to go out to eat. Tirrell didn't argue. He would find a way to talk to Tasha later.

Pat walked in the house to find Kevin slouched on the sofa in front of the television, with his bare feet propped up on the coffee table, munching on potato chips. Unshaven and unwashed, he had on a pair of pajama bottoms and a loose-fitting T-shirt, which was an indication to her that he'd probably been in that same spot most of the morning.

Micah climbed into his father's lap and reached his hand inside the greasy bag.

"Uh huh," Pat chided. "You're gonna mess up your clothes and ruin your dinner." She took the bag out of Kevin's hands. "Go on upstairs and change."

Micah pouted and poked out his lips.

Kevin picked him up and sat him down on the floor, patting him on the rear. "Go on and do what your mother said. Come back down when you're done."

Micah stuffed the chips in his hand into his mouth and darted up the stairs. Kevin snatched the potato chips back from Pat. She chuckled.

"I should make you go up there and change your clothes too."

"How was church?"

"You'd know if you had gone," she snapped.

"Did you see Noonie?"

"Yes, and I saw Tirrell, too."

Kevin ignored her and turned up the television volume. Pat took the television remote from his hand and clicked it off.

"What are you doing? I was watching that."

"Don't act like you didn't hear me, Kevin."

"Give me back the remote."

"No."

"I'm serious, girl. Quit playin'."

Pat laughed and ran toward the kitchen. "You want it, come and get it."

Kevin smirked, jumped up from the sofa, and chased after her. He trapped her up against the sink and they playfully grappled for the remote. He tickled her until she surrendered.

"You've been smokin', haven't you?" Pat observed.

"I had one cigarette."

"Kevin, you said you were gonna stop."

"I just had one and I didn't smoke it in the house."

"Kevin."

"You know how I get when I'm stressed."

"Stressed about what?"

"Tirrell. What else?" Kevin leaned on the island in the center of the room and folded his arms. "I found out why he's really here. He was booted out of the Army for fighting."

"What? Did he tell you that?"

"No. I found out on my own."

"How?"

"I knew he was hiding something, so I went over to Noonie's and looked through his stuff. I found his discharge papers."

"Kevin, no, you didn't."

"I feel pretty shitty about it."

"Well, you should. You wouldn't want anyone scrounging through your personal stuff."

"He lied, baby. He lied to all of us."

"So, that gave you the right to do what you did?"

Kevin scratched his beard. "We had a fight—right in front of Noonie. I was just so damn mad. I just wanted to hurt him."

"Kevin."

"You should have seen the way Noonie looked at me. All this time I felt like he was the outcast. Maybe it was me all along."

Pat sighed and stepped between Kevin's legs and hugged him. "Baby, you are not an outcast. But, you can afford to be the bigger man."

"The bigger man would avoid the conflict all together and just stay away from him."

"And what exactly will that solve? Are you just gonna stay away from Miss Betty, too?"

Kevin shook his head.

"You're bound to see each other, especially if he's stayin' in town. You may as well find a way to deal with him."

"Maybe we should move to California. Micah could be closer to Mama."

"I hope that's a joke. I like your mother, but having her on the other side of the country works just fine for me."

Kevin buried his face in Pat's shoulder and held her tightly. "I'm never gonna do to you and Micah what my father did to me. I promise you that."

"I know you won't." Pat laughed as she pulled away and picked up a paring knife on the counter. "Because if you ever do I'm gonna cut your nuts off."

12

Tirrell was eager to see Tasha. When he and Betty returned home he tried to convince her to let him borrow the car to go and see her. Given his DUI and pending court date she was naturally reticent.

"Please, Noonie, please. I promise I'll be careful. I'll go and I'll come right back."

"You know I can't do that."

"Then can you drive me over there?"

"Tirrell."

"Please, Noonie. Please. I swear I'll be extra careful. I have to see her."

After several minutes of seeing Tirrell sulk, Betty relented and handed him the keys. "No drinking. You go and you come straight back, you hear me?"

He heartily embraced her and dashed out the door. En route his cell phone rang—it was Bobby again.

"Man, I called you last night. I thought we were gonna hook up."

"Yeah . . . sorry about that. Somethin' came up at the last minute."

"Well, look . . . you want the stuff or not?"

Tirrell licked his lips and his jaws clenched as if he'd sucked on a lemon.

"T, you there, man?"

"Yeah."

"So, you ridin' through or what?"

Tirrell blew a cleansing breath. "Naw, I think I'm gonna pass."

"Man, you bullshittin'."

"Sorry, Bobby. I gotta go."

The security gate was up at Tasha's complex and Tirrell drove right through. He saw her car parked in front of the building, and thankfully Darnell's was not. With his eyes shielded behind a dark pair of sunglasses, he climbed the stairs to her apartment. He knocked and waited. He could hear her moving on the other side of the door, but she didn't answer.

"Tasha, please. Open the door. I know you're in there. I'm not drunk," he teased. "C'mon, baby. Open the door. We need to talk. You heard the reverend this mornin'. Love your neighbor like you love yourself." That was nowhere near what the pastor preached, but he wasn't really listening.

After what seemed like forever, the door opened. "No gas station flowers?" Tasha cracked.

"Can I come in? Please?"

She stepped away from the door. Tirrell apprehensively entered and closed it behind him.

"You looked really good this mornin'." He smiled.

She pulled at her bathrobe uncomfortably and pushed her hair away from her eyes. "What do you want?"

"I want to apologize for the way things went down the other night. I'm sorry I ruined your birthday. I wanna make it up to you if you give me another chance."

"I've given you a million chances, Tirrell. We're not gettin' anywhere. I don't wanna keep ridin' this merry-go-round. I messed up. God knows you messed up. I was tryin' to convince myself that someday . . . I finally woke the hell up and realized that this situation was not gonna get any better. I need what you can't give me, and I don't want to settle anymore."

Tasha went to the bedroom, and when she returned she had a box of his things he'd left behind.

"Baby, c'mon, don't do this."

"I should've done it a long time ago."

"Okay . . . I love you," he exclaimed. "I love you. Is that what you want me to say?"

"No. Don't you get it? If you don't mean it, saying the words isn't enough. Just take your stuff and go."

Tirrell sneered and snatched the box. "When did it start?"

"What?"

"You and this other dude. When did it start?"

"There is no *other dude,* Tirrell."

"Didn't seem that way to me."

"What difference does it make now?"

"He's the real reason you wanna end this, right?"

"No, Tirrell. You are."

"Where did you meet him?"

"Why?"

"Because I want to know."

Tasha sighed. "We met at the gym."

"The gym? Did you screw here or at his place?"

"That's none of your business."

"It is my business."

Tasha turned toward the window and paused before answering. "It was just one time, that's all."

Tirrell threw the box of his belongings on the floor. He violently yanked Tasha by the arms. She yelped.

"So, you been lyin' to me all this time, huh?"

"Let go," she said through clenched teeth.

"No, not until we settle this."

"It is settled. We're done."

She tried to pull away. He held fast.

"You're hurtin' me."

"You gotta listen to me."

"What are you gonna do, Tirrell? Huh?"

He backed her up against the wall. His rage was palpable.

"See, this is why I didn't wanna . . ."

"You didn't wanna what, Tasha?"

"Nothing."

"You didn't want to what?"

Tears burned hot in her eyes. Her lips trembled. It was time for the truth, no matter how painful.

"I didn't wanna have your baby."

It was as if he'd been hit in the throat. The shock of what she said ripped through him like knives. He shook her. "What are you talkin' about? Tell me or I swear I'll—"

"You'll what, Tirrell? Hit me? Push me out the window? What?"

He shoved her away and sank down on the sofa. "Is this what you meant when you said you weren't givin' up any more of yourself? Are you pregnant?"

"No," she whimpered.

He looked up at her. "Were you pregnant?"

She closed her eyes and cried, "You weren't any more ready to bring a baby into this madness than I was."

He pressed his fingers to his eyes to keep from crying. "What did you do?"

"I found out I was pregnant when I came back from visiting you in January."

"You got an abortion?"

"I wasn't sure what I was gonna do."

"Did you get an abortion?"

"I was scared. I made a mistake."

"Answer me, dammit!"

"Yes!"

"It was just that easy."

"Hell no, it wasn't easy. But it was what I had to do."

"You just made the decision all by yourself. You didn't think I needed to know. You didn't think I wanted to have a say?"

"Can you honestly tell me that you would have wanted to have a baby?"

"You didn't give me a chance, Tasha."

"You were in the Army. You could have been deployed. You could have been killed. I may never have seen you again. You never wrote. You hardly called. What was I supposed to do?"

"You could have told me. You could have let me decide whether I wanted to be a father." He sprang up and she shrank back. "How can you tell me that you love me after doin' some shit like that? And to top it off you messed around with some other dude."

"You slept around too."

"But I never said I loved you, and it's a damn good thing I didn't! How do I know it was even my baby?"

"Because you were the only one I was with when it happened."

He laughed at the irony. "Damn."

"Tirrell, I'm sorry."

"Yeah, you sorry all right."

"I didn't mean for—"

"You know what, fuck you, Tasha!"

With that he picked up the box of his stuff and stormed out. He jumped in the car and tore out of the parking lot.

Learning that Tasha took it upon herself to have an abortion was not what he needed to hear. If he had second thoughts about getting high they were gone. Betty called him, but he didn't answer. He couldn't talk to her now.

***

Tirrell circled the block a few times before finding a parking space outside Bobby's Midtown apartment. Once he got inside he discovered why it had been hard to find a parking spot. He could hear the music pumping—vibrating the walls.

"Yo, T. I thought you wasn't comin'."

"Yeah, so did I."

Bobby threw his beefy arm around Tirrell's neck—a glass of Patrón sloshed around in his free hand. "C'mon in. Join the party."

Tirrell offered no resistance. He licked his lips and wiped his mouth with heady anticipation.

"Yo, dude, Crystal is here—somewhere."

"Crystal?"

"You don't remember Crystal?" He held his hands out from his chest signifying her attributes.

Tirrell recalled the blonde he'd awakened next to when he and Bobby had gone out a few weeks earlier.

"Damn, what happened to your eye?"

"Nothin'." Tirrell remembered the sunglasses in his shirt pocket and slipped them on.

"You gotta go into the kitchen and fix yourself a drink." He tapped his index finger on the side of his nose. "And there's plenty of dust."

Tirrell didn't feel like partying. "Look, Bobby. I just wanna get the stuff and go, a'ight?"

"C'mon, man. You can hang out for a minute."

"No," Tirrell insisted. "I'm serious. I can't stay."

The man scratched his bald pate. "Okay, let's take care of business."

Tirrell followed Bobby to his bedroom, where a couple of his guests sought privacy. A woman had her blouse off and the man she was with snorted cocaine from her exposed breasts. They were surprised by Bobby's abrupt entrance. The woman grabbed her blouse from the bed to cover herself and the man leapt to his feet, buttoning his shirt and zipping up his pants. Bobby nodded toward the door and they hastily exited the room.

He closed the door and locked it behind them, something the couple had forgotten to do. He then proceeded into a closet. Tirrell tried to see what he was doing. Bobby threw a sharp look over his shoulder and Tirrell turned around to face the opposite direction. This room, like the rest of the apartment, was decorated in such fashion to bring into question exactly what Bobby did to make a living. Selling drugs was the obvious answer, Tirrell surmised; after all, that's why he was there. He took note of the primitive African masks that adorned the walls, examining them as if he were in a museum.

"They're prosperity masks," Bobby said as he stepped up beside Tirrell. "This one is from Nigeria."

"Do they work?" Tirrell asked.

"Look around. You tell me."

Bobby handed a packet to Tirrell, and Tirrell reached in his pocket for money.

"Is this all you want?"

"For now," Tirrell replied. "Sorry I can't stay. Maybe next time." Tirrell opened the door and headed for the exit, hoping to avoid Crystal altogether.

It had been a long day. He sat in the car in the driveway of his grandmother's house, staring at the powdered substance in his hand. He was beginning to feel the profound effect of the loss of a baby he didn't know he wanted. Tasha may have unburdened her soul, but this would be yet another weight he'd carry for the rest of his life. He opened the plastic pouch and tapped a bit of cocaine on his closed fist and snorted. A sudden and unexpected wave of emotion gushed forth from the pit of his stomach, causing him to cry out. He could feel the darkness closing in around him. After several minutes, emotionally depleted, he gathered himself and went into the house. He hadn't expected to find Betty still awake.

He quietly opened the door, slipped off his shoes, and tiptoed across the hardwood floor. He then slumped down on the sofa, set his box aside, and laid his head back. A light switched on from the back room.

"I thought I heard you come in," Betty said.

"Noonie. I thought you'd be asleep."

"And I thought you'd be back with my car hours ago."

"I'm sorry. I didn't get stopped or nothin'. It's just that me and Tasha . . ."

"You and Tasha what?"

Tirrell wiped his hand over his face. "It's late. I'm tired and I really don't feel like talkin' about it right now, okay?"

Maternal instinct kicked in when Betty looked at the distress in his eyes. "Tirrell, what happened with Tasha?"

He shook his head and teared up.

Betty looked down at the box next to his feet. "What's all this?"

"Stuff I picked up from Tasha's. It's over. We're done. For good this time."

Betty moved to him and wrapped her arms around him.

"She killed my baby."

"What?"

"She was pregnant, and she had an abortion without tellin' me."

"Oh, Lord no."

"Yeah, your little *nice* girl turned out not to be so nice after all. And you were worried about me hurtin' her."

Betty held on to him as he mourned. It was the first time she felt his heart break since his mother died, and it broke hers too.

It had been two days since Tirrell discovered that Tasha had an abortion. He hadn't gone to work and Betty hadn't forced the issue. She crept quietly around the house, making sure she had everything she needed. After collecting her purse and keys she hustled into the kitchen for her thermos of coffee. Tirrell was there and dressed in his uniform.

"Can you drop me off at the garage?"

"Baby, are you sure you're feelin' up to it?"

"I'm fine." Tirrell inhaled deeply to ensure the maximum effect of the cocaine he'd ingested before coming into the kitchen.

"You don't look fine," Betty noted.

Tirrell discerned the pinched concern in Betty's expression, and kissed her cheek in a vain effort to reassure her that he was better than he let on. "I don't wanna talk about Tasha anymore, a'ight? What she did was really foul. But, maybe it was for the best. I don't know that I could have been any kind of father."

"I can't say whether it was for the best. I'm just sorry that she hurt you."

"I'm dealin' with it."

Betty took Tirrell's hand and gave it a squeeze. "You know I'm here for you."

"I know. But, I just need to process right now. Is that okay?"

She nodded and smiled.

"Tirrell, what the hell are you doin'?" Marquis shouted.

"What?"

"You were gettin' ready to put oil in that radiator."

"Oh, shit," Tirrell spat, realizing his mistake. "I must've grabbed the wrong hose." He immediately righted himself and checked to make sure that he hadn't spilled any oil.

"What's wrong with you, man?"

"Nothin'. I'm just a little distracted."

Marquis recognized the look in Tirrell's eyes. "Man, you high as hell."

"No, I'm not."

Marquis grabbed him by the arm and spun him around. "Yes, you are. I can see it."

Tirrell yanked his arm back and threw the funnel down that he was holding. "Get off me, man."

"T, what's up with you, man?"

Tirrell looked around to see who was in earshot. Drills, hydraulic lifts, and jacks distributed enough noise to keep anyone from overhearing. "Tasha had an abortion."

"Get the fuck outta here. Tasha? It was yours, right?"

"I don't know. Maybe."

"What do you mean *maybe?*"

"She said it was mine, but I found out she was screwin' this dude while I was in North Carolina."

"Who was it?"

"I don't know him."

"Damn."

"He showed up the other night when we were at Bone's, all friendly and shit."

"So, he gave you that black eye?"

"Hell no. I kicked his ass. Tasha got pissed and left me at the restaurant, so I went to a bar and had a little too much to drink."

"So, what happened?

"I got arrested for DUI."

"Damn, T."

"Whatever you do, you can't tell your pops. I can't afford to lose this job."

"Then you need to get your shit together, man. You can't be comin' up in here high every day. That just ain't cool."

"I know," Tirrell said, properly contrite. "It won't happen again. I swear."

Coke, flake, girl, dust, blow, toot, snow. It didn't matter what it was called, or how he may have thought he could handle it. The insidious lure of cocaine was pulling him closer to the edge and that was the most dangerous place for someone like Tirrell Ellis to be.

13

"Travis, it's Alex . . . Did the caterers call? Do they have what I asked for? Are they going to have them on time or not? Look, call them back and tell them if they don't want me to cancel the contract they will . . . Dammit! I think I just hit something . . . I'll have to call you back."

The woman slowed down and pulled her Yukon Denali over into the far left lane of the interstate. She looked up into the rearview mirror to see that other cars were swerving to avoid a piece of plywood lying in the center lane. Pressing a button on the OnStar device in the dashboard of the vehicle, she called for the location of the nearest mechanic. She discovered there was one just off the exit she was approaching.

The sign read Crawl's Service and Repair; this would have to do until she could get to the dealership.

The sight of the pearl-colored Yukon Denali pulling up on the lot didn't garner much attention, but when the curvaceous red-boned driver stepped out from behind the wheel, everyone noticed.

The woman leaned over into the passenger seat to retrieve her purse as lascivious eyes watched. She pushed her Versace sunglasses up on her nose and adjusted her navy-blue pencil skirt, as two of the mechanics at an open bay closest to her fought to be the first to assist her.

"Can I help you?" Marquis leered, his glance sweeping her from head to toe.

The woman stepped toward the back of the vehicle as Marquis turned to the others with a roguish grin on his face and followed.

She stooped to examine the back tire on the driver's side. "I may have a nail in my tire. I think I ran over a piece of wood or something." She stood up, almost bumping into Marquis, who had leaned in close enough to tell what perfume the woman was wearing, if he'd known what it was. Annoyed by his immaturity, the corners of the woman's mouth curled into a grimace. "Do you think you can check it out? The tire I mean."

Marquis cleared his throat. "Yes, ma'am."

"How long do you think it will take?"

"I can pull you right in . . . Your car. I can check it now."

"I knew what you meant."

"You can step inside and wait while I take a look," Marquis said, pointing to the lobby of the shop. "There's a soda machine if you want somethin' cold to drink."

"Thanks. The keys are in the ignition." The woman offered a half smile and started toward the lobby as Marquis and a couple of the others ogled her.

When she stepped inside she spied Tirrell bending down to retrieve a soda from the machine's receptacle. He had his work shirt off, tied around his waist, and his wife-beater T-shirt slighted soiled with grease and oil. His biceps glistened with perspiration. She pulled her designer glasses down and they made eye contact. "Hi." She smiled.

"How's it goin'?" he responded, popping the top of the can of cola.

The woman took a seat facing a frumpy house frau fussing with an unruly child, and leered as Tirrell chugged the cold drink. She flicked her French-tipped nails through her highlighted spiky bangs and pixie-cut tresses, suggestively crossing her legs when he looked in her direction. He stuck his tongue out just far enough for it to graze his upper lip, sucking in the excess of soda.

Her cell phone rang. Without taking her eyes off him she fished into her bag and pulled it out. "Travis . . . What did they say?"

As the woman chatted on her cell the other woman, noticing the nonverbal exchange between Tirrell and the leggy temptress, interrupted.

"Do you know when my car is gonna be finished? I have to go," she directed to Tirrell. "Excuse me . . . Excuse me . . . Did you hear what I said?"

Tirrell shot the woman a side-glance. "I'll go see how much more they have to do on it."

He exited through a side door that led to the work area of the garage, and the irritated customer cut her eyes across the room toward the other woman as she ended her call and put her phone back in her purse.

Within minutes Marquis came in to let the woman know that a nail had been found in her tire. "We patched it up. You're good to go."

"I don't believe this," the unnerved customer scoffed. "I've been sittin' here for almost an hour. How come you got done with her car so fast? I knew I should've taken my car somewhere else. You try to support your own and look how they treat you."

"Ma'am, all we had to do was take a nail out of her tire," Marquis said evenly. "There was more to do on your car."

The woman rolled her eyes. "Well, y'all need to hurry up. I can't be sittin' up in here all day."

Marquis escorted the fashionable beauty out to her vehicle.

"How much do I owe you?" the woman asked, looking around for Tirrell.

"Don't worry about it." Marquis smiled. "We didn't have to do much. But those are pretty expensive tires so if you got a warranty you may wanna take your car back to the dealer."

"Thank you. I intend to do just that."

Preparing to get into the Denali, she spotted Tirrell under the carriage of a truck. To Marquis's disappointment, but not surprise, the woman strode over to him. Tirrell poked his head out from under the truck, scanning the length of her legs. She smiled and removed a card from her purse and pressed it into his grimy hand. She then turned on her Gucci heels, being careful to sidestep the grease stains on the ground, and sashayed back to her vehicle. As she drove off, a couple of the guys, including Marquis, gathered around Tirrell to see what she'd given him.

"Event Planning, by Alex," Tirrell read aloud.

Marquis was peeved. "Ah, man. She gave you her phone number."

One of the others asked. "You gonna call her?"

"I don't know." Tirrell smirked.

"Shit, dude. That babe was fine as hell. If you don't want to call her give me the number."

He reached for the card and Tirrell slapped his hand away.

"She don't look like the type of woman who would be into corn-fed white boys, Scotty. Besides, you wouldn't know what to do with a woman like that."

"Man, shoot. I'd climb up in that and—"

"Cry like a little girl."

They all laughed.

***

"Hello. Can I speak to Alex?"

"This is Alex. Who is this?"

"This is Tirrell. I was the guy at the garage earlier you gave your number to."

"Your phone came up with a nine-one-oh area code. I almost didn't answer."

"It's a North Carolina area code. I've been meanin' to get that changed."

"You're from North Carolina?"

"Somethin' like that. I could tell you about it if you want to get together some time."

There was silence on the phone.

"Hello . . . Alex . . . You still there?"

"You should know, Tirrell, that I'm not a beer and wine cooler kind of girl."

"Yeah, I kinda figured that out already."

"Do you know where the Omni Hotel is?"

"Down by Centennial Park?"

"That's the one. Would you like to meet me at the Overlook Bar at nine tonight?"

"Yeah, I can do that."

Tirrell hung up the phone and stripped. He dashed into the bathroom for a quick shower, taking extra time to scrub the grease and dirt from his hands and under his fingernails. The water beat down on his flaccid erection, causing it to stiffen with anticipation. Following the shower he rummaged through his inadequate selection of clothes like a nervous teenager getting ready for the prom. There wasn't a thing suitable enough for him to wear to meet a woman like her. "Dammit," he spat, trying to decide between the one good suit he owned and his favorite pair of slacks. He opted for the suit. He checked himself in the mirror, glad that he at least had a fresh haircut.

It was Friday night and Betty hadn't made it home yet or he would have begged her to use the car again. He thought about calling Marquis, but he didn't want to add salt to his wound, given his reaction when the woman chose him. He ultimately decided to catch the MARTA.

There are several significant holidays throughout the year when the energy and the pulse of Atlanta comes to a frothy head—Labor Day weekend is one such occasion. There would be hundreds of parties, reunions, festivals, and cookouts, and the clubs and bars are overrun with locals and tourists alike.

The Overlook Bar in the south tower of the Omni Hotel offered a spectacular view of the hustle and bustle of the park below, but it could have overlooked the city dump for all Tirrell cared. Having only arrived just minutes before his date, he was seated at the bar trying to pull himself together when she walked in, dressed in a royal-blue silk sheath of a dress that complemented her buttery, smooth complexion. It hung loose around her shoulders and clung snugly to her hips, the hemline cut just below her pleasure zone, a look that could have made any other woman look cheap, but Alex Solomon had the poise and exuded the confidence to pull it off.

"Hi." She smiled.

"Hi." He smiled back.

"Have you been waiting long?"

"No, not really."

"So, how about that drink?"

"Lead the way."

They commandeered a table near one of the windows where a male server quickly approached them.

"May I get you something from the bar?"

Tirrell deferred to Alex.

"Grey Goose on the rocks with a twist of lime."

"Make that two," Tirrell added.

"Are you trying to impress me, or keep up with me?"

"Both."

Alex inhaled. "What's that cologne you're wearing?"

"Egyptian musk. It's not cologne, it's actually an oil."

"I like it. It smells like sex."

Tirrell's dimples popped when he smiled and he blushed.

"Too direct for you."

"Not at all."

"How old are you, Tirrell?"

He thought about the tired dictum "how old do I look," but decided this wasn't the game he wanted to play with her. "I'll be twenty-three in November."

"Young and hard, just like I like 'em."

He covered his mouth to keep from laughing aloud.

"You're not embarrassed, are you?"

"Should I be?"

"If you are, then you're not the man I thought you were."

"And what kind of man is that?"

"The kind who can appreciate a woman like me."

The server returned and put their drinks down on a table. Tirrell reached into his pocket for his wallet.

"We'd like to start a tab, please," Alex said to the man.

"Certainly," he responded, noticeably and shamefully eyeing Tirrell.

"He must know a good thing when he sees it," she teased as the server left the table.

Tirrell scoffed. "I'm not gay."

"Don't be so defensive. You're a very handsome man, but you know that already. Your eyes alone probably get you a lot of play, and those dimples don't hurt either."

"Is that what attracted you?"

Her eyes smiled and scanned him. "That and a few other things."

"So, why would a classy woman like you want anything to do with a grease monkey like me?"

She ran her manicured nails up his thigh. "I'm willing to bet that there's a lot more to you than meets the eye."

"You know you caused quite a commotion today when you came into the shop ridin' in that big Yukon."

"What can I say? I like riding big things." She picked up her drink and they toasted.

There was no doubt in Tirrell's mind where this evening was going to end up, and he was enjoying the journey just as much as he was sure to benefit from the destination. They chatted for over an hour, each seemingly feeling the other out.

"So, you have a North Carolina phone number?" she noted.

"I used to live there."

"For how long?"

"A couple of years."

"Is Atlanta your home?"

"Yes."

"What brought you back?"

"Family."

"No girlfriend? No wife?"

Tasha briefly crossed his mind, but she wasn't worth mentioning. "Not anymore. What about you?"

"No. I don't have a girlfriend or a wife either."

He laughed. "That's not what I meant."

"I know. I was just teasing you. I'm currently single and I'm not seeing anybody."

"You from here?"

"New York."

"So, why are you here?"

"I needed a change of scenery."

"I feel you."

"Not yet, but you will."

He licked his lips and smiled.

"I don't like to play games, Tirrell. I see what I want and I go after it—usually. I haven't gotten this far in life sitting on the sidelines waiting for things to happen." Alex paused and took another sip from her glass. "I want to have sex with you, but you already knew that too, didn't you? I don't want to talk about it. I don't want to analyze it. I just want to do it."

Tirrell swallowed hard. He hadn't encountered a woman so candid before. It scared him a little and stimulated him a lot.

She removed a key card from her purse and handed it to him. "I'm in room nine-thirteen. If you want to join me, use the key. If not, no hard feelings."

"How do you know I'm not some kind of psycho killer?"

"How do you know I'm not?"

Tirrell's heart beat faster. The invitation or the alcohol, possibly a combination of both, made him light-headed. He wished he had cocaine to help enhance the whole of the experience. He flipped the room key in his hand, wondering if he should take her up on her offer. Maybe she really was playing some sort of game. Maybe she was married and this was her hideaway. Her mystery intrigued him and he felt he owed it to his manhood to find out more.

Once Alex exited the bar he got up to pay—cringing at the near hundred dollar tab. "This ass better be worth it," he whispered on his way to the elevators.

He slid the plastic card key in the door lock and it clicked open. Alex stood naked at the large uncovered window with her back to him. There was no need for questions—the answers lay bare in front of him. He anxiously undressed and stepped up behind her—their reflections mirrored in the glass. He pressed his rigid penis into her backside and cupped her ample breasts in his hands. She was shorter without heels. Her petite frame fit nicely in his arms.

"You're a little freak, aren't you?"

"No, sweetheart. I'm a big freak. Is that going to be a problem?"

He inhaled with anticipation. "Not for me." His hands caressed her, and his lips found delight in the taste of her skin.

She moaned appreciatively when his fingers explored her inner walls. "I want you to tie me up." She sighed.

"What?"

"You heard me."

"You like rough sex?"

"Tie me up," she repeated.

Tirrell grabbed her, needing no further incentive, and threw her on the bed. He kissed her deeply, passionately, and then he found silk scarves on the nightstand and went to work. He was gentle initially, tying her wrists, trying to find something to secure them to. The scarves were long enough for him to anchor them to the bed railing.

"No. From behind," she insisted.

"Damn, girl."

She turned over and raised her hips up ever so slightly, yielding to his touch. "Take it."

He was emboldened. It almost sounded like a dare. He deftly slid into a condom and unhurriedly mounted her. He held his breath and almost lost it as he eased into her, shuddering with each thrust. The sensation was mind blowing.

Forcing her to her knees he worked his fingers back into her vagina and skillfully massaged her to climax. Alex bucked, jerked, and cried out with total abandon.

"Bite me," she screamed.

"Huh?"

"Bite my neck."

On the verge of ejaculation, Tirrell sank his teeth into the back of Alex's neck just hard enough to gratify, but not to break the skin. A primal cry exploded from his gut as his loins spewed forth equal amounts of pain and pleasure.

Alex had an insatiable appetite. "Don't worry. I won't hurt you."

It didn't take much coaxing for him to venture into a sexual exploration that lasted well into the night. He had more of an affinity for her hunger than he would have thought. Just before the smoldering dawn broke over the downtown Atlanta skyline, they collapsed in a heap of satisfied, sweaty flesh.

"Wow," she sighed, her fingernails gliding over the perspiration on his chest and tracing the scar on his arm. "I didn't think you had it in you."

"Most of the time *you* had it in you." He panted and laughed.

The rapid beat of his heart slowly returned to normal. His heavy breathing eased into a shallow snore. Nestled in his embrace, she drifted off as well.

When her internal body clock sounded, Alex opened her eyes and slid out from under Tirrell. She was showered and dressed by the time her cell phone rang and gave him a start. She clicked it off.

He rose up on his elbows, yawned, and wiped his eyes. "What time is it?"

"Checkout time," she threw over her shoulder as she continued to gather her things.

He glanced at the clock next to the bed and fell back on the pillows. "It's seven-thirty."

"It's time to go."

"Give me a few more minutes."

She moved close enough to the bed for him to reach up and grab her.

"Come back to bed."

She recoiled and forcefully pushed him away. "I said it's time to go."

"What's wrong with you?"

Realizing that she may have come off a bit too terse, she relented. "Look . . . I'm sorry. I just can't lie around all day."

"I thought . . ."

"Last night was last night. We kicked it. It was fun, but I got a business to maintain."

"I was hoping . . ."

"You were hoping what, Tirrell? We were going to be boyfriend and girlfriend, or something?"

Her cell phone rang again. She stepped over toward the window to answer.

Maybe it's her husband calling, Tirrell thought. She was cold and distant now compared to how strong she'd come on to him before. He had to laugh to himself when he thought about how many times he'd acted much the same way after a one-nighter. *Who's the bitch now?*

Alex continued her hushed conversation, not looking at him. He threw the covers back and sluggishly rolled out of bed. He pulled on his boxers and grabbed his pants as she ended the call and turned to face him.

"Aren't you going to shower?"

"I thought you were in such a big hurry," he said; the words came out sounding poutier than he intended.

"Awww," she said as she moved toward him. "Did I hurt the baby's *wittle* feelings?" She took the pants from him and tossed them onto the bed. She wrapped her arms around his neck and kissed him. "I've got some things to take care of. Maybe we could get together later."

He smiled, feeling a little less dejected. "I gotta go to work anyway, but my brother is havin' a barbeque later this afternoon if you wanna come with me."

"That's a little more than I want to commit to right now."

"Tell me the truth. Do you have a husband you're creepin' on?"

"I told you I was single."

He'd chastised Tasha for encroaching in his life; now here he was inviting a woman he just met to a family gathering. He could just see his grandmother grilling this woman and putting her on the defensive.

Alex kissed him again. "Why don't I just call you and we'll play it by ear, okay?"

"She did what?" Marquis shrieked.

"I'm not kiddin'. It was like she was some sex-crazed vampire. She was givin' me head and the next thing I knew she had her tongue in my ass."

"Dude, that's nasty."

"Hey, don't knock it 'til you try it, bruh."

Marquis hung voyeuristically on Tirrell's every word, trying not to show how envious he was. Over the years he'd become quite adept at suppressing the little green monster. He wasn't bad looking, and he too had his share of trysts, but the vicarious exploits of his friend seemed many times the things he only fantasized about. Much of what he shared was the exaggeration of truth: the tales men brag about with each other when one attempts to best another in an effort to keep their pride and masculinity intact.

"So, you seein' her again?"

"I told her that I was busy, and I'd call her when I got the chance," Tirrell boasted.

"You itchin' to call her, ain't you?"

Marquis was right, but Tirrell wouldn't give him the satisfaction of knowing that a woman had captivated him so quickly. "Naw, like I said, I'll call her when I get the chance."

"So, we still goin' out to Kevin's after work?"

"I don't really want to, but I guess I will for Noonie. I know it was her idea anyway. And it's a good thing I got a little help." He extracted a joint from the pocket of his work shirt and grinned devilishly.

"Where did you get that?"

"Scotty gave it to me. You know that white boy always got somethin'."

"T, c'mon, man."

"Not here. Later. Before we have to deal with all of Kevin's shit."

"Naw, man. I'm good. Besides, I don't want my moms to smell it on me. The woman's got a nose like a bloodhound."

"C'mon, Markie-Mark." Tirrell playfully threw his arm around Marquis's neck. "You gonna take a shower before we ride out anyway, right?"

"Yeah, I guess."

"A'ight then. Loosen up. It's the holiday."

14

The air around Kevin's house was thick with the smell of charbroiled meat. He stood out in the backyard turning slabs of ribs, chicken, and bratwursts over an open flame, while Pat busied herself in the kitchen finishing up potato salad and other side dishes to complement the cookout.

"Baby, can I get you anything?" she yelled from the open patio door.

"I could use some more water," he responded.

Pat filled a glass with ice and water from the freezer and took it out to him. She wiped the beads of perspiration from his brow with a paper towel—he took the glass and chugged down the water.

"Where's Micah?"

"He's upstairs trying to get your mother to play another video game with him."

"He must be driving her crazy by now."

"No, I think she's all right. You know it's been forever since she's seen him. She's havin' the time of her life, and I think the merlot helps a lot."

"She's drinkin' around Micah?"

Pat laughed. "She told him it was Kool-Aid."

"That's not funny. She might just give him a taste."

"She damn well better not, or she and I are gonna have words."

"Have you heard from Noonie?"

"She called a few minutes ago. She and Tirrell are on their way."

Kevin's cheeks tightened.

"Baby, c'mon now. You promised Miss Betty."

"I'm not going to do or say anything to upset Noonie. And after what she told us about Tasha, I'll even try to be nice to Tirrell."

Pat kissed him. "I know you said you wanted to keep your distance, but I'm glad you're makin' an effort."

"Yeah, well hold the applause. If Tirrell starts acting stupid I'm gonna have to get in his ass."

Kevin and Pat looked up to see his mother opening the screen door. "Oooh, something sure smells good out here."

Gloria Patterson tucked her forty-nine years discreetly behind a box of Dark and Lovely hair color, giving a natural sheen to the short copper curls that framed her freckled, cinnamon complexion. The medium-framed woman, who routinely shaved at least ten years off her age, stepped out onto the patio dressed in a form-fitting pair of hot pink Capri pants and a low-cut white cotton blouse.

"Hey, baby," she said, with a smooth, honey-toned lilt in her voice. She greeted Kevin with a kiss on the cheek.

"Everything all right in there, Mama?"

"Everything's fine. Why?"

"Micah's not bothering you, is he?"

"Not one bit. I just needed to come down and freshen my . . . Kool-Aid." She laughed.

"Mama, you're not letting Micah have any of that, are you?"

"No, boy. Why would I do that?"

"I'm just checking to be sure."

"Your sister called. She wanted me to tell you again that she was sorry that she couldn't make the trip. That new boyfriend of hers gets all her attention these days."

"Jacqui could have brought him."

"I told her that, but her and some of her other friends had already planned to go off to Vegas for the weekend."

"You live in Oakland, Mama. Jacqui can go to Vegas anytime. I think I know why she didn't want to come."

"You don't think she's going there to get married, do you?" Pat teased, diverting the direction of the conversation.

"Not if she knows what's good for her," Gloria said. "If I get back to California and she tells me she had one of those tacky weddings I will shoot her and that boy."

Betty called from the interior of the house. "Anybody home?"

"Noonie," Micah shouted as he bounded down the stairs.

"I hope she didn't bring Tirrell with her," Gloria sneered.

"Mama, I already told you he was coming."

"I know what you told me, but maybe he did us all a favor and changed his mind."

"Be nice," Kevin warned.

She sucked her teeth, slid open the patio door, and stepped back into the kitchen. Pat followed.

"Hey, Betty," Gloria oozed with a plastered smile, embracing her. "How've you been?"

Betty set a hefty pan of macaroni and cheese on the counter. "I've been fine, Gloria. How 'bout yourself?"

"Couldn't be better."

"You remember Anne Crawl, don't you?"

"Of course." Gloria nodded. "How are you, Ms. Crawl?"

"I'm doin' real good," the spirited woman replied. "You know, Kevin, my mouth has been watering for some of your barbeque all day. Here, I made one of my pineapple coconut upside-down cakes."

"That was nice of you, Miss Anne. I'll take it," Pat said, finding counter space for it.

"Hail. Hail. The gang's all here," Tirrell proclaimed as he entered, his eyes hidden behind a dark pair of sunglasses. "Hey, sister-in-law." He shot Gloria a side-glance. "Ms. Patterson."

"Tirrell." She nodded coolly.

They all stood there, oddly uncomfortable. Tirrell hadn't seen his brother since their altercation, and he hadn't seen his shrew of a mother for nearly three years. Clearly, as in Kevin's case, there was no love lost between them.

Tirrell looked around. "Where's Jacqui?"

"She didn't want to come," Gloria responded. "She found something better to do."

Kevin cut his eyes toward his mother and cleared his throat.

"I really need to use the facilities. I've been taking these water pills and seems like I've been having to go every five minutes," Anne Crawl blurted, pushing her glasses up on the bridge of her nose and flattening the windblown strands of her hair back into place.

Kevin pointed the woman in the direction of the half bath off the side of the kitchen, before he turned to go back outside to tend the grill.

"Where'd that Micah get off to?" Betty asked.

"He's out front with Marquis," Tirrell replied and flopped down in a chair at the kitchen table. He helped himself to a handful of mixed nuts from an open container.

Betty absently washed her hands at the kitchen sink, not thinking about the times she'd chided others about doing the same.

Gloria leaned against the counter with a guarded eye on Tirrell. "Kevin tells me you got put out of the Army?"

He stopped chewing and ran his tongue over his salty lips. "I'm thirsty. Pat, do you have any beer?"

Pat turned to address him—Gloria cut her off.

"I heard you got a court date coming up next week for a DUI. Do you really think you should be drinking?"

"I can hold my liquor just like you can."

"Apparently not," Gloria shot back.

Enmity stirred like the fragrant hickory that rose from the grill.

"I'll just take some water," Tirrell said.

Pat pulled a bottle of water from the refrigerator and passed it to him. He kicked back from the table and went outside to join Marquis and Micah, who had made their way to the backyard.

"Gloria, was that necessary?" Betty asked, drying her hands on a paper towel.

"What? I just didn't think drinking was appropriate for somebody who's already facing a DUI charge."

"You don't have to be so ugly about it," Betty chided.

Gloria's voice rose with condescension. "Ugly? I was just stating a fact."

Betty shook her head. "Look, we all know how you feel about Tirrell. You have made that clear more than once. That's why Jacqui and Kevin could never accept him."

"I know you're not putting this on me."

"Who else?" Betty sneered, tossing the towel into the trash. "Don't you think it's long past time for you to put all that nastiness that went on between you and Junior all those years ago behind you?"

"Every time I look at that boy he reminds me of what Junior did," Gloria shrieked. "He didn't just walk out on me; he walked out on his kids. Tirrell has played you from the day he moved into your house, Betty. Keep on protecting him like you always have, just like you stuck up for his no-good daddy, and see what happens."

Pat attempted to run interference. "C'mon, y'all, don't do this, not today."

Anne Crawl, who was coming back in from the bathroom, decided to go in the other direction to stay clear of the escalating family drama.

"I never defended Junior," Betty protested. "I didn't like what he did to you and those children, and I told him so. But, there ain't nothin' none of us can do about that now."

"Not as long as you keep throwing Tirrell in our faces."

"You know, Gloria, it's been a long time and a lot has happened. You need to stop bein' so petty. Blamin' Tirrell for somethin' he had nothin' to do with."

Kevin threw open the sliding glass of the patio door and stepped back inside. "What the hell's goin' on?"

Pat shook her head. Her eyes darted between the two women. Kevin knew instantly that his mother's liquid indulgence aided in loosening her tongue and she must have said something to set them off. He went over to her and tried to take the wineglass from her hand.

She withdrew. "Kevin, what do you think you're doing?"

"You've had enough *Kool-Aid*."

"I'm the mama. You don't tell me when I've had enough. I'm just speaking my mind. Somebody has to. I'm sick of my son always bein' dragged in to clean up after Tirrell."

Betty put her hands on her hips and slowly walked toward her. "Is that what you think?"

"You called him to go bail Tirrell out of jail, didn't you? He's forever into somethin'. When are you goin' to cut him loose, Betty?"

"I would no more cut Tirrell loose than I would these other children. I wish to hell everybody would stop treatin' him like a pariah!"

"Then maybe he needs to stop acting like one," Gloria seethed.

Betty stormed out of the kitchen and Pat ran after her.

Kevin scratched his head and wiped his hands over his face. "Mama, why'd you do that?"

"For the life of me I don't understand why Betty favors Tirrell over you and Jacqui. You went to law school and Jacqui's a programmer. Tirrell can't seem to tie his own damn shoelaces without Betty's help. I can't stand the fact that you keep taking the back seat to your father's bastard. Now, I'm sorry if I hurt Betty's feelings, but I gotta look out for my children and Tirrell is not one of 'em."

Betty was seated on the sofa with her face in her hands when Marquis bounded in with Micah riding on his shoulders. She raised her head and Anne handed her a tissue. Pat took Micah in her arms.

"Mommy, what's wrong with Noonie?"

"I'm all right, baby," Betty said, flashing a half-hearted smile. "Where's Tirrell?"

"He uh . . . he heard y'all arguin'," Marquis replied. "He took off."

Micah scrambled out of his mother's arms and climbed into Betty's lap.

"Took off? Where?"

"I don't know. I tried to stop him, but I couldn't."

Micah wrapped his arms around his great grandmother's neck and kissed her cheek. "He's okay, Noonie."

Kevin entered the room, forcing his mother to follow. "Baby, can you, uh, take Micah upstairs?"

After Pat left the room Anne Crawl stood up and asked Marquis to join her in the kitchen.

"Betty, I'm sorry," Gloria began.

"Are you?"

"Not for saying what I said, but how it came out."

"Then I don't think you're sorry at all." Betty stared at the floor, not looking up at the woman. "From day one you directed your anger at the wrong person, Gloria. Junior ain't here, and neither is Tirrell's mama, so he's an easy target. But, he was as much a victim in all of this as any of you, and you don't have no call to keep spewin' your poison on these kids."

"Now wait a minute," Gloria protested.

"Let me finish," Betty interjected. "You know I don't feel no better about what my son did to this family than you do, but I never went around cussin' him and callin' him out of his name. A lot of damage was done. Him dyin' like he did was a horrible thing. Maybe if y'all didn't push Tirrell away like you do he wouldn't feel like such a burden and he wouldn't act up. He lost his mama and his daddy. She didn't have no family to speak of, and all he had was me. So, if I showed him a little more attention than Kevin and Jacqui that's just because he needed it more."

"So you've said, over and over again, and just look how good he turned out," Gloria sneered.

"Now, see. That's exactly what I'm talkin' about."

"Betty, you ain't got to put up with me too much longer. I'm just gonna be here 'til Tuesday. When I leave I'll take my poison with me."

***

Tirrell walked a mile before coming to the nearest MARTA station. The platform was virtually empty. His T-shirt was soaked through with perspiration. An unexpected cool breeze blew in from the east. It appeared that the rain that had been threatening for days was finally rolling in as well.

He removed his outer shirt and wiped his brow with the driest part of it. He called Alex as he sat and waited for a train. She didn't answer. He dialed Bobby.

"What's crackin', T?"

"I need to see you."

It took over an hour to get the train out of Alpharetta. There was a steady downpour falling over Midtown by the time he arrived at Bobby's door. Another of Bobby's infamous gatherings was in full swing. Smelling of salty perspiration and now drenched by the rain, Tirrell had misgivings about knocking, but he had traveled too far to turn back. A quick in and out, just like the last time, and he would be on his way.

After several minutes a man answered the door. Tirrell recognized him immediately. It was the same man he fought at the restaurant the night of Tasha's birthday.

"Well, I'll be damned," the man scoffed. "Looks like Bobby will invite any lowlife to his house."

Tirrell's jaws tightened. "I guess you ought to know." He peered over the man's shoulder and caught a glimpse of Tasha.

The man gave Tirrell the once-over. "You know I should've pressed charges against your ass. You fucked up a three hundred dollar suit. Looks like it would have been a waste of my time. You don't look like you got a pot to piss in anyway."

Tirrell rubbed his hand over the moisture on his face. "Rickey, right?"

He nodded.

"Look, I don't want no trouble. I didn't come here to see you. I came to see Bobby."

The man backed away from the door to allow Tirrell entry. When he stepped inside he saw Tasha laughing and chatting up a couple of other people near the bar. A lump formed in his throat when she glanced in his direction. She looked better than he remembered. The pounding music swallowed them up as she awkwardly averted her gaze.

"Yo, T," Bobby called out as he came out from the kitchen. "It's about damn time you got here. What took you so long?"

Tirrell shook his head and watched haplessly as Rickey Hicks made a show of kissing Tasha. He knew he had no right to be angry.

"Damn, dude," Bobby injected. "Every time you come to my place you look a hot mess."

"Just got caught in the rain, that's all. Look, I don't wanna impose or nothin'. Let's just get to it and I'm out."

"Okay, cool. Let's do it."

Bobby stepped outside, past Tirrell, onto the landing shielded by the eaves. Tirrell took one last look at Tasha before joining him.

"So, what's that dude's story?" Tirrell asked. He slipped the pouch of cocaine into the pocket of his jeans and handed Bobby a tightly folded hundred dollar bill.

"Who, Rick? He's all right, one of my best customers and he brings in a lot of business. Hey, but did you check out who he was with? Didn't you used to tap that?"

"Ancient history."

"Damn! Ol' girl gets around, huh?"

"Yeah, a little more than I thought."

"That ass was lookin' good, though," Bobby noted. "No disrespect."

Tirrell ignored the comment. "Look, the rain is easin' up. I'm gonna take off. Catch you later."

As he darted up the rain-drenched street Tirrell wondered if Tasha might be using. Maybe, like so many, she really didn't know what kind of business Bobby was into and was just there for the party. Still, she was there, and if her new man was into recreational narcotics, how could she not be a partaker? Or was she as blissfully ignorant of Rickey Hick's foibles as she had been of his?

Tirrell stumbled home after one in the morning. Betty awoke and sat up in her recliner.

"S . . . sorry I woke you up. I always seem to keep doin' that."

"Tirrell?" Betty rubbed her eyes. "What time is it?"

"It's late."

Betty picked up the remote and flipped off the television. "I was tryin' to wait up."

"I just needed some time alone."

"Are you hungry? I brought you a plate back from Kevin's."

"No. I just wanna go to bed." Tirrell swayed and bumped into the coffee table.

"Tirrell, what's the matter with you?"

"Nothin'. I'm just tired."

Betty went to him and took hold of his arm. He looked away. She cupped his chin and turned his face back to her. "Are you high on somethin'?"

"No." He pulled away from her.

She grabbed his arm again. "Tell me the truth."

He yanked back more forcefully. "Why are you on me? Why is everybody on my case? Can't y'all just leave me alone?"

He stormed to his room and slammed the door. Betty followed him.

"Tirrell, open this door." She rattled the locked handle. "Open this door, right now. Do you hear me?"

She stood for several seconds and pressed her ear to the door—there was little movement on the other side. Realizing that she wasn't getting in and he wasn't coming out, she shook her head and retreated to her room.

Either the smell of brewing coffee or the need to relieve himself lured Tirrell from his room early that Sunday morning. He found Betty in her bathrobe, in the living room, seated in her leather recliner facing the window.

"You're not goin' to church?"

She didn't look at him. "No, not today."

"How long have you been up?"

"I haven't really been to sleep."

Those were six words he hadn't heard in a long time. The last time he remembered causing her to forfeit a night's rest was just before he went off to basic training. He, Marquis, and a few others had gone out to celebrate and he staggered in at nearly dawn, completely trashed. He recalled getting sick and vomiting all over the bathroom floor before passing out and leaving Betty to clean it up.

He sat down on the sofa facing her, cloaked in shame. He didn't say anything. He just watched her wring her hands. Her desperate agony was apparent, even to someone as self-absorbed as he. The heartache he didn't want her to feel was the very thing he continued to dispense. His eyes burned with sorrow.

"I was sittin' here thinkin' about your grandfather," she began. "I was wonderin' what he would make of all this foolishness still goin' on after all this time. You know Curtis never did say a whole lot, but you could look in his eyes and tell how he was feelin' about a thing. Your daddy was like him in that way. Junior was a lot of things, but underneath it all he was a good man. Even when he failed he still tried to do right—like you—most of the time. I've tried to show you how important you were to this family in spite of what anybody said. Maybe this is all my fault. I've been too lenient. You've been too willful. And I need to stop coddling you. I know you been through a lot, including all this mess with Tasha. But, you're not an outsider. You don't have to keep actin' like one."

It was killing Tirrell that Betty couldn't look at him while she spoke. She could have whipped him until welts showed up on his hide like ripe cucumbers, but to hear her pain was unbearable.

"I know I hurt you," Tirrell said, choking back tears. "I know it may not mean nothin', but I love you, Noonie. All I ever wanted was for you to be proud of me."

"Just be the man I know you can be. Do that, and that will be enough for me."

"You want me to move out?"

"I didn't say that."

Stillness assailed them—neither moved until the ringing telephone perforated the silence. There was no hurry to answer. Betty stood and moved to Tirrell. Her soft, warm touch caressed his wet cheeks.

"You know I love you, don't you? I'm here for you. If you ever need to doubt anything you don't ever have to question that."

Tirrell nodded. Betty caressed the top of his head and sighed. She then went on to her bedroom, ignoring the ringing phone.

She puttered around the house with busy work the rest of the day. Kevin called again to check on her and to see if she wanted to come to his house for dinner.

"Noonie, I've been calling you all morning. You weren't at church."

"I wasn't really up to it, baby. Just a little heartburn is all."

"Can I bring you something?"

"No, I don't need anything."

Betty was intent on avoiding another scathing discourse with Kevin's mother. She thought it best to wait until the woman was well on her way back to California. Gloria Patterson's spiteful, wine-fueled assertions were on target for the most part. Betty could do without being caught in the crosshairs of any more of her former daughter-in-law's injurious commentary.

15

The following Tuesday morning, Tirrell was to stand before a judge at the DeKalb County Courthouse to answer for the DUI charges. He was glad that Betty took the morning off to be with him. He looked up to see Kevin enter the courtroom, certain that he was only there to revel in his demise.

As case after case was presented and met with harsh penalties, Tirrell wondered if there was any need to worry about a place to live.

The bailiff's booming voice resonated in the gallery. "Ellis, Tirrell C."

Tirrell glanced at his grandmother and stood up.

The judge perused his file. "Mr. Ellis, you were arrested Saturday night, August 9, 2008, at exit 33, Interstate 285 East. Your BAC tested at .18, and you've entered a plea."

"Yes, Your Honor," Tirrell answered.

The judge looked up at him. "This appears to be your first offense. I understand that you were cooperative the night of your arrest, and ADA Ellis has spoken to me on your behalf. So, here's what I'm going to do: I'm still going to suspend your license, effective immediately. You're also ordered to pay a fine of five hundred dollars. We will revisit your suspension in thirty days on the proviso that you complete a mandatory defensive driving class that is scheduled to commence on the eleventh of this month. If you do not successfully conclude this mandate your license will be revoked for the period of no less than a year, and you can look forward to some jail time. Am I clear?"

"Yes, ma'am."

"See the bailiff for the necessary information and paperwork on your way out." The judge rapped her gavel. "Next case."

Both Betty and Tirrell breathed a collective sigh of relief. He then turned to look at Kevin, surprised by his intervention.

The bailiff confiscated Tirrell's license and gave him the paperwork he needed to present to the instructor at the defensive driving school. He found Betty with Kevin waiting in the corridor outside the courtroom.

He extended his hand to his brother. "Thanks."

Kevin hesitated, and reluctantly returned the gesture. "I didn't do it for you."

"I know."

"Just make sure you do what you need to do to get your act together."

"I will." Tirrell knew it was past time for him to do right by them all. He needed to man up.

Kevin embraced Betty. "I've got to get back over to my office. I'll talk to you later."

"Thank you, Kevin," Betty responded. "I need to be gettin' to work myself."

Kevin walked up the bustling hallway toward a bank of elevators, and Tirrell escorted Betty to the parking garage.

"Are you goin' into work today, Tirrell? Do you need a ride?"

"No, thanks. I didn't know what to expect, so I got the whole day off. I'll catch the train back. I don't wanna make you any later than I already have."

"All right, I'll see you at home later."

Tirrell kissed Betty's cheek and watched her drive off. He then walked out of the garage and inhaled the sweet smell of leniency. Standing on the sidewalk outside the courthouse he pulled out his cell phone and dialed Alex's number. He wanted to talk to someone who knew nothing about his current dilemma. He hadn't spoken to her in days and she hadn't bothered to call. The phone rang through to voice mail. "Hey, Alex. It's Tirrell. I've been tryin' to call you. I'm not workin' today. I was thinkin' that maybe we could do lunch or somethin'. Call me." He flipped the phone closed and rubbed his hand over his mouth, frustrated and unable to believe what his encounter with the elusive vixen had done to him. He was never prone to chase after a woman, but in her case he was willing to make an exception.

"Operator . . . do you have a listing for Event Planning by Alex?"

Tirrell hopped the bus to the Buckhead location he was directed to. Tacked on the granite walls inside the twelve-story building he found an embossed plate that confirmed there was indeed such a business. He took the elevator to the third floor and made his way through double glass doors at the end of the hallway. The space was bathed in the sunlight pouring in through the large plate glass windows. A couple of hefty green rubber trees and palms stood decoratively in opposing corners, and lively impressionist prints hung on the walls.

A fastidiously dressed African American man talking on the telephone, seated behind an Isotta desk with a frosted glass top, pulled the receiver away from his ear. "Can I help you?"

"I'm here to see Alex Solomon."

The man looked at Tirrell in his dark gray three-button suit and leaned back in his chair. "Are you here about an upcoming event?"

"No."

"Do you have an appointment?"

"No."

"I'll have to call you back," he said, directing his attention back to his call. "Unfortunately, Ms. Solomon isn't here."

"I can wait. Do you know when she'll be back?"

"Let me explain something to you, Ms. Solomon is very busy. If you want to see her you need to make an appointment. Should I pencil you in for next week?"

Tirrell moved to the chairs in the reception area, sat down, and picked up a magazine. "I'll wait."

The man picked up his phone and whispered into the receiver. Seconds later, Alex came out from the back office.

"What are you doing here?"

Tirrell got up and walked over to her. "I wanted to see you. If you didn't want me to be here maybe you should've returned my calls. Or maybe you shouldn't have given me your card in the first place."

Alex grabbed Tirrell's arm and pulled him toward the exit. "I'm working. You have to go."

He leaned into her and whispered seductively, "I brought your lunch." He took her hand and tried to pull it toward his crotch. "You remember how good it tasted, don't you?"

"Woooo hoooo, I can hear you," sang the man from behind the desk.

Alex yanked her hand away. "Travis, can you go in the back and make the call I asked you to make earlier?"

"What call?"

"Travis!"

"Fine." The man grabbed a notepad and exited the reception area.

"You need to go, Tirrell."

"Oh, you remembered my name. Funny you couldn't remember my number."

"Look, I don't have time to play with you. We had sex. That's it. No more, no less."

"It was good though, wasn't it?"

"It did the job."

"You got off several times that I recall, and you loved every minute of it."

"I hate to burst your bubble, Tirrell, but I'm not one of the obsequious tricks you're used to tripping all over themselves to get to your dick. How many times have you gotten with a woman and never called her back? Men aren't the only ones with game."

"I thought you didn't have time for games."

"Go away. I'm serious."

"You want me to take it again, is that it?"

Without warning, Tirrell grabbed Alex and wrestled her against the wall, shoving his hand up under her skirt.

"What the hell do you think you're doing?"

"If I recall you like it rough, don't you?"

He pressed his mouth onto hers and pulled at her panties with his fingers. She pushed at his chest, trying to fight him off. He became more forceful.

Her associate sailed back into the room. "I called Ush . . . Ooops, didn't mean to interrupt."

Alex slapped Tirrell across the face. "Get out!"

Tirrell backed off, rubbing his cheek. He licked his fingers and walked out laughing.

"You're breathing awfully hard. You look a little flustered," Travis remarked. "You want me to get you a glass of water, or maybe something stronger?"

"Shut the hell up, Travis."

***

Tirrell sat on the train, calculating his next move. He recalled the look in Alex's eyes. He knew that he'd gotten to her. The Ellis charisma rarely failed him when he needed it. He was sure he wouldn't have to wait long to hear from her the next time.

His cell phone rang, playing his ring tone "Stronger."

"Bobby, what's good?"

"I can't call it. You tell me. You still workin' at that little rinky-dink garage?"

"I'm off today. Why? What's up?"

"How would you like to put some dead presidents in your pocket?"

Tirrell hesitated. Money was exactly what he needed if he was going to move forward. He would be able to get his own place and stand on his own two feet once and for all. He thought about Bobby's apartment and imagined his own. He thought what he could do for his grandmother with the extra cash. And he thought about how he might impress a woman like Alex Solomon.

"T . . . You there, man?"

"Yeah . . . I'm here."

"Did you hear what I said?"

"Yeah, what did you have in mind?"

"Why don't I swing by your place and pick you up and then I can tell you all about it. I can be there in an hour."

"A'ight, bet."

Tirrell rushed home with just enough time to change clothes. He heard, then saw, the Escalade and ran to meet it before Bobby had a chance to loiter in front of the house.

"You ready to make that paper?"

"Hell yeah."

Merging on to the interstate, Bobby began to lay out his plan to bring Tirrell into his lucrative venture. Dollar signs were all Tirrell envisioned.

"What do you need me to do?"

"We gotta make a run to Miami."

"When?"

"Tomorrow night."

"What's in Miami?"

"You'll know when we get there."

Tirrell pondered this for a minute. "What am I gonna do about my job?"

"Call in sick."

"Just like that?"

"Yeah, just like that."

Tirrell coughed. "Yeah, I guess I do feel a cold comin' on."

They laughed.

"We'll be back in a couple of days. No worries. But, if I'm gonna bring you into this I need to know I can trust you, 'cause if I can't, this ends now."

Tirrell pondered a decision. "You can definitely trust me, but . . ."

"But what?"

"You should probably know that I was in court today. I got a DUI on my record. I can't afford to fuck up and get caught up in anything illegal."

Bobby signaled and pulled over to take the next exit.

"What are you doin'?"

"Takin' you back home. I don't think you're gonna work out."

"Wait, I just—"

"You just what, T? You're either in or out."

Tirrell sighed, contemplating what he considered to be all the implications.

"What's it gonna be?"

"I'm in."

"A'ight then. Cool."

Bobby drove to an area of town near Hartsfield-Jackson International Airport, and parked the Escalade in back of an abandoned warehouse on a sparse parcel of land overgrown with dense weeds and dried grass, scored with the boisterous soundtrack of massive jets taking off and landing.

Tirrell was uneasy but tried not to show it. "What are we doin' here?"

"You'll see."

While they waited Bobby pulled out a Glock 9 mm and aimed it at Tirrell.

"Man, what the fuck!"

He drew down and laughed.

Tirrell caught his breath. "What the hell's the matter with you?"

"You said I could trust you."

"You can."

He handed Tirrell the gun. "Prove it."

"How?"

Bobby pointed to a husky older African American man skulking around the corner edge of the building. "You see that fat muthafucka over there?"

"Yeah."

"He owes me a couple of stacks for some product that he was supposed to turn around. His ass is probably gonna try to pull a fast one. I need you to have my back on this. You feel me?"

"Are we gonna have to . . . You want me to kill him?"

"If it comes down to that hell yeah."

Tirrell's throat went dry.

"You in or out, T?"

Bobby started the ignition.

"In. I'm in."

"That's what's up, T."

Bobby jumped out of the Escalade and approached the man. Their altercation quickly escalated. Tirrell's eyes flushed wild with panic when the man abruptly pulled a gun on Bobby and fired without a moment's hesitation.

"Oh shit." Tirrell gasped. He scrambled over into the driver's seat and realized that Bobby had taken the keys with him. "Shit!"

Another shot rang out as a plane flew overheard. "Hey, you," the shooter yelled. "Get out of the car."

Shaking, Tirrell grabbed the 9 mm that Bobby left him with and slowly opened the door. Keeping it close to his side he stepped out into the open.

"Sorry, kid. It's just business," the man sneered as he raised his gun.

Tirrell leveled the 9 mm. "I don't wanna kill you. I just wanna get outta here."

"I don't think I can let you do that, boy. Looks like what we got here is an old-fashioned standoff."

"I ain't got nothin' against you, dude."

"So, you just gonna let me off your boy and not do nothin' about it. That's fucked up."

The man fired off a shot toward Tirrell and missed. Tirrell took aim and squeezed off a round. The man grabbed his chest and tumbled to the ground.

Tirrell heaved and ran over to see about Bobby. "I can't believe this shit."

"I can't either." Bobby laughed and opened his eyes.

"What the fuck," Tirrell spat.

"Congratulations, killer. I think you passed."

"What?"

"'Don't make me kill you, dude. I just wanna get outta here,'" the other man mocked as he got up off the ground. "Boy, if you could've seen the look on your face." He lifted his shirt to show that he was wearing a bulletproof vest. "Good thing we took precautions. If you had better aim you might'a did some serious damage."

Tirrell was shaky—bewildered.

"Boy, I think you shit yo'self."

Bobby took the gun and showed him the clip. "Dude, the gun is loaded with blanks."

Tirrell's anxiety shifted to anger. "You son-of-a-bitch!"

"Calm down, man. I had to know if you were really willing to do whatever it takes."

Tirrell fell against the wall of the building. "Asshole."

Bobby removed a wad of cash from his pocket and tossed it to the man. They bumped fists and he brushed himself off and left in the direction he came from. Bobby headed back to the Escalade.

"Yo, T. You comin'?"

Tirrell shook his head and waved him away.

"T, c'mon, man. I'm sorry I had to do that to you, but I needed to be sure."

"Fuck you, man."

"C'mon, T. We way out here by the airport. You just gonna walk home?"

Tirrell collected himself and got back in the Escalade.

"That was foul, Bobby."

"Yeah, I know. But you in, right?"

Tirrell glanced up at Bobby and nodded.

"My man. I gotta make a couple of other stops."

"Some more of your bullshit?"

"Naw, man. There're some people I need to introduce you to, on the real." Bobby looked over at Tirrell, who still seemed put off by the whole ordeal. "T, you a'ight, man?"

Tirrell stared at his trembling hands. "Yeah, I'm a'ight."

They drove to an inconspicuous residence on the southwest side of Atlanta. To the unsuspecting eye, the house fit perfectly into the domesticity it conveyed from the outside. There were trees in the front yard, and children running and playing up and down the block, but inside revealed a different story. There were enough furnishings to give the place an air of legitimacy, but there was no mistaking that a lot more went on here, given the men he met brandishing semi-automatic weapons. As a stranger in this environment, Tirrell was thoroughly checked and his cell phone was confiscated and examined.

"They just want to make sure you're cool," Bobby assured him.

Cameras were mounted in every corner of the house and followed every movement like the eyes of a painting in an art museum, which gives one the illusion they're being watched. Tirrell was certain this elaborate setup was no illusion.

They all snorted cocaine while conducting business and laying out plans for the next transport. Tirrell joined in, putting into perspective the disdain of what had transpired earlier —almost as if it hadn't happened at all. Given the seriousness of the security in and around the house and the all but veiled threat of death, Tirrell felt he had no choice now but to swear his allegiance.

When they left the house he and Bobby found a soul food restaurant and grabbed something to eat before continuing downtown. They ended up outside a renovated high-rise overlooking Centennial Park.

"Damn." Tirrell gasped. "Who lives here?"

"C'mon. You'll see."

Bobby rang the intercom outside the building and announced himself before he was buzzed in.

Nervous energy coursed through Tirrell's body as they approached the apartment. He didn't know it, but he was about to be introduced to a key player in Bobby's operation—somebody who would change the rest of his life. When the door opened there was a surprise waiting on both sides.

"What the . . ."

"T, this is my cousin, Alex."

Tirrell suppressed his delight. "Nice to meet you."

The woman stood speechless.

"Yo, Alex, you gonna let us in or what?"

"Bobby, what the hell's going on?" she spat.

"This is my guy I was tellin' you about. C'mon, let us in."

Alex's brow arched and her jaw clenched as she moved back from the door. Tirrell couldn't keep his eyes off of her.

"T, have a seat, man," Bobby directed, as if it were his house. "You want somethin' to drink?"

"Bobby." Alex was visibly annoyed.

"Relax, girl. It's cool."

"No, it is not cool," she retorted. "You know what, we need to talk; right now."

Irritated, she left the room. Bobby shot Tirrell a look before following her.

Tirrell perched on the end of the plush cream-colored sofa, afraid to move—afraid to touch anything. Surrounded by abstract art and mahogany fixtures, overstuffed furnishings and marble floors, he shook his head and laughed quietly at his good fortune. "Oh yeah, that ass was definitely worth it."

"Bobby, what the hell," Alex seethed. "Why did you bring him here?"

"Whoa, chill out, girl. We talked about this, remember? I told you I was gettin' somebody to replace Jay."

Keeping an eye on Tirrell, Alex peered through a crack in the kitchen door. "Why him?"

"He's cool. We can trust him."

"How do you know that?"

"Let's just say if we get him in, we got insurance."

Alex turned away from the door. "What are you talking about?"

"His brother works in the DA's office."

"What is he, a clerk?"

"No. Kevin Ellis. He's an assistant DA."

"Oh, shit. Are you serious? Have you lost your damn mind? You may as well have brought a cop up in here."

"Slow down and think about it for a second, a'ight? We can use him, and if he gets out of line"—Bobby fixed his fingers as if he were holding a gun—"we put a bullet in his head."

Alex paced nervously. "I don't like it. It's too damn messy. I got too much on the line."

"Alex, have I ever let you down? I've been watchin' this cat for a long time. He's cool."

"I don't like it, Bobby."

"Let's give him a chance, and if he fucks up I'll take care of him."

"One chance—that's it. We can't afford any missteps."

Alex sent Bobby on an errand so that she could be alone with Tirrell. When he left the apartment, Tirrell smugly leaned back on the sofa. Alex, too, appeared more at ease. She moved to the bar set up in the corner of the room, stocked with everything a proper bar should have, and poured Grey Goose in a glass with a couple of cubes of ice.

"You look pretty pleased with yourself, Mr. Ellis."

"It's a nice coincidence." He smiled.

"Maybe it's more like providence," she countered.

"So, why all that business in the hotel? Why not just bring me here?"

"I don't bring every man I meet to my place."

"Do you screw every man you meet?"

She sashayed over and straddled him. "Only the ones I like."

"So, you like me?"

"That remains to be seen."

Tirrell took the glass from her hand and took a drink. "How am I doin' so far?"

"I haven't thrown you out, have I?" Alex took her drink back, finished it, and set the empty glass on the table next to the sofa. "Bobby tells me that you'd be a valuable asset."

She sat up and pulled her silk blouse over her head, exposing her bare breasts to him. She could feel his manhood pressing against her. He gently squeezed and sucked her jutting mounds of flesh.

"You better not become a problem for me, Tirrell Ellis."

"Well, I'm willing to give you a chance if you're willing to give me one," Tirrell replied. "That is, unless you're afraid you're gonna become . . . What was the word you used? Oh yeah, *obsequious*."

Clothes fell away as they worked their way back to her bedroom. Tirrell needed no prodding. Ardent, angry sex ensued. Her thirst called to the animal inside him.

"You want it. Take it," she demanded.

Their eyes locked as he threw her legs over his neck and plunged deeper between her thighs. He clasped his hand to her throat and grunted like a wild boar. He teasingly withdrew several times; she begged him not to stop. He reveled in her yearning. Unable to sustain his prolonged torture he gasped and released.

"Damn," he cried, pulsing and jittery.

Once he'd been satisfied, his tongue found delight in the sweet nectar of her juices. Her body shuddered with an equally electrifying orgasm.

Tirrell wanted to linger, but Alex had no intention of allowing Bobby to return and find him in her bed. "You have no idea what you're dealing with here," she said as she slipped into a silk robe.

"Maybe I do and maybe I don't," he responded. "But in case I missed somethin', why don't you fill me in?"

"I guess you'll find out soon enough. For now you need to get up and get dressed. Bobby should be back soon."

Tirrell got up and she directed him to the restroom. She smiled, watching his swagger from behind, and bit down on her lip. When he emerged he found Alex dressed and putting the bed back together. He pulled on his boxers and blue jean shorts and sat on the side of the bed to pull on his socks and Timberlands.

Alex noted the scratches on his back. "I meant what I said earlier. You better not become a liability, otherwise, what happens to you will be a lot worse than a few fingernail scratches."

"That sounds like some kind of threat."

"Just a warning, but you can take it however you like."

16

It was a tepid September day. Tirrell left work early so he could get home to shower, change, and pack in order to meet up with Bobby. He was surprised when Bobby pulled up in a blue Chevy Malibu instead of the comfort he'd expected to cruise to Florida in.

"What happened to the Escalade?"

"This is less conspicuous," Bobby replied. "We're doin' the speed limit all the way. I'll drive part of the way and you can take over."

"Uh, no license, remember?"

"Oh, yeah, right. I guess it's all on me then. So, what did you tell your grandmother about you leavin'?"

"She ain't home. I left her a note tellin' her that I was goin' out with this new girl." It wasn't that far from the truth.

Bobby shot him an odd look. "You screwin' Alex, ain't you?"

Tirrell didn't answer.

"I ain't stupid. I knew somethin' was up when I came back to her place the other night. Watch your back, playboy. I look out for mine. I don't want her gettin' hurt. Not like before."

"Before? What do you mean?"

"Nothin'. I shouldn't have said anything."

"Well, it's too late now. So, tell me."

"Never mind. Forget it."

"C'mon, man. Tell me."

Bobby was silent for a few miles before finally opening up. "Alex was married to my cousin, Ray, back in New York."

"Was?"

"He died."

"How?"

Bobby glanced at Tirrell. "Overdosed. Had a heart attack."

"Damn. So, you and Alex aren't blood relatives?"

"We're related in every way that counts. We watch out for each other."

"Okay. I feel you."

"Alex was really into Ray. It hurt her a lot when he died. That's why I'm gonna keep my eye on you. You mess over her and it's yo' ass, nigga."

Miami, Florida: land of perennial sunshine, beaches, and beautiful people. Despite the twelve-hour ride Tirrell was invigorated by cocaine and the lights of Biscayne Boulevard as they entered the city. Bobby was energized as well. "T, as soon as we get to where we're goin' we'll rest up, take care of some business, and there may be some time to get in a little fun before we head back."

"That's what's up."

They continued up the coast for several miles until they came upon an isolated beach house (more of a compound) bordered by a sentinel of palm trees and secured behind an iron gate and monitored by cameras. An armed man accompanied by two black pit bulls greeted them. Even though he recognized Bobby, he still checked him for concealed weapons and sequestered his Glock.

Despite Bobby's declaration, the man was more suspicious of Tirrell. Once they both checked out, the man jumped into his Jeep and drove up to the house. Bobby and Tirrell followed.

Tirrell took in the balmy morning breeze and the impressive surroundings of the opulent center of operations. As they entered the foyer a tall, strapping Latino with dark wavy hair, dressed in a white linen shirt and pants descended the spiral staircase. He and Bobby embraced.

"*¿Qué tal, mi amigo? ¿Cómo era su viaje?*"

"*¿Bueno,* Xavier. *¿Cómo está?*"

"*Bien gracias.*" He stepped over to Tirrell. "You must be Señor Ellis," he said with a heavy Colombian accent. He extended his hand. "Welcome, my friend. Welcome."

Tirrell returned the gesture.

"*¿Este chulo es muy hermoso, la verdad?*" The man smiled, holding on to Tirrell's hand a little longer than necessary.

He didn't have to speak Spanish to understand the man's intent. He flinched and pulled away.

"Xavier, *deje al hombre en paz.*" Bobby laughed. "*Él no es maricon.*"

The man laughed and nodded. "*Siento,* señor. Just having a little fun."

Tirrell smiled uncomfortably and cut Bobby a look, gritting his teeth to arrest a caustic comment.

"You must be hungry and exhausted after your long trip. Carmen will show you to your rooms. Once you settle in, please join me for brunch on the terrace." The man snapped his fingers and a portly subservient woman appeared and escorted them up the stairs.

It was all very gangster, Tirrell mused.

While they dined on plantains, chorizo, and fresh fruit, Tirrell's cell phone rang. It was Marquis. Tirrell had called and left a voice mail message for Mr. Crawl already; this was not the time to talk. He clicked the End button on the phone and then turned it off.

"Sorry about that," he said.

"It's quite all right," their host responded. "Just don't let it happen again."

Tirrell swallowed nervously at the man's intimidating overtone. He could actually picture him saying the words, "Say hello to my little friend."

The man laughed. "You must learn to relax, amigo." He turned to Bobby. "Señor Ellis takes himself too seriously, but I like him."

On the surface Xavier Rivera seemed friendly enough, but Tirrell was certain there was a more sinister side to him, one that he knew he didn't want to encounter. Men like Rivera didn't get to be who they were by playing nice.

Tirrell remained cagey in the two days he and Bobby spent in Miami. He enjoyed the beach and sunning by the pool. At the invitation of his host, he indulged his cravings for some of the finest cocaine money could buy. But he denied himself the pleasures of the various scantily clad women lounging about the house, for fear that his exploits would reach Alex before he had time to sneeze.

This was routine for Bobby: a monthly or bi-monthly excursion to Florida for the supply that would support the habitual addiction of the masses in and around Georgia. Tirrell was being groomed for more than he realized.

With a street value of just over $1 million, twenty kilos of cocaine were stored for transport in the hollow of a spare tire in the trunk of the Malibu. Bobby and Tirrell made the trek back to Atlanta and drove straight to the house on the southwest side of town. Bobby pulled his Glock from under the car seat and holstered it. He then removed one of the packages and carried it into the kitchen. One of the men Tirrell saw earlier, and a woman he hadn't met, were seated at a glass table.

Tirrell was fascinated watching the process. Pots of water boiled on the stove as the pair mixed small amounts of water with equal parts of cocaine and baking soda into glass mason jars. Each jar was submerged into the water and cooked. Once calcified, the rock-like substance was removed from the jars and placed on paper towels to dry completely before being cut and packed for distribution.

While they waited, the woman brought glasses and a bottle of Patrón from the freezer. They all drank to their mutual and prosperous venture.

"Here's to runnin' this bitch," Bobby toasted. "It's on and poppin' now."

"So, what's gonna happen to the rest of the stash?" Tirrell asked as they left the house.

"We save it until we run low and then we process the rest," Bobby responded.

"What do we do in the meantime?"

"We sit back and wait for the money train. Supply and demand, T. We got the supply and there's definitely a demand."

They bumped fists in agreement.

"Can I ask you a question about this Rivera dude?"

"Yeah, okay."

"What's his deal? Is he gay, or what?"

Bobby laughed. "He's tri-sexual. That crazy-ass Columbian will *try* just about anything. A couple of those fine-ass women you saw back at his place in Miami weren't born that way."

"Shut the fuck up."

"I'm serious. I found that out the hard way—no pun intended. You ain't got to worry about Rivera messin' with you, unless you get down like that."

"Hell, naw." Tirrell laughed.

"You sure? 'Cause you were squeamish like a little girl when you had that gun in your hand back at the airport that day with ol' dude."

"Man, fuck you. I can handle my shit. Hell, I thought yo' ass was toast and I wasn't tryin'a be next."

"I'm just playin' with you, dawg. I know if it came down to it you'd know what to do."

"Damn straight."

It was after seven when Bobby pulled on to Eastland to drop Tirrell off. He extracted twenty hundred-dollar bills from his pocket and handed them to him.

"What's this for?"

"Consider it a bonus from Rivera. Buy yourself some damn clothes. Keep this on the low, for real. You feel me?"

Tirrell took the money, stuffed it into his pocket, and jumped out of the car. Bobby pulled off just as Marquis was motoring up the street in the opposite direction. He blew his horn to get Tirrell's attention.

"Markie-Mark, whud up, yo?"

Marquis got out of his De Ville still dressed in his uniform from work. "Was that Bobby I just saw?"

"Yeah."

"That explains what the hell you been doin' for the last few days. I thought you was supposed to be sick."

"Yeah, well that wasn't exactly true."

"So, what were you doin' with Bobby?"

"Nothin' for you to get all twisted about."

"Oh, so that's how it is, huh? You miss two days of work to hang out with that son-of-a-bitch and you just gonna blow me off."

"Man, quit trippin'. We ain't fuckin'."

Marquis scoffed. "That's uncalled for, T. I thought we were supposed to be boys. I thought we had each other's backs."

"Look, I'm sorry, man. I didn't mean—"

"You know what . . . to hell with it. You wanna waste your time with that thug I can't stop you. Just don't come cryin' to me when he gets you into some shit you can't get out of."

Marquis darted into his mother's house. Tirrell shook his head and continued into Betty's.

She was seated at the dining table, finishing dinner. "Well, look who's home."

"Hey, Noonie."

"Where've you been?"

"Uh, didn't you get my note?"

"Yes, I did. Awfully considerate of you, but you could've returned my calls."

"I wasn't gettin' a good signal where I was."

Betty sucked her teeth, pushed away from the table, and took her empty plate to the kitchen. "You hungry, or did this new girl cook for you?"

"Let me get cleaned up first."

Tirrell took his bag to his room, tossed it on the bed, and went to the bathroom to wash his hands. When he came back into the dining room Betty had already piled a plate with mashed potatoes, a vegetable medley, and baked chicken.

She sat down in a chair facing him, slowly peeling the plastic wrapping of a Moon Pie. "So, tell me about this girl you all excited over enough to miss work."

"Nobody you know." He continued to talk as he shoveled food into his mouth.

"How do you know who I know?"

"Well, I don't think she goes to Big Bethel."

"Don't be smart," Betty sneered. "I know more than church people."

Tirrell grinned. "I've been thinkin'. Maybe it is time for me to move out and find my own place."

"Boy, don't talk with your mouth full."

He swallowed and then took a swig from a glass of tea. "I think it's about time for me to have my own space."

"For you and this new girl?"

"No. She's got a place of her own."

"Really? Does she have a name?"

"Alex."

"Alex?"

"Alexandra. She's an event planner."

"Uh huh."

Tirrell put down his fork. "What's that look for?"

"Is this event planner person the reason you're in such a hurry to move out after I already said you didn't have to?"

"I'm just doin' what a man is supposed to do. Ain't that what you wanted?"

"Men work. How're you gonna afford a place of your own if you start missin' more days from your job because of this new girlfriend of yours? She ain't gonna be takin' care of you, is she?"

"It was just two days, not the end of the world. And it's not gonna be like that. C'mon, be happy for me, please. It's about time for me to get out from under my grandmother, don't you think?"

"I'm just concerned that you barely got over what Tasha did to you and you're already with somebody else."

Tirrell jumped up and ran around the table, embraced Betty, and planted a sloppy kiss on her cheek. "Don't worry, *Moonie*. You are still my best girl."

She laughed despite herself and playfully pushed him away.

Tirrell fished $300 from his pocket and handed it to her. "Here. If this doesn't prove that I can take care of myself I don't know what will."

"Where did this come from?"

"I got paid before I left."

"Baby, I told you I don't need your money."

"Take it. If you don't wanna pay a bill, buy yourself somethin' crazy."

"Tirrell."

"I just wanna take care of you for a change."

"All I need for you to do is take care of yourself. And I want you to be careful, you hear me? Don't rush into nothin'."

"Don't worry. I know what I'm doin'."

"I hope so, Tirrell. I really do."

17

A chilly reception awaited Tirrell at the garage the next morning. He stuck to his story about being sick. Marquis scoffed but didn't rat him out, although he steered clear of him most of the day, which did not go unnoticed by his coworkers.

"T, what's up with yo' boy?"

Tirrell shook his head. "I don't know, Scotty. He trippin' on somethin'."

"You two have a lovers' quarrel?" the man quipped.

"Man, you better go somewhere with that."

Scotty doubled over laughing wildly as Marquis rounded the corner toward the bay they were working in. He quickly fell silent.

"What?" Marquis inquired.

"Nothin'," Scotty replied.

Tirrell went back to the engine he was tuning.

"What the hell did you say about me?"

"Why you so paranoid, Marquis? I didn't say nothin' about you," Tirrell snapped.

"Then what's so damn funny?"

"Why don't you ask Scotty?"

"I'm askin' you."

Tirrell pulled his head from under the hood of the Oldsmobile. "You ain't said two words to me all day and now all of a sudden you wanna ask me questions?"

"Forget it, man." Marquis grabbed the wrenches he came for and turned to leave.

"Punk ass," Tirrell sneered.

Marquis spun around sharply, dropped the wrenches, rushed over to Tirrell, and shoved him. "I'm sick of your shit."

"What the hell is your problem, Marquis?"

"You are!"

"You know what, you really are a li'l bitch."

Marquis swung. Tirrell blocked his fist and clocked him in the jaw, sending him flying backward into a rack of diagnostics tools. The noise brought two other mechanics running to help. Marquis shook them off and stood up on his own.

"Why don't you go run and tell your ol' man that I hit you?"

"I don't have to tell him shit. I'm assistant manager, remember? Get the hell out of here. You're fired."

Tirrell looked at the men standing around salivating, and jeered. He picked up a towel and wiped the grease off his hands. "To hell with you, Marquis, and this damn job."

He threw the towel in Marquis's face and went into the locker area to retrieve his things. He discarded his uniform, quickly dressed, and left the shop. He called Alex and asked if he could come over; she told him that he could.

Alex's bathroom was aglow with candlelight. The sultry vocals of Floetry's "Say Yes" helped set the mood. Tirrell sat sulking in a garden tub of suds with her legs wrapped around his waist while she gently washed his neck, back, and shoulders.

"So, are you ready to talk about what happened with you today?"

Tirrell sighed deeply. "Not really."

"Do you feel like talking at all?"

"We can talk about anything but my day."

"Okay, let's see. Tell me something about yourself that I don't already know."

"Like what?"

"For starters, why do you live with your grandmother? Why don't you have a place of your own?"

Tirrell shrugged his shoulders. "I don't know. My grandmother raised me. It's just always been like that."

"Where's your mother and father?"

"They're dead," Tirrell answered sullenly. "They died when I was a kid. Sometimes I close my eyes and I try to see my mother's face and I can't anymore. I look at an old picture and wonder what she'd be like if she were still around. I just wanna talk to her sometimes, you know?"

Alex was suddenly sorry she broached the subject.

"What about you? Are your parents still alive?"

"My father died after I graduated college," Alex answered. "My mom still lives in New York."

"Are you close?"

"Yeah, I try to go up to see her as much as I can." Alex reached for a bottle of Riesling that sat outside the tub, and refilled their glasses. "If you had the money and could go anywhere in the world, where would you go?"

He shrugged his shoulders again. "Never really thought about. Maybe Puerto Rico or someplace like that."

"Why there?"

"My mother was Puerto Rican. I don't know a whole lot about the culture."

"Do you have relatives there?"

"Hell if I know. I don't remember my mother ever talkin' about brothers or sisters."

"Wow."

"So, where would you go?" he countered, trying to sound less morose.

"I would go to Nigeria; that's where my parents are from. I've only seen pictures, but I've always wanted to go."

He turned and kissed her. "Maybe we could go there together."

"I think we should get to know each other a little better before we talk about taking trips and making space in my closet for your clothes."

"Who said anything about movin' in? You were the one who brought up travelin'. I just thought it would be fun to do somethin' like that together."

Alex chuckled. "Like a couple?"

"What's so bad about that?"

"Because we're not," she countered.

"What do you call this?"

"Two people taking a bath together."

Tirrell pulled her into him. "We could be a couple."

"Is that what you want?"

"What do you want, Alex?"

"I want to change the subject."

"Why? I like you. I think you like me. All you gotta do is 'say yes.'"

"Yes. Yes. Yes," Alex teased breathlessly, and splashed water in his face.

He splashed her back and they laughed.

"How about we start with a road trip to Savannah before we commit to an excursion to the other side of the world, Mr. Ellis?"

"That's cool, but you might have to do all the drivin'."

"Oh, right. Bobby told me about your DUI."

"My brother stepped up and the judge took it easy on me, but I gotta go take this stupid class next week before I can get my license back."

"I thought you and your brother didn't get along."

"We don't. The only reason he did what he did was because of my grandmother."

"So, you're her favorite," Alex teased.

"No."

"There's nothing wrong with that. Everybody shows favoritism every now and then."

"Are you your mother's favorite?"

She stroked his erection. "I'm everybody's favorite."

He titled his head for a kiss and turned over and took her in his arms. Their wet bodies intertwined and slid together like puzzle pieces.

"I think the train wants to come into the station."

Alex laughed. "What are you—twelve?"

"Do I feel like a twelve-year-old to you?"

Tirrell slid a hand between her legs. Alex's body submitted completely to his touch. She threw her head back and moaned as she opened up, allowing his fingers access. Kissing and licking her neck and sucking her nipples, he worked her into a frenetic climax. Relaxed and content she pushed him away and climbed out of the tub.

"Alex, what are you doin'?"

"The water's getting cold."

"You just gonna leave me all hard like this?"

She wrapped a towel around herself. "You can either finish without me, or you can join me in bed."

Tirrell sighed and lay back in the tub. "Damn."

After Alex left the bathroom he leaned over to dry his hands, grabbed his pants, and pulled out a packet of cocaine. He tapped some on his closed fist and snorted up both nostrils.

"What are you doing?"

He looked up to see Alex.

"Where did you get that?"

"I got it from Bobby."

She snatched the packet out of his hand and flushed it down the toilet.

"Alex, what the hell?"

"I don't want you putting that shit up your nose. Do you hear me?"

"Alex?"

"I'm serious, Tirrell."

"Have you lost your damn mind?"

"No, but apparently you have."

"What's the matter with you?"

"Get out of my house!"

Stunned by her reaction, Tirrell jumped out of the tub and chased after her. He grabbed her arm and spun her around to face him. "What's goin' on with you?"

"What are you doing with that shit?"

"It's just a little blow. What's the big deal?"

She jerked away. "If you don't know then you already got a problem."

"What are you talkin' about? You sell it!"

"I don't use it!"

"I'm not an addict," Tirrell insisted.

"Then if you want to be with me stop using."

"Bobby uses. He works for you."

"I'm not fuckin' Bobby. And if you don't stop, I won't be fuckin' you either."

"This is really about that dude you were married to, ain't it?"

"What the hell are you talkin' about?"

"Bobby told me about you and his cousin."

"He shouldn've have done that. That's my business."

Tirrell reached out to her, trying to hold her. "Alex, I'm not him."

She attempted to pull away again.

He held on. "I'm not him."

Realizing the futility of her struggle, she calmed down and he relaxed his grip. "I hate this," she cried. "I hate losing control like some damn weak-ass female. I promised myself after Ray that I would never let another man get the best of me."

She furiously rubbed her temples and sat down on the bed. Tirrell eased down next to her. He took her chin in his hand, turned her to face him, and kissed her.

"Don't."

"I'm not Ray."

"Fuck you, Tirrell."

"I'm not gonna die on you, baby."

He kissed her until he wore down her resistance and slid her bathrobe away from her shoulders. Laying her back on the bed he spread her legs apart, eased on top, and entered her. She gasped. He thrust deeper—slowly—tenderly. He put his mouth to hers, his lips and tongue asserting his desire as their bodies locked in a synchronized rhythm. Alex was more vulnerable in that moment than she'd been since they'd met. Tirrell felt her release, which made his all the more gratifying.

In the wee hours of the next morning Tirrell awoke to find that Alex was gone. He rolled out of bed. When he opened the bedroom door he found her seated at the dining room table. She abruptly closed her laptop and pulled out a jump drive she was saving to.

He slipped his arms around her. "What are you doin' up so early?"

"I couldn't sleep, so I thought I'd get some work done. I got this party coming up in a couple of weeks and I need to make sure that everything is perfect."

He kissed her neck. "Come back to bed."

"In a minute, okay?"

He went to the bathroom to relieve himself and left the door ajar. Moments later Alex came into the bedroom. He spied her through the mirror slipping the jump drive into a small locked hideaway drawer in her bureau and placing the key in her jewelry box.

They climbed back into bed and she laid her head on his chest. Neither closed their eyes.

"Tell me about Ray?" Tirrell asked while gently caressing her back.

She paused. "Why?"

"I wanna know why a woman like you is in a business like this."

"I like the lifestyle it affords me."

"But you don't like users."

"Good salesmen don't have to use the product."

"So, you doin' this has nothin' to do with this cat you were married to?"

Alex sat up, pulled her knees to her chest, and stared blankly out the window facing the bed. Tirrell propped up on his elbow and comfortingly stroked the inside of her thigh.

"I loved Ray. I met him when I was in college. Bobby was dating a girlfriend of mine. He introduced us. Ray was smooth and cocky—a lot like you. I was really naïve back then. I used to go on drops with him and before I knew it I was doing the drops for him. There wasn't much he could have asked me to do that I wouldn't have done. I didn't get any scholarships or anything, and I needed help with school and with my dad because he was so sick."

"So, dealing never bothered you?"

"It did at first, but I adapted. Ray was good to me. My parents liked him, and the money came in handy and covered what insurance wouldn't. We got married a few months after my father died. We were together almost three years and I never realized Ray was as strung out as he was. Maybe I did, and I just pretended not to notice because I liked the things he bought me. I didn't know he had a bad heart, though. When he died, Xavier Rivera called to offer condolences and the rest, as they say, is history."

"So, you inherited the business like some kind of Mafia bride, huh?"

"Yeah, something like that."

"You ever been to jail?"

"No, and I don't intend on going. Came close once a few years ago. That's when I decided to relocate and set up shop here."

"You carry a gun?"

"You ask a lot of questions."

"You don't have to answer."

"I don't know why I'm telling you any of this. But yes, I have a gun and I know how to use it. We live in a dangerous world, Tirrell. A girl's got to protect herself."

"You ever kill anybody?"

She stared into his eyes intently. "Have you?"

His silence spoke volumes.

Alex got up and moved toward the bathroom. "I know your brother's an ADA, so I'd advise you to consider the consequences if you ever think about being disloyal to me, or Bobby. I will do whatever I have to do to take care of myself."

Tirrell thought about something Kevin told him when he first got back to town. *"Let me make something clear to you. However long you're going to be here, you need to make sure that whatever other business you got goin' on doesn't come back on Noonie."* What if he'd already put his family in danger? Lying there, he contemplated exactly how far he would go to protect them if he had.

***

The morning sun seeped in through the window. The ringing telephone reverberated in the room. Alex had slept much longer than she'd intended.

"Hello . . . Travis, what is it? They did what? How much more is it going to cost to get it fixed? Why can't you take care of it, you know I'm not coming into the office today. Where are you? Well, come on up. What do you mean there's no place to park? All right . . . all right . . . Circle around the block. I'll be down in a minute."

Alex leapt out of bed, went to her closet and threw on a pair of jeans and a sweater, and picked her fingers through her spiky coif.

Tirrell sat up. "What's wrong?"

"Something to do with the rooms we booked at the hotel for the party. Travis is downstairs. I need to go deal with this." She slid into a pair of flat-heeled shoes. "I'll be right back." She darted out of the room.

Tirrell lay back into the pillows, but suddenly sprang up when he realized he needed to seize this opportunity. Checking to ensure Alex was out of the apartment, he booted up the laptop on the dining room table. He hurried back into the bedroom and searched her jewelry box for the key to open the hideaway drawer. He found a jump drive atop a passport and some other papers. He wasn't sure how much time he had before she came back and he needed to see what, if anything, was important enough to lock away.

"Okay, Ms. Mafia, let's see what other kind of secrets you got."

Tirrell plugged the drive into the side of the laptop and opened a file called "Solomon's Temple." Xavier Rivera's name appeared at the top of a list of names on a spreadsheet along with dates, dollar amounts, and product quantity.

"This definitely ain't got nothin' to do with event planning."

He entered his e-mail account and copied the file to himself. "Sorry, baby. I gotta look out for my family, too."

When the file was sent he yanked the drive out of the laptop and shut it down. He then returned the jump drive to its hiding place, locked the drawer, and put the key back inside the jewelry box. He then jumped back into bed just as he heard the apartment door open.

"I swear, I have to do everything," Alex huffed, coming back in and kicking off her shoes.

"Is everything a'ight?" He followed her eyes as she noticed her bureau drawer stood slightly ajar. "Baby, is everything cool?"

She looked at him as if she sensed something was amiss. She moved to the bed, sat down beside him, and put her hand on his chest. "Why are you breathing so hard?"

"I did some sit-ups and pushups while you were gone." He flexed his muscle. "You know I gotta keep my shit tight."

Her brow furrowed slightly. If she suspected anything she didn't let on. She smiled wryly. "I'm hungry. What do you say we get something to eat?"

"That sounds good. I'm starvin'."

"Get dressed. We've got some things to do to get you ready for this function."

Tirrell threw back the covers. "What do you mean?"

"Sweetheart, you're fine and all, but you definitely need to upgrade your appearance."

"Alex."

"Don't argue with me. I want my man to look nice. Is that a crime?"

"So, I'm your man now?"

"If we're going to be together you got to look the part. I can't be seen with just anybody. I got a reputation to maintain."

"I'm not for sale, and I'm not your project."

"I never said you were, but saggy jeans and Timberlands aren't going to cut it."

"So you want me to change?"

"You don't have to do anything you don't want to do, Tirrell. The door's right there."

"It's just clothes, right?"

Tirrell could have easily taken offense, but he wasn't going to make it on hubris and looks alone. He didn't much care for the pampering of manicures and pedicures, but he really got into the designer suits and shoes. The stakes were higher now. His game had to be on point if he was going to play with the big boys. It all seemed well worth the price of his compromised integrity.

Travis was in charge of the transformation over the next week. Although he would never admit it, Tirrell actually had fun and felt as entitled as any other shopper in Phipps Plaza as he spent lots of Alex's money in stores like Saks Fifth Avenue, Nordstrom, Hugo Boss, and Armani. He happened on a purple amethyst pendant with a sterling silver chain in Tiffany's jewelry store that was just within his price range. So he wouldn't feel like a complete whore, and to thank Alex for her generosity, he purchased the charm for her with his own money.

All of the shopping and primping was tempered by forty tedious hours of a melancholy instructor droning on about vehicle safety, while showing horrific slides of wreckage at the hands of drunk drivers on Georgia highways.

Tirrell knew he was just marking time—getting a slap on the wrist. Unearthing his real demons would take courage. Denying their existence and disguising them behind expensive suits and shoes was a less daunting task.

18

Betty stepped outside to retrieve the mail as a Yukon pulled up to the curb. There wasn't much she could make out through the tinted windows. She moved closer to the edge of the porch to get a better look. She didn't know whether to smile or scowl when Tirrell exited the passenger side of the vehicle. Her face made up her mind when she spied Alex in the driver's seat. She pursed her lips and her hands rose simultaneously to her hips. Even though he'd called to check in, it had been almost two weeks since he'd come home, and this woman had to have been what kept him.

"How's my girl?" Tirrell beamed, throwing his arms around her and kissing her cheek.

"Boy, where have you been? I haven't heard from you since you called me to tell me that the DUI school was over with."

"Noonie, I told you everything was okay when I called the other day."

"Hearin' your voice and seein' your face are two different things."

"Well, I'm here now. See, it's all good."

"Look at you," Betty observed. "Fancy. Marquis told me you quit the garage. I wonder how you can afford these new things."

Alex stepped up behind Tirrell.

"Noonie, this is the woman I told you about. Alexandra Solomon, this is my grandmother, Betty."

Betty took her in with one wary glance.

Alex extended her hand. "Nice to meet you, Mrs. Ellis."

"Likewise," Betty responded evenly. "Well, come on in. It's a little cool out today."

"I'll be right back," Tirrell said, hurrying from the room and leaving the two women alone.

"Won't you have a seat," Betty offered as she stood in the arch between the dining room and living room.

Alex cleared her throat and eased into Betty's favorite chair. "I love your house. It's . . . charming."

Betty retained a distant demeanor. "Thank you. Would you like something to drink?"

"No, thank you." Alex scanned the room, taking note of all the framed snatches of family history. She stood up and moved to the credenza when she spied a picture of Tirrell.

"He never told me he was in the Army."

"Considering you all haven't known each other that long I'd imagine there's a great many things you don't know about my grandson. Just as I'm sure there are things he doesn't know about you."

"It takes time, but we're getting there."

"Don't you think he's a little young for you?"

Alex glared at Betty with a forced smile. The contrived pleasantries were becoming tiresome. "Age is relative, don't you think?"

"I guess that depends on who you ask. I have to admit when Tirrell told me that he was seeing someone, I expected a girl a little closer to his own."

Alex put the picture down. "How old do you think I am, Mrs. Ellis?"

"Maybe just a little too old."

Alex scoffed. "Do you have a problem with me? Other than the fact that you think I may be too old for Tirrell?"

"I don't really know you well enough to have an opinion."

"Really? Because I think you had an opinion from the moment you saw me."

"Well then because you're a guest in my house I won't be rude. I'll just keep it to myself—for now."

Tirrell had to dig deep into his underwear drawer to find what he was looking for. "Shit," he spat, noting that the plastic pouch didn't contain enough cocaine for a respectable high. His heart pounded; he practically salivated for its taste. The physical reactions he felt due to his involuntary withdrawal were telling. He sat down on the edge of his bed. Betty knocked at his door.

"You all right in here?"

He jumped up and started picking up the clothes he'd strewn about and stuffed them into a bag. "It's all good, Noonie. I was just lookin' for somethin'."

"From the looks of things I hope you found it."

He shook his head.

"Well, what is it? Maybe I can help you."

"No. It's okay. You know what; maybe I don't need any of this stuff after all." He put the bag away.

Betty put her hand on his shoulder and he turned to face her.

"I can see that something's botherin' you. Tell me what it is."

"It's nothin' that I can't handle."

"Why don't I fix you somethin' to eat? We'll sit and catch up."

"Sorry, I don't have the time. I promised Alex that I would help her with some stuff she's tryin' to get done for this big party she's puttin' together."

Betty grimaced.

"You don't like her, do you?"

"I don't know her."

"But you still don't like her."

"I didn't say that."

"You didn't have to."

"Tell you what; will you at least come to church with me in the morning? Pat's cookin' dinner afterward and I'm sure Micah would love to see you."

"I don't think I'm gonna be able to."

Betty's countenance soured all the more.

Tirrell acquiesced. "Okay, I'll try to make it. But, I can't promise anything."

Betty pulled him into her embrace and held him as if the mere act itself would keep him. "I love you."

"I know you do, Noonie. I love you too." Tirrell gently nudged her away and caressed her face. "You don't need to worry about me, Noonie. Everything's all right."

Betty stood and watched them through the glass storm door as they drove off. In spite of what he said, her intuition informed her that things were certainly not all right.

"My grandmother wants me to come to Big Bethel in the morning. I think we should both go."

"Church." Alex scowled.

"Yeah, I haven't spent a lot of time with her lately, and I promised I'd try to come."

Alex cut her eyes at him.

"What? You never been to church before?"

"Yes, I went to church a few times when I was growing up in New York."

"C'mon, it'll be good. You can spend some time gettin' to know my grandmother."

"I don't think your grandmother has any interest in getting to know me."

"Why do you say that? You talked for five minutes."

"After she made a crack about my age, it wasn't that hard to figure out."

Tirrell laughed. "She was just bein' protective."

"Protective is not the word I'd use."

"You just have to get to know her, that's all. She just takes a minute to warm up to you."

Alex cut her eyes again. "Look, I'm sure your *Noonie* is a lovely woman, but maybe it's best that I keep my distance."

Tirrell noted her dig. "You don't have to be like that. I don't even know how old you are."

"You know enough."

Tirrell reached for her purse. "I could just look."

Alex took one hand off the wheel and popped him. "Keep your damn hands off my purse."

"Fuck it then," he pouted.

They continued in silence until Alex tried to change the subject. "So, where're the things you said were so important you had to get from the house?"

"I couldn't find 'em."

"You know you really didn't have to go to Grandmother's house for anything. I told you that I would buy you what you needed."

"Has it occurred to you that maybe there are some things I need you can't buy me?"

"Like what?"

"That's my business," he snapped. "Can you let me out at the next corner?"

"Why? Where are you going?"

"Just let me out, a'ight?"

"Fine." Alex pulled over and slammed on the breaks.

"I just need some time by myself," Tirrell offered. He leaned over and tried to kiss her.

She pulled away.

"I'll call you later."

"Whatever."

He jumped out of the Yukon. Alex sped off.

His body craved a fix that he knew he wouldn't be able to get as long as Alex was around. Bobby was instructed not to provide him any more cocaine. He needed to find another source to placate the beast.

He walked until he happened on a well-known haunt that catered to his particular perversion. Within a few blocks, the mostly familial neighborhood morphed into urban squalor. Many of the businesses had either moved away or closed. Other than a dry cleaners and a barber shop at the corner of the block, the only establishments that appeared to be thriving were a chicken wing shack and a liquor store. Abandoned buildings were prevalent, surrounded by vacant plots of land where even grass refused residency. A storefront church held up the other corner, but even its faith didn't keep the windows from being barred.

Tirrell seemed uncomfortable and out of sorts—a more fashionable replica of his former self. Still, his crisp white shirt and camel-colored suede jacket could not mask the fact that inside he was still the same man.

It didn't take long for him to engage someone.

A dark-hued man with twisted locks and a deep scar on his face came out of the liquor store. They sized each other up before the man approached.

"Yo, Dorothy. I don't think you're in Kansas anymore," the man cracked. "But I think I know you from somewhere?"

"I doubt it." Tirrell scratched his head and wiped his hand over his mouth.

A perceptive glint filled the man's eyes; he knew why he was there. He looked around to see who might be watching. "Is this what you lookin' for?"

Crack cocaine: a derivative of the pure that was secreted back from Miami. Tirrell flashed on the process and wondered if this was one of the many foot soldiers dispatched throughout the city to subvert the war.

"How much?"

"You ain't no cop, is you?"

"Naw, man. I ain't no cop."

The man leaned into Tirrell and took a sniff.

"Naw, you don't smell like one. I got a place around the corner. We can work somethin' out."

Tirrell sheepishly followed the man, giving little thought about what he might be walking into.

"I'm Calvin."

Tirrell spied the etched tattoo on the man's neck and remembered their encounter on the MARTA months before. He was willing to overlook it for the certain embrace of a mistress that would not be denied.

"Kevin," Tirrell said without missing a beat. "You say you live close?"

"Yeah," the man replied. "Just up the street."

When they got to the man's house a mangy mutt ran howling to greet them. The man picked up a rock and pelted him with it and the dog scampered away. They stepped around the decaying bricks of the front stoop. A muffled stereo could be heard before the door was opened. The meager furnishings notwithstanding, Tirrell could see that the house was somewhat affected by a woman's touch.

"Come on in," the man said. "Yo, Stacey, where you at?"

A sallow Caucasian woman with strawberry-blond shoulder-length hair emerged from the bathroom, drying her hands on her short denim skirt. "What Cal . . . Oh, damn. You didn't tell me we were havin' company."

"Kevin, this is my girl, Stacey."

Tirrell nodded. "Sup."

"You are, apparently. Come on in. Have a seat."

Tirrell sat pensively on the edge of an overstuffed chair whose decorative flowered pattern had long since faded from years of use. The smell of bacon grease assaulted his nostrils. From the looks of what he could see in the kitchen, no one had bothered to wash the breakfast dishes.

"You want a beer?" the man asked as he stuck the case he carried into the refrigerator.

"Naw, I'm good."

"Kevin, chill out, dude. Stacey ain't gon' bite—unless you want her to."

Tirrell laughed at his angst. "A'ight, okay. I'll take one."

"Me too," the woman said, curling up lasciviously on the sofa.

The man pulled out three beers and passed one to Tirrell. He then lit incense and sat down on a mismatched sofa next to the woman and handed a beer to her.

"That's some nice shit you wearin'," the man said. "Where you shop? D&K or someplace like that?"

"Yeah," Tirrell agreed, taking a swig from the bottle. He didn't think it was necessary to tell the man his clothes probably cost more than his rent.

He eyed the drug paraphernalia on the coffee table between them and rubbed his chin. The man pulled a plastic Baggie out of his pocket and laid it down on the table next to pieces of Brillo pads, a roach clip, and a glass cylinder no bigger than a cigarette with a bowled tip. "I thought you might wanna sample a li'l bit of this shit before you buy it."

He cut a small piece of one of the pads and burned off the chemicals before rolling it into a ball and packing it into the tip of the glass pipe. He put a cocaine rock on top of the pad and lit a fire underneath to melt it into the pad. The pungent aroma of something akin to burnt plastic and a Bic pen with a twinge of sweetness filled the room. As the substance dissolved, the man put the pipe to his lips and inhaled. Tirrell's throat tightened. The man passed the pipe to him.

Following suit, Tirrell packed in another rock, lit the fire, and inhaled. The sensation caused his blood pressure to rise. His head felt as if it were engulfed in the clouds. The powerful rush was intoxicating. This was what he'd longed for.

"Kevin, you all right?" the woman asked.

"Yeah, it's all good."

"You ain't done this before, have you?" Calvin asked.

Tirrell shook his head and leaned back.

"You startin' to chase that rabbit now—ain't cha, boy." Calvin laughed. "The first time is always the sweetest. You ain't gon' never get this one again."

It didn't take long for them to polish off all twelve bottles of beer, and they smoked enough to be considered sufficiently "tweaked." With his defenses relaxed, Tirrell slipped off his jacket, closed his eyes, and savored the bliss.

Calvin went to the bathroom. When he came back he found his girlfriend topless and on her knees between Tirrell's legs. She had worked his zipper down and fished out his penis.

"What you doin'?" Tirrell muttered.

"Take it easy, baby," she whispered. "Stacey's gonna take real good care of you."

"Hell, yeah," Calvin encouraged her. "Do that shit."

A part of Tirrell fought to resist, but not the part the woman now held in her mouth. Turned on by her performance, Calvin dropped his trousers and joined in.

Even in a disoriented state this was a little more than Tirrell wanted to deal with.

"Stop," Tirrell heaved, and pushed at her.

"Suck it, girl," Calvin said enthusiastically.

"I said stop," Tirrell yelled, shoving the woman more forcefully.

She fell backward, bumping her head on the end of the coffee table. "What the hell!"

Calvin pulled up his pants. "Hey, man. We just havin' a li'l fun."

"Just back the fuck up off me," Tirrell slurred. He wobbled upright.

"Calvin, just get your money and put this limp-dick asshole out."

"Limp dick!"

The woman leapt to her feet. "That's what I said."

Tirrell pulled his clothes together and grabbed his jacket. "Y'all a bunch of damn freaks. I'm outta here."

Calvin seized Tirrell's arm. "You ain't leavin' here 'til I gets my money."

The woman reached for his jacket, trying to get into his pockets. Tirrell spun around wildly and knocked her to the floor. Calvin punched him in the back, nearly sending him to his knees. Tirrell's violent fury ignited. He elbowed the man in the face, took a handful of his locks, and rammed his head into the wall.

"Shit! You done broke my nose," the man yelled.

"You motherfucker," the woman screamed.

She scrambled to her feet again and retrieved a small-caliber handgun from under the sofa cushions. The first shot she fired whizzed by Tirrell's ear and lodged in the doorjamb behind him.

She took aim again and Tirrell picked up an empty beer bottle and threw it at her. He tore out of the house before either had a chance to retaliate. He ran until he was back in familiar territory. His heart raced and he was sweating profusely. Lightheaded and woozy, he fell against a lamppost for balance. Betty's house was just around the next corner.

He knocked instead of using his key. A lump formed in his throat when she opened the door and he looked into her eyes.

"Tirrell."

She welcomed him home without question. There was no judgment.

19

Whether or not he intended to honor his promise, the next morning Tirrell found himself at church, seated several pews behind his grandmother, who sat next to Anne Crawl. Marquis wasn't there. Thankfully Tirrell still had a few things he could wear left hanging in the closet of his bedroom. Being in church again was disquieting; still, he sought absolution. Tears formed in his eyes at the thought of possibly losing his life the day before. Shaking it off, he looked around, half expecting to see Tasha—he hoped he would. He caught a glimpse of Kevin and Pat on the other side of the sanctuary trying to quiet Micah, who seemed to be bursting at the seams to get to his uncle.

Tirrell felt a tap on his shoulder as he flicked at the loose lint that clung to his pants. He was floored when he looked up to see who it was.

"Alex?"

"Is there enough room for me?"

He stood and allowed her to squeeze by. A beautiful woman dressed in a form-fitting two-piece suit was bound to attract attention. Her legs alone stirred the interest of several of the men around her.

"What are you doin' here?"

"Isn't this where sinners belong?"

Tirrell smiled and shook his head in disbelief. "How did you know I'd be here?"

"I just assumed you would be. Besides, if I want your grandmother to like me, I gotta put forth a good effort, right?"

A crescendo of music signifying the beginning of the service swept through the edifice as parishioners stood to their feet. It didn't take a mind reader to see what Betty was thinking when she turned to see Alex standing next to Tirrell. Alex took Tirrell's hand and winked.

After service Micah broke from his parents and bolted over to his uncle. Betty made a beeline to him too.

"Hey, li'l man, what's good?"

Alex smiled. "Who's this handsome boy?"

"This is my nephew, Micah."

Tirrell turned to see Kevin and Pat walking toward them and remembered Alex's warning. His cheerfulness dissipated as his worlds collided. He handed Micah off to his father.

"Aren't you going to introduce us to your lady friend?" Kevin asked.

Tirrell swallowed nervously. "Alex, this is Kevin and my sister-in-law, Pat."

Alex nodded. "Nice to meet you."

"Nice to meet you too," Pat responded. "Did you enjoy the service?"

"You know, I really did. I am going to have to come back."

"We should get goin'," Tirrell injected.

"Oh, no." Betty sighed. "I thought we'd be together today—just the family."

Tirrell took Alex's arm and squeezed. "We have to go. Remember all that stuff you said you had to do that I was supposed to help you with?"

"Right," Alex agreed. "Maybe we can get together another time."

Tirrell rubbed his hand over Micah's head and tick-led him. "I'll see you later, li'l man." He kissed Betty's cheek. "I'm sorry, Noonie. Thanks for lettin' me stay last night. Later, Kev."

He hurried Alex out of the sanctuary, leaving them all standing there baffled.

"What was that about?" Pat queried.

"Whatever it is, it's got something to do with that woman," Betty sneered.

Kevin scratched his beard. "I know her from some-where. I just can't put my finger on where."

Pat looked at Betty. "Are you all right?"

Betty shook her head. "Lord, help me. I know we're in church, but there's just somethin' about that woman I don't like."

"Let's go," Tirrell demanded as he and Alex jumped into the Yukon.

"Why were you in such a hurry to get me out of there?"

He leaned into her. "You threatened my family. You think I want you to spend any time around them?"

"You were the one who invited me to come to church."

"Yeah, what the hell was I thinkin'."

"You sure you don't want to go running back to your grandmother's apron?"

"You leave her out of this, or I swear—"

"What? What will you do, Tirrell?"

"You know what, I don't need this. I'm out." Tirrell reached to open his door and Alex hit the power locks to stop him.

"I'm sorry. We just got out of church. I shouldn't be acting like this."

"Damn right you shouldn't be."

"And I'm sorry you feel I threatened your family."

"You did threaten them."

Alex sighed. "Can we just let that go?"

Tirrell shook his head and scratched his brow.

"I'm thirty-three," Alex blurted.

"What?"

"You wanted to know how old I am. I'm thirty-three."

Tirrell lay back on the headrest and took a moment to calm down. "So, why are you tellin' me this now?"

"I stayed up half the night waiting for you. You never called. I was . . . I was worried."

"You were worried?"

"Look, this is hard for me. I like you. I really do. I wouldn't have come to church if I didn't . . ."

"If you didn't what?"

She sighed. "I don't like feeling what I'm feeling. I don't want you to go."

"Then what do you want?"

"I don't want to fight. This all just scares me a little, you know."

"It scares me too."

She kissed him.

"You need to stop," Tirrell said. "We're still in the church parking lot."

"Can you think of a better place for consummation?"

"Watch it. Your horns are showin'."

"As soon as we get back to my place I'll show you my tail, too."

"Alex."

"Please. Let me make it up to you."

Everyone has an Achilles heel. If it came right down to it she knew exactly how to exploit Tirrell's, and she wouldn't hesitate a second to do so.

20

The Georgian Ballroom of the majestic Biltmore Hotel with its crystal chandeliers, Palladian windows, and marble floors served as the facility for the extravagant event that Alex had been planning for months. Over the years Atlanta had come to be known as a premiere mecca of R&B and hip-hop entertainment. Red carpet events were drawn by its Southern hospitality and big-city charm. No expense was spared for her renowned client's birthday celebration. She and Travis checked into their suites early in the day to ensure that every meticulous detail had been attended to.

Accompanying sumptuous entrées of steak, lobster, and chicken dinners would be bottles of Cristal for the men and boxes of Godiva chocolates for the women. And the entertainers scheduled to perform were sure to please the most discriminating listener. The invitation-only gala would be the talk of any- and everybody in the know.

"Excuse me," Alex said, trying to get the attention of one of the workers. "This table linen has a stain on it."

The woman closely examined the tablecloth. "You can barely even see it."

"I can see it," Alex barked. "Now change it."

The woman pursed her lips and moved to make the change.

Alex then addressed the florist. "You. Put another centerpiece on this table. These orchids are wilted."

"Alex, calm down before you give yourself a stroke," Travis admonished.

"Don't tell me to calm down. You know how I get when I'm working. If it's not right, I'm going to say something."

"You don't want these people walking out of here before the guests arrive, do you?"

"They wouldn't dare, if they know what's good for them."

"Well, saying *please* and *thank you* would go a long way."

"How about I just say *unemployment* or *green card*? Would that get their attention?"

"Pump your breaks, Alex. Everybody's doing their job. We got at least three hours before anybody is supposed to get here. Why don't you go up to your room and relax. Maybe get Tirrell to work off some of your stress."

"Remind me to fire your ass when this is over," Alex snapped.

"You wouldn't make it without me," Travis countered.

"If it's all the same to you, I'll just stay here and make sure everything gets done the way I want it to."

"You're the boss."

"Damn right."

Paparazzi descended on the hotel as the stars came out to play. Alex dazzled in a gold-beaded mini Nalini Vermuri and led the applause when the Grammy-winning Usher and his companion stepped out of their limousine.

"Alex, the place looks great."

"Nothing but the best," she said enthusiastically.

"Are Terry and Jimmy here?"

"Right over there." Pleased with herself, Alex looked around and enjoyed her victory.

Tirrell slipped his arms around her from behind and kissed her neck. "You did an amazing job, baby."

She moved away uneasily. "Tirrell, don't. Not here."

"What did I do?"

"Nothing. I'm just very busy."

"Fine," he sulked.

She stroked his cheek. "C'mon, don't pout. I'll make it up to you later when we get back to the room, okay? By the way, Mr. Ellis, did I tell you that you look very handsome and dapper tonight?"

Tirrell spun around and mugged in his tailored Armani suit. "Well, you know. I gotta represent."

"I see somebody over there I need to talk to. Behave yourself, baby." With that, Alex whisked away to the other side of the room.

Tirrell shook his head. "Behave myself? What the hell does she think I'm gonna do—pee on the carpet?" He stepped over to the bar.

"What can I get you?"

"Corona," Tirrell said. "On second thought, make it Grey Goose with a twist. May as well make the most of this Cinderella bullshit." When he turned around he bumped into Tasha, almost spilling his drink on her.

"Tirrell, what are you doin' here?"

"I could ask you the same thing." Tirrell glanced over her shoulder and found his answer. "Oh, I see. That's your boy, *Dickey*."

"His name is Rickey," Tasha asserted.

"Looks like a dick to me," Tirrell sneered.

"He's here for a client."

"Client?"

"Rickey's an entertainment lawyer."

"Damn, girl. You look good," Tirrell noted, tracing the spaghetti straps of her dress with his fingers.

She blushed and lowered her gaze. "Thank you. So do you."

"I'd ask you how you've been, but I can see you must be doin' all right for yourself."

"Rickey's a nice guy, believe it or not."

"I wasn't talkin' about him."

"Can I get you something, miss?" the bartender asked.

"Long Island."

When she reached for her drink Tirrell spied the diamond tennis bracelet he'd given her. It made him smile.

"How's Miss Betty?"

"She's good."

"She stopped comin' to the shop. I know she hates me for what I did."

"How do you know I told her?"

Tasha shot Tirrell a look that suggested she knew that he had. "I should be gettin' back to Rickey."

Tirrell glanced over her shoulder again to see her date engaged in a lively conversation with someone else. "He doesn't look like he's missin' you. So, why don't we go somewhere and talk?"

"We are talkin'."

"You know what I mean."

"I don't think it's a good idea. We don't really have anything else to say to each other."

He reached out and caressed her bare arm. "Tasha, c'mon. I'm not gonna do anything to you."

She turned around to see if Rickey Hicks was looking in her direction, and followed Tirrell to the terrace.

"It's a little chilly out here," she said.

He removed his jacket and wrapped it around her shoulders. "Is that better?"

"Armani? Kind of pricey for a mechanic."

"Who said that's all I know how to do?"

"It just doesn't seem like you, that's all."

"Maybe this is the new me."

Tasha took a sip of her drink. "So, who is the *new* you here with?"

"You." Tirrell leaned in for a kiss.

She backed away. "What are you doin'?"

He pressed his cheek up against hers. "It hasn't been so long that you forgot, has it? I know a lot of shit went down between us, but we had a good thing once. We could again."

"No, Tirrell. We can't."

"If you wanted to move on you wouldn't be wearin' my bracelet."

He leaned in again. This time the kiss was reciprocal.

"So, this is where you ran off to."

They jerked apart and turned to see Alex.

"I don't believe we've met," Alex said.

"Um . . . this is Tasha," Tirrell injected. "She's an old friend."

"Hi, Tasha. I'm Alex. Tirrell's *new* friend."

Tasha slipped Tirrell's jacket off and handed it back to him. "I think I'd better get back inside."

"Don't rush off on my account. Looks like the two of you were just getting reacquainted."

Tasha breezed by, leaving Alex and Tirrell alone.

Alex stepped to Tirrell and wiped a smudge of lipstick from his mouth with her thumb. "The party's inside."

He brushed her hand away. "You know what, I think I'm gonna just hang out here for a while. I'll be in later."

"Tirrell, I don't think your *old friend* is coming back."

He pulled a cigarette from a pack inside his jacket. "Can I have a little time alone, please?"

"Fine." Alex reluctantly stepped back inside.

Tirrell closed his eyes and leaned against the building. The nicotine in the cigarette wasn't as agreeable as he'd hoped it would be. *You startin' to chase that rabbit now, ain't cha, boy.*

"Travis, have you seen Tirrell?"

"I didn't know I was supposed to be babysitting."

"Don't be a smart ass."

Alex scanned the ballroom and saw Tasha, so she knew that Tirrell wasn't with her. She went back to the terrace to check. He was gone.

Saturday night traffic in Midtown was as lively as ever. Tirrell shoved his hands in his pockets and walked briskly up West Peachtree Street. Knowing what he was looking for, but not sure where he'd find it, he rounded the corner of Cypress Street and unearthed a treasure of nefarious intent.

He stood rubbing his hands together and observed the cars that cruised by and slowed for a better look. After a time it felt as if he were on exhibit—like a puppy in a pet store window waiting for someone to claim him.

The prowlers who paraded up and down the block, stroking themselves provocatively, broadcast exactly what was for sale. Tirrell studied their scurrilous behavior for as long as he could before shaking his head and walking away. When he crossed the street he heard a horn blaring to get his attention; he didn't look up, he didn't turn around.

"Tirrell!"

He was alarmed when he heard his name. "Scotty?"

An F-150 truck pulled up to the curb. The sandy-haired man leaned out the window. "What the hell are you doin' down here?"

"I uh, missed the last bus," Tirrell responded.

"Bus? Forget that, man. C'mon."

Tirrell jumped in and they took off. "Thanks, Scotty."

"Man, look at you. What have you been up to? You hit the lottery?"

"No, I was at a party. What are you doin' down here?"

He scratched the scraggly hairs on his chin and laughed. "I was supposed to be meetin' this chick, right. We've been talkin' online for a while. We exchanged pics and let's just say she misrepresented herself."

"It didn't look like her?"

"In the face maybe. The body belonged to somebody else."

They laughed.

"I'm serious. She was fat."

"So, you got somethin' against a healthy woman?"

"No. I like a woman with a little meat on her—more cushion for the pushin', you know what I mean? I just don't want her to look like a side of beef."

"Aw, man. That just ain't right."

"So, what kind of party were you at?"

"Peep this. I was at a birthday party . . . for Usher."

"The singer?"

"Yep."

"Damn, how you get invited to something like that?"

"You remember that fine-ass woman who gave me her number?"

"You hit that?"

"Knocked a hole in it."

They laughed again.

"Must not have been that great a party if you lookin' for a bus."

"It wasn't as social as I wanted, you feel me?"

The man reached into his inside pocket and extracted a bag of marijuana.

Tirrell licked his lips. "I . . . uh . . . I was sort of lookin' for somethin' with a little more kick to it."

"Well, why didn't you say so?" Scotty asked. "You ever lace your weed with cocaine?"

"No, but I ain't opposed to tryin' it."

"Trust me. You're gonna love this shit."

Scotty invited Tirrell back to his place in Decatur. There was no fear of an unwanted sexual advance; he had only pacification to look forward to.

21

A cold rain subsided by the time Tirrell got off the train and crossed through Centennial Park toward Alex's condo. His buddy, Scotty, provided him with a change of clothes. It had been two incomprehensible days since he walked away from the Biltmore. He was prepared to face the firing squad, or so he thought.

He wavered as he reached out to press the button on the intercom. He stepped back a few paces and tried to shake off the anxiety. His first instinct was to forget about Alex and cut and run back to the warmth of his grandmother's home, but he couldn't leave things as they were between them. If he did, there would be no telling how she would react. "Man up, T," he told himself and he pressed the intercom.

"Who is it?" Alex's tone was sharp and agitated.

Tirrell swallowed. "I . . . It's me."

"Who the hell is 'me'?"

"C'mon, Alex. It's Tirrell."

There was no immediate response. Seconds lumbered by before the buzzer sounded and the door clicked open. Tirrell's heart beat furiously, magnifying the blood pumping in his ears as the elevator ascended to her floor. The door was ajar as he approached. He slowly pushed it open to find her seated at the dining room table, facing him. Owning up to what he'd done propelled him forward.

"I would have packed your shit and thrown it out the door. But, everything in that closet I bought, and you don't get a consolation prize for fucking me over," Alex snapped.

Tirrell couldn't make eye contact. He stared down at the floor. "I'm sorry."

"Yeah, you are. Too bad I refused to see it before now."

He forced himself to look at her. "Just let me explain, a'ight?"

"Explain what, Tirrell? How you decided to embarrass me and take off without so much as a good-bye? Or, how you stayed away for two whole days and couldn't even be bothered to call."

"Alex."

"You know what, I don't want to hear it. Get the hell out. I don't know why I let you in here in the first place. You're pathetic!"

He started toward her and she eased up from her chair.

"I said, get out. I don't ever want to see your sorry ass again. You could have had a good life with me, you know that? There was no limit to what I would have done for you."

"Maybe I didn't want you to do anything. You ever think about that? I'm a man. Maybe you buyin' me every goddamn thing was more than I could handle."

Alex laughed callously. "You are many things, Mr. Ellis. But, a man is not one of them. So, why don't you run your little raggedy ass back across town to your precious *Noonie*. I'm sure there's still some milk left in those healthy breasts of hers for you to nurse on."

He angrily slammed her into the wall and clutched his hand to her throat. It was a recognizable but unexpected response. "You wanna be nasty, bitch, huh?"

Her eyes teared up. She remained eerily calm. "Get . . . your . . . damn . . . hands . . . off me!"

He withdrew, shuddering. She slapped him. He recoiled. She slapped him again.

"Are you high?"

He turned away. She yanked him back around and looked in his eyes for confirmation.

"Get out of my house." She snatched the amethyst from her neck and threw it at him. "You can take this cheap piece of shit with you. And don't even think about telling anybody what you think you know about me, or you know what will happen."

"What I *think* I know?" Tirrell countered. He pointed his finger in her face for emphasis. "Bitch, if you come near my family I swear you'll be the one who's sorry."

She smacked his hand away. "Don't you ever put your hand in my face again."

"I got all the proof I need to blow your little operation to hell. And if anything happens to me or mine, it's all over for you."

"You're full of shit."

"You wanna go to prison and have some big dyke shove a stick up your pretty little ass, just try me."

"You better be careful who you try to intimidate. I'm not the only menace to your family."

"Then you better make damn sure that no one else comes after them either."

Tirrell backed out the door slowly, afraid to turn around.

Alex massaged her throbbing neck muscles and racked her brain, thinking about what Tirrell could possibly have that could be used against her. Other than the fact that he'd been to Rivera's house, what else could he know? She replayed every conceivable time since meeting him that she could have slipped up. It suddenly dawned on her what it could be. She raced into her bedroom, fumbled for the key in her jewelry box, and threw open the bureau drawer. She breathed a sigh of relief to find that the computer jump drive was where she'd left it. "What does he know?" She moved to her bed, sat down, and picked up the phone. "Bobby, it's me. You need to get over here, right now. I don't care that you have company. We've got a big problem that we need to make disappear."

Alex hung up the telephone and went to the living room and poured herself a double shot of vodka. Bobby made it to her apartment within the hour; by then, she was nursing her second drink.

"I fucked up," he said.

"We both did," she admitted.

"I thought he could handle it. I never expected him to go ape-shit. Are you sure he was high?"

"I looked into his eyes and all I could see was Ray."

"He wasn't gettin' that stuff from me, I swear."

"Unfortunately, we're not the only game in town. He could have gotten it from just about anybody."

"You wanna call Rivera?"

"No. We can't do that. He can't know that we were that stupid and careless. You know he would eliminate every possible connection to him."

"So, what are we gonna do?"

"We have to find out what Tirrell has, and we have to stop him before he can use it against us."

"You think we'll have to kill him?"

"I'm not going to jail, Bobby. We have to protect ourselves." Alex poured another drink and poured one for Bobby. "Remind me again how his brother being an ADA and the threat against his family was supposed to keep him in line."

***

Tirrell castigated himself as he walked toward downtown. *How the hell could you be so stupid? Why did you tell her that you had proof that could put her in jail? Why the hell didn't you just leave well enough alone? If she hurts Noonie it's gonna be on you.*

He stopped and leaned against a building, pounding himself in the forehead with his fists until tears flooded his eyes. It was nearing seven o'clock in the evening. He had to know if Betty was all right. He patted his pockets for his cell phone and then remembered he must have left it at Scotty's apartment. He reached in his pants for change and searched for a payphone. When she answered a wave of relief washed over him.

"Hello. Hello. Is anyone there?"

"Noonie."

"Tirrell?"

He sucked in a mouthful of air to arrest his anguish.

"Tirrell, what's the matter? Are you all right?"

"Yeah, I'm fine. I just wanted to call . . . and . . . and tell you that I love you."

"I can hear that somethin' is wrong, Tirrell. What is it?"

"Nothin'. I'm okay as long as I know you are."

"Do you need to come home?"

"No." He couldn't let her see him like this.

"I made dinner. I could warm somethin' up for you."

"I'm okay . . . I'll talk to you later, a'ight?"

After ensuring that she was definitely all right, Tirrell sank to the ground in a puddle of shame and sobbed. A sudden storm burst through the clouds and forced him from the sidewalk. He darted into a building where it appeared some sort of gathering was going on. Everyone inside turned toward the door.

"C'mon in. You're among friends here," said the man at the front of the room.

Tirrell took inventory of the varied faces of the men—old—young—black—white—battered—tired—distressed—hopeful; most seemed homeless.

"You're just in time. We were just gettin' started."

All the men stood up, eighteen in total, and together they joined in a litany they recited verbatim.

"God, grant me the serenity to accept the things I cannot change, courage to change the things I can, and wisdom to know the difference."

Damn, Tirrell thought. *This is some kind of AA meeting.* He turned to leave.

"Where you goin', man? No need to feel ashamed. None of us is here to stand in judgment of nobody else. We've all been where you are at one time or another."

Tirrell glanced around and saw heads bobbing in agreement.

"What makes you think you know where I am?"

"You're here, aren't you?"

"This was a mistake."

Tirrell headed for the door, but stopped in his tracks as the rain beat down harder. He turned back around and the man leading the meeting stared at him. It made him uncomfortable.

"Maybe it's time for you to come in out of the rain, literally and figuratively, bruh."

Tirrell pulled tightly at the windbreaker he wore and took off. He ran as if he could somehow dodge the pelting raindrops, but his efforts were futile. He was soaked by the time he made it to the MARTA station.

"Why are you breathing so hard?"

"I did some sit-ups and pushups while you were gone. You know I gotta keep my shit tight."

Alex opened her eyes. She shot straight up in bed and turned on the lamp on the nightstand next to the bed. She found her briefcase in the living room, pulled out her laptop, and booted it up. She looked at the browsing history and found a site that she was sure she hadn't visited, and no one else, not even her assistant, should have accessed; that would be easy enough to verify. Clicking on it brought up Flexmail—this was not her e-mail service. "Dammit. When the hell would he have been on my computer?"

Alex called Tirrell. He didn't pick up. She opted to leave a voice message. "Whatever it is you think you have, if you're thinking about giving it to the police or to your brother, you better think again. What I could do to you is nothing compared to what Xavier Rivera will do when he finds out."

22

Bad dreams shook Tirrell awake. He gasped and looked around the room to get his bearings. He inhaled the smell of cheese from a half-eaten pizza that lay in a box on the table in front of him, surrounded by empty beer cans. He threw a blanket back, sat up on the sofa, and rubbed his face. The alarming sound of sirens drew him to the window. It was barely daybreak. The cold autumn sky looked as if it were gearing up for another downpour.

"Damn, that noise wake you up too?"

Tirrell turned to see Scotty plodding out of his bedroom, yawning and scratching his pinkish bare chest. He proceeded to the refrigerator.

"You want a beer?"

Tirrell shook his head. "How the hell can you drink beer this early in the morning?"

"I just think of it as coffee." Scotty popped the top of the beer can, leaned against the kitchen counter, and chugged it. "What's so interesting out there?"

"Nothin'," Tirrell said as he moved away from the window and sat down. "Hey, Scotty. I wanna thank you, man, for lettin' me stay here."

"No sweat, T. You're welcome to the couch at least until my roommate gets back next week." He belched. "Oh, man. I gotta take a dump. I think that pizza we had didn't agree with me."

Tirrell chuckled. "Aw, dude, that's nasty. Thanks for sharin'."

When Scotty left the room Tirrell moved the pizza box and found the CD he'd made. He recalled getting in and using Scotty's computer to access his e-mail account. Before they got trashed and everything became a blur, he'd burned Alex's file on to it. He needed to stash it somewhere safe, someplace where someone could find it in case anything happened to him. For a split second he thought about Kevin, but how could he bring himself to tell him that he'd potentially put the entire family in peril?

His cell phone rang. It was Bobby. He ignored the call. The phone rang again—this time it was Betty.

"Hello."

"Tirrell, are you all right?"

"Yeah, I'm good."

"You had me worried after you called last night. Are you sure you're okay?"

"Yeah, I'm sure."

"I couldn't rest thinkin' about how you sounded on the phone. Are you in some kind of trouble?"

Tears stung his eyes. This was a predicament that he caused and somehow he was going to have to fix it.

"Are you with that woman? Is that why you can't talk? You know you can always come home, Tirrell. If you're not ready to—"

"Noonie, I'm fine. You don't have to worry about me, okay?"

"I'm gonna worry until I can see for myself that you're okay, you hear me?"

"Yes, ma'am."

When he ended the call with Betty he dialed Kevin. It rang to voice mail—he didn't leave a message. He listened to the one Bobby left:

"You done messed up now, T. You're gonna be real sorry."

It was peculiar that Tasha should cross Tirrell's mind at a time like this; Marquis did, too. Even if they were speaking to him he couldn't drag them into this. He was completely alone and needed an escape if only for a little while. Shuffling through the mess on the table he found the pipe and just enough crack to assuage the foreboding.

On his way back to the Inman Park transit station, Tirrell found a pawn shop. He went in and produced the amethyst in his pocket.

"How much can I get for this?"

The grouse proprietor behind the glass enclosure looked at Tirrell and examined the pendant. "The clasp is busted. Did you steal this?"

Tirrell wiped his mouth. "No . . . Me and my girl got in a fight and she broke it pulling it off her neck."

"Uh huh," the man grunted, doubting the validity of the story. "You got a receipt?"

"Nah, man. I gave it to my girl as a gift. I don't have the receipt anymore."

"I'll give you ten dollars."

"Ten? C'mon, man. I paid three hundred. I got it from Tiffany's."

"Where's the receipt?"

"I don't have it."

"Ten dollars. Take it or leave it."

"C'mon, bruh. Do me a solid. I really need the cash."

"I'm not runnin' a charity."

The look in Tirrell's eyes implored the man to reconsider. He rang the register open and handed him twenty dollars.

"Get out of here before I change my mind."

Tirrell thanked the man and hustled to the exit. He vacillated between finding a dealer and continuing to his grandmother's house. He chose the latter.

"I'm glad you decided to come home," Betty said enthusiastically, embracing him tightly.

How many times had this scene played out whenever he found himself with no one else to turn to? She knew him better than anyone else. She loved him harder than anyone could.

"You come over here and sit yourself down. I'm gonna fix you something to eat."

"I'm not really hungry," he said.

"Nonsense," Betty insisted. "You are gonna sit down and eat and I'm not gonna take no for an answer."

"Let me just go get cleaned up, okay?"

Tirrell went into the bathroom, closed the door, and braced himself on the ledge of the counter. He examined himself in the mirror. He looked haggard. He knew that Betty saw it, too. He opened the linen closet and pulled out a towel to wash his hands and face. It wasn't much of an improvement, but he felt better.

The mouthwatering aroma of pork chops and fried corn caused his stomach to grumble, indicating that he was a lot hungrier than he thought. He sat down to a heaping plate of love, and ate until he could feel the pressure in his stomach. When he finished he discovered that Betty had gone into his old room and changed the sheets and made the bed for him.

"How's work?" he said, forcing conversation as he helped her put away the food and clean the kitchen.

"It's fine. I had somebody quit on me last week, though. If you're lookin' for a job I could talk to the head of housekeeping and put in a good word for you." She smiled and winked.

"I just might take you up on that," he responded.

When the dishes were dried and put away Betty went into the living room and turned on the television. She sat down in her favorite chair and scanned the channels until she came across a movie she'd wanted to see.

Tirrell went to his room and hid the CD on an upper shelf in his closet inside a shoebox. He then joined his grandmother and sat down on the sofa to watch with her.

"I can find somethin' else," Betty said.

"No, this is cool," Tirrell responded, noting how much Sanaa Lathan reminded him of Alex.

It wasn't long before he drifted off to sleep. A truck backfiring jarred him awake.

"Tirrell, why don't you go on and get in the bed."

He didn't argue. He was exhausted. It would be the first non-drug-induced sleep he'd had in several days.

The next morning, after Betty went off to work, Tirrell found himself back downtown, peering through the window of the building he'd stumbled into a few nights prior. He saw an elderly man sweeping the floor.

The man poked his head out the door. "You lookin' for somebody?"

"Yeah, I was here the other night and there was some kind of group thing goin' on."

"Oh, you mean the NA meetin'?"

"NA?"

"Narcotics Anonymous," the man clarified.

Tirrell swallowed nervously. "Yeah. There was this black dude. He was about this tall. He had a gray patch in the middle of his 'fro."

"You must be talkin' about Charlie Preston."

"Yeah, I guess that's him."

"He works at The Mission over there off Ivan Allen. They come here two or three times a week for them meetin's."

Tirrell nodded. "Thanks."

He walked up Marietta Street and crossed over Luckie Street until he found The Mission. He wasn't sure why he felt compelled to do it—something in him just knew that he had to. When he got to the door he was directed where to find Mr. Preston.

After a few minutes the man came out from the back office. "Can I help you?" His eyes were piercing, but kind. His voice was deep with a resonating Southern drawl.

"I uh . . ."

"You're the young man from the other night, ain't you?"

"Yeah."

"What brings you in here?"

"I'm not exactly sure."

"You do know what this place is, don't you?"

"Yeah."

"So, you are lookin' for *that kind* of help after all?"

"I don't have a drug problem. I was maybe thinkin' . . . I'm not really sure what I was thinkin'."

"What's your name?"

"Kev . . . Tirrell." He sighed. "Shit, this is crazy. I don't know what the hell I came here for. Sorry I bothered you."

"Tirrell, wait," the man said. "Here. Take my number. Call me if you figure out what it is you're lookin' for, or even if you just wanna talk."

The man gave Tirrell his card with the name and address of The Mission on the front of it and his phone number written on the back.

Once outside, Tirrell felt like his lungs had opened up and he could breathe again. "This is crazy. I'm not an addict. I'm not like the rest of those dudes." He tossed the man's card in the street, pulled a cigarette from his pocket, and kept walking. He returned a few seconds later to retrieve it.

23

Another week passed and there had been no backlash from Alex or Bobby. Tirrell was nervous, given the fact that they hadn't called again or sought him out. He was sure they weren't going to let this go. And if they'd gotten Xavier Rivera involved there was undoubtedly a lot more to worry about. He questioned the wisdom of keeping Kevin in the dark. He was, after all, in the DA's office and could marshal the entire police force to protect Betty and the rest of the family if he had to.

"Hey, Kev . . . it's me, Tirrell. I know you don't wanna hear this, but somethin's happened. I may have gotten us all in some really deep shit. I could use your help, man. This is serious. Please call me back as soon as you get this message."

Kevin clicked his phone off and shook his head. He didn't want anything to ruin the evening that he and Pat had planned, especially not Tirrell.

"Noonie, you sure you don't mind taking care of Micah?"

"No, baby. You and Pat go on and enjoy your concert. Don't worry about Micah and me."

"Okay. He's already had his dinner. Don't overdo it with the sweets."

"Boy, are you tellin' me how to look after my great-grandson?"

"No, Noonie. I know you know what you're doing."

"If you're worried about Tirrell bein' back home, don't. Micah is goin' to be just fine."

"Kevin, we need to go or we're going to be late," Pat said after kissing Micah good-bye.

Kevin picked Micah up. "You be a good boy and mind Noonie, understand?"

"Yes, Daddy."

"I'll be back in the morning to pick you up."

"Okay."

"Gimme a kiss."

Micah threw his arms around his father's neck, puffed his cheeks with air, and blew, making a sputtering noise as he kissed him. Kevin tickled him and he laughed and squirmed hysterically.

When Kevin put Micah down he scurried off to Betty's room to play. He then hugged Betty, thanked her again, and he and Pat exited. Betty waved them off and closed the door.

"Micah, would you like some cookies and milk?"

Scampering little feet following her into the kitchen was all she needed to hear. She took two chocolate chip cookies from the jar on the counter and put them on a napkin, and poured a half cup of milk and set it on the table in front of him.

Micah hummed and swung his legs and feet, enjoying his snack. Betty sat down next to him with a Moon Pie.

"Noonie, is Uncle Tirrell comin' home soon?"

"I don't know, baby."

"Can I stay up until he comes so we can play?"

She glanced at her watch. "Well, your daddy told me to have you in bed by eight, but we'll see."

***

A souped-up black Mustang with dark tinted windows cruised by Tirrell as he walked toward the house, and made him uneasy. He lowered his gaze and picked up his pace.

"Yo, Q. Slow down, man," the passenger inside the car barked.

"What for?" the driver asked.

"That was that muthafucka I was tellin' you about who came to my place the other week. He jacked Stacey and busted my damn nose."

"Do you think he lives around here somewhere?"

"I don't know. Let's get his ass."

Another car pulled up behind the Mustang as it idled at a stop sign and blew its horn, prompting them to continue through the intersection. The Mustang quickly turned off into a neighboring driveway and spun around.

Tirrell spotted Marquis driving up to his mother's house and called to him. Marquis got out of his car and Tirrell started across the street just as the Mustang careened toward him. The quick flash of a gun barrel sticking out of the passenger window was all Tirrell saw before rapid fire rained down like a hail storm. Marquis ducked for cover. With scarcely enough time to react, Tirrell dove into a bank of hedges in front of the house.

"T!" Marquis yelled as he came from behind his car and hurried over to him.

The Mustang tore through the four-way stop at the end of the block and disappeared.

The commotion brought skittish neighbors to their windows and doors, and Anne Crawl raced screaming from her house.

"Marquis! Oh my God, are you all right?"

"I'm all right, Mama." He went to Tirrell and helped him up out of the bushes. "T, are you all right?"

"Yeah."

"Oh my God," Anne shrieked. "You're bleeding."

There were cuts and scratches on Tirrell's face from the prickly sticks and brambles. He was in shock and didn't feel the shot that had torn into his left thigh. When he saw blood spewing from the open wound, reality came crashing in. He turned to see the glass in the storm door and front window of Betty's house shattered and the house riddled with bullets.

"Noonie!"

He pushed Marquis aside as he tripped up the concrete steps and limped to the door. The horrifying sight that greeted him took his breath away. Betty was slumped over in her recliner.

Tirrell swept her up in his arms and wailed. They were all stunned when they looked up to see Micah coming from her room crying. Anne Crawl picked him up, shielded his face, and tried to calm him down. Marquis called 911.

Spectators swarmed the house on Eastland Avenue like ants at a picnic; some even dared to come up on the porch to get a better look inside as emergency vehicle lights flashed and lit up the street.

Tirrell wept vehemently. "Don't die, Noonie. Please don't die."

Micah fought, screamed, and reached out for his uncle when Anne Crawl tried to take him out of the room.

Tirrell choked, "It's okay, Micah. Go with her."

Police arrived and attempted to control the pandemonium. Anyone not directly involved was ordered to move away from the house while the EMTs hurried in and went to work.

"There's a lot of blood here," a female EMT reported to her partner. "As far as I can tell she's been hit in the abdomen."

"Let's clear the area," her male counterpart responded.

He moved a lamp and table. Marquis offered assistance setting aside any obstruction. Tirrell hovered, refusing to budge.

"Sir, you're going to have to step back so we can do our job."

"She's my grandmother," he cried.

"What's your name?"

"Tirrell Ellis."

"Okay, Tirrell, we're going to help your grandmother, but you're going to have to give us some space."

Marquis pulled Tirrell back.

One of the paramedics noticed Tirrell's blood-saturated pants when he winced. "Can I take a look at your leg?"

"No," Tirrell countered. "I'm all right. Fix my grandmother."

"What's your grandmother's name?"

"Betty."

"How old is she?"

Tirrell rubbed his blood-spattered hand over his face. "Uh . . . sixty-three . . . sixty-four."

The male EMT radioed for a backup unit and returned to his partner. "Her breathing is shallow. Pulse is weak and thready. Blood pressure sixty over forty. We need to intubate."

There was an alarming back and forth exchange between the two paramedics as they furiously worked to bring Betty around.

"She's having arrhythmias. Start two large-bore IVs."

"Get some pressure on the wound."

"She's in v-fib!"

"Shock her at two hundred."

The female technician ripped open Betty's robe, grabbed a pair of defibrillator paddles, and pressed them on to her chest. "Clear!"

Betty flailed like a ragdoll. After a few more attempts she began to respond. Another team arrived soon after and tended to Tirrell. Tearing open his pant leg it was easy to see that the bullet had ripped into the meat of his thigh, but it couldn't be determined whether it had caused any damage to an artery.

Tirrell grunted and spewed expletives as pressure was applied.

"You're goin' to need an X-ray," one of the technicians declared.

"No shit," Tirrell countered.

His leg was cleaned, packed with gauze, and bandaged while he waited to be transported to the hospital.

The tranquil Ellis living room became a frenzied crime scene within a matter of minutes. Tirrell glanced around to see a police officer in the kitchen talking with Anne Crawl, who was still trying to pacify Micah. Another was in the dining room questioning Marquis.

There was absolutely no doubt in his mind who had perpetrated this calamity. Tirrell was already formulating a plan for revenge.

Once Betty was stable enough to move, the EMTs put her on a stretcher and loaded her into the back of the ambulance.

"I'm goin' with her," Tirrell demanded, ignoring his own injury.

"Mr. Ellis, we've got some more questions for you," one of the officers said.

"To hell with that. I'm goin' with my grandmother."

Marquis helped Tirrell to the ambulance. The male EMT looked at the police officer for his consent.

"I gotta get checked out anyway, right?"

The officer nodded and they pulled him on board.

The police followed directly behind the ambulance with Marquis, his mother, and Micah in tow.

"Dispatch, we have an African American female, approximately sixty-four years old, GSW to the abdomen. There is massive internal bleeding. Patient is in and out of consciousness and diaphoretic. We started two large-bore IVs of normal saline, wide open, and patient was shocked at two hundred. We also have a male on board . . ." The EMT turned to Tirrell. "How old are you?"

"Twenty-two."

"African American male, twenty-two years of age, GSW to the left quadrate muscle of the thigh. We're about ten minutes out. Please have a trauma team standing by."

Tirrell leaned into Betty and gently took her hand. "Hold on, Noonie. Everything's gonna be all right. I swear. Just hold on."

Betty was wheeled into the ER where a surgeon promptly assessed the extent of her injuries. "Let's get an X-ray of her chest and abdomen to see if there is any other damage. I want her blood type crossed and matched for ten units." The surgeon took a scalpel to open her up and discovered the cause of the hemorrhaging. He stuck his hand inside her chest to put pressure on the hole in her aortic valve. "Get the vascular surgeon on call to meet me in the OR, stat!"

Tirrell's wound was treated in the ER, but he knew that all the antibiotics and stitches in the world would not be enough to save him once Kevin found out what happened.

***

Kevin checked the messages on his cell phone as he and Pat walked out of the Civic Center. He scowled after finally listening to the one Tirrell left earlier. He was panicked by the one left by Anne Crawl.

"Kevin, what is it?"

"There's been a shooting."

"What?"

"Noonie's been taken to Grady Hospital."

"What about Micah?"

"I don't know. We gotta go."

Kevin grabbed Pat's hand and they pressed through the crowd in the lobby and dashed through the parking lot to their car. Unnerved by the sea of cars jockeying to exit, he laid impatiently on his horn as if by doing so they'd move any faster. While Kevin cursed and cut other drivers off, Pat called Anne Crawl for an update.

"Micah's with Miss Anne," Pat relayed. "He's all right. Tirrell was shot."

"What the hell happened?" Kevin snapped.

"Some sort of drive-by. Miss Betty's in surgery."

Kevin turned to his wife with a stricken look on his face. "Tirrell had something to do with this. I know he did."

As usual the burgeoning Atlanta traffic didn't bow to the urgency of the situation. Despite risking an accident, and defying the police to stop them, they managed to make it to the hospital in less than twenty minutes. They bolted through the ER doors and found Anne Crawl and Marquis sitting among the many others waiting to be seen by a doctor. Micah, who had cried himself to sleep, woke up and leapt into his father's arms.

"Where is she?" Kevin barked.

"She's still in surgery," Anne replied. "I was going to go up to check on her, but I thought I should wait down here with Micah."

Kevin passed Micah to Pat. "Where's Tirrell?"

"He's in with the doctor," Marquis piped up. "The police are in there too."

Kevin's public manner of poise and decorum gave way to ire as he stepped to the nurse's desk and raged on about being with the DA's office, demanding to know where to find Tirrell. He barged through the double doors and hurried past a bank of curtain-shrouded examining rooms.

"You son-of-a-bitch," he yelled when he found Tirrell. He lunged at him and grabbed him by the collar. The police officer questioning Tirrell pulled him off.

"What the hell did you do this time, Tirrell?"

"Mr. Ellis, you need to calm down," the officer cautioned.

"I don't have to do a damn thing. My grandmother and my son could have been killed, all because of this no-account muthafucka!"

"I didn't know," Tirrell cried. "I didn't know Micah was in the house."

"Is that supposed to make me feel better?"

"I didn't want Noonie to get hurt."

Kevin lunged toward Tirrell and again the police officer moved between them.

"God help your sorry-ass if she dies," Kevin spat.

It had been over an hour and no word had come regarding Betty's condition. Kevin paced anxiously while Micah slept in his mother's lap. Anne Crawl and Marquis also waited.

The surgery team emerged around one in the morning. The small-framed, bearded surgeon who had taken the lead on the operation found the family.

"Mr. Ellis?"

Kevin raised his head from Pat's shoulder and snapped to attention. "I'm Kevin Ellis."

"I'm Dr. Stone. Your grandmother made it through surgery."

"Is she going to be all right?"

"We're just waiting for the anesthesia to wear off before we can assess any further. She sustained a significant amount of damage. The cardio-vascular surgeon repaired the aortic valve, and we had to remove a lacerated spleen."

"When can we see her?"

"She's in ICU. We're keeping an eye on her. It'll be a few more hours before she comes around. Why don't you and your family go on home, get some rest, and come back later. The nurse will call you if there's any change."

"I'm not going anywhere," Kevin insisted.

The doctor tried to be conciliatory. "There's really not a whole lot you can do for her right now."

Pat touched her husband's shoulder. "Kevin."

He looked at her and sighed. "Fine."

Pat thanked the doctor and Kevin scowled. They all sluggishly started to the elevator. Tirrell hobbled up the other end of the corridor. In spite of the blame and accusation in their eyes he continued toward them.

"How is she?"

Without saying a word Kevin charged at him and punched him in the mouth. Marquis shook his head and joined them on the elevator, leaving Tirrell standing alone.

24

Sensing that Alex was standing over him, Tirrell lurched from a restless sleep. He gingerly moved his bandaged leg from the chair that he'd positioned in front of another for a makeshift bed, and cringed. He stretched out from the uncomfortable position and slowly stood up. He then walked out into the hall to see if there were any nurses lurking who would keep him from sneaking into the ICU.

His heart ached looking into Betty's ashen expression. The beeping and hissing of the monitors and machines echoed off the sterile walls. Tirrell glanced over his shoulder before moving closer to her bed. Remorse spilled out of his eyes and down his face. He pulled up a chair, eased into it, and caressed her forearm. "I know who did this to you. I swear I'm gonna make 'em pay if it's the last thing I do."

"What are you doing in here?"

Tirrell jumped as a nurse entered the room. He wiped his eyes on the sleeve of his shirt.

"You're not supposed to be in here."

He clumsily got up and pushed past her.

The Eastland Avenue shooting was the lead story on the local news the entire day. The police were on the lookout for the black Mustang that Marquis described. Tirrell had no intention of waiting until they found it. He was obsessed with meting out his own justice.

***

Alex was glued to the news reports when her telephone rang. It was Bobby.

"Did you hear?"

"Yeah, I'm watching it right now."

"Looks like somebody did us a favor," Bobby callously responded. "T should be scared shitless right about now."

"He's going to think we did this."

"You think it could have been Rivera?"

"No. I didn't tell him anything."

"I wonder who we have to thank," Bobby said.

"I don't care," Alex replied. "I just want that file back. I tried calling him but his cell phone's been cut off."

"If this shooting doesn't bring him around, maybe paying a visit to the rest of his family will get his attention."

Bobby ended the call with Alex and put his cell phone into the inside pocket of his leather jacket. He then checked his gun and secured it in the waistband of his pants. When he opened the door to leave he was struck in the face by a 2x4, causing him to stumble back into the apartment and flip over a chair. Tirrell stormed in, wielding the 2x4 like a baseball bat as Bobby went for his gun. Tirrell smacked the Glock away and it flew across the room. Bobby growled, charged, and rammed him into the wall. A plaster bust fell from a shelf, hitting Tirrell, and gave Bobby enough time to pick up the board. He swung—Tirrell ducked and leapt toward the gun. Bobby grabbed his legs and they both hit the floor, grappling like rabid dogs, trading bone-crushing blows. Tirrell butted Bobby in the head, rolled over to the gun, took aim, and fired, dropping Bobby like a massive tree.

Tirrell slowly stood heaving and coughing. "Well, will you look at that? It wasn't loaded with blanks that time, was it?" He wiped the perspiration and blood from his face with a handful of paper towels he pulled from a rack in the kitchen, and stuffed them in his pocket while simultaneously checking outside to see if anyone was around who had heard the shot. "You ain't gonna hurt nobody else in my family." He moved as quickly as he could into Bobby's bedroom and searched through his closet, looking for his stash, frustrated that he only found a safe he couldn't open. He took a towel and frantically ran about the apartment, trying to wipe clean anything he remembered touching. Then he picked up the gun and tucked it into his blue jeans. Bobby's cell phone rang and startled him. Tirrell pulled off Bobby's leather jacket and slipped it on. Then he pulled the hoodie he was wearing over his head and bolted.

He discovered Bobby's wallet in one of the pockets and removed the cash once he made it to the MARTA platform. Just before the train arrived he tossed the cell phone and wallet on the tracks. He jumped into the last car and sat huddled in the back with the collar of the jacket pulled up around his face. A sharp pain shot through his leg and he looked to see that his stitches had opened during the skirmish. He took the towel he had in his pocket and pressed it against his leg. Adrenaline coursed through his body, making his head throb. He wanted to get high, and thanks to Scotty, he knew exactly where to find what he needed.

He made his way to an abandoned house in the seediest part of the West End area, and nested in the dank basement among a host of drug-addled strangers.

"Y'know dat coat looks mighty warm," a toothless indigent said to him. "Why don't you let me wear it for a li'l while."

"Get the hell away from me, dude."

"C'mon, man. I'll give you somethin' for it."

"Back up off me, Gumby."

The man cursed and moved to the other side of the room, watching Tirrell as he eventually nodded off. His head bobbed—fighting sleep—chasing vice—facing apparitions.

You could have been a halfway decent soldier. Instead, you're a goddamn disgrace!

When he woke up his jacket was gone, and so was the gun. "Shit," he sighed. "I only closed my eyes for a few minutes."

He moved off the soiled couch and recoiled. The anesthesia of crack had run its course and reminded him of the horrors that had taken place. There were a few people lying around on the floor, in the corners, but he couldn't find his things, or the vagrant he assumed had taken them.

Tirrell couldn't tell what time it was, but it was dark and cold when he limped from the building. He needed a hot shower, food, and medical attention. He reached down into his shoe and dug out twenty dollars left from the $200 he'd taken from Bobby. Pulling tight the dirty denim jacket he had on underneath the leather one, and bowing his head against the assault of the October wind, he made his way toward a corner diner for some food.

After scarfing down a cheeseburger and fries he found a payphone and called Scotty—he wasn't home. "What am I gonna do now?"

The unassuming man from The Mission crossed his mind. He pulled the card with the man's phone number from his back pocket.

"Hello."

"C . . . Can I speak to Mr. Preston?"

"That's me. Who's this?"

"It's Tirrell Ellis. I came by to see you the other day."

"What can I do for you?"

"You said if I wanted to talk I could call you. I'm in trouble, man."

"What sort of trouble?"

"It's bad."

"How bad? What did you do?"

"Can we meet somewhere?"

There was no immediate response from the other end of the line.

"Hello? Mr. Preston, are you there?"

"Yeah, I'm here. Where are you?"

Tirrell looked around for a street sign. "Lee Street in the West End—near the mall."

"Is this the kind of trouble you need the police for?"

"No police. I just . . . I just need to talk."

Mr. Preston sighed. "I'll be there in a few. Wait for me."

"How will I know you?"

"I'll be drivin' a dark blue Silverado with a dented right fender."

Tirrell shoved his hands in his pockets for warmth and loitered in the shadows, hoping not to attract any undue attention. Just as he'd promised, the man pulled up and found Tirrell standing on the corner.

"Hop in."

They drove back to the diner where Tirrell had been earlier. Mr. Preston ordered coffee and invited Tirrell to get whatever he wanted. Having just eaten, Tirrell asked for coffee too.

"You live around here?" Tirrell asked.

"Why do you need to know that?"

"What? You think I'm gon' rob you, or somethin'?"

"I don't really know what you're capable of," Mr. Preston responded.

"So, why'd you come?"

"I'm a sucker for lost causes. I was one myself once not so long ago."

The server returned with coffee for them both.

"So, Mr. I Don't Have a Problem, why did you call me?"

"'Cause you said I could."

"You said you were in trouble. What did you do?"

"When you hear those guys in that place tell you all their stories in those meetin's you ever tell anybody?"

"No."

"Can I trust you?" Tirrell continued. "I'm sayin', are you like a priest or somethin'?"

Mr. Preston smirked. "Are you Catholic?"

Tirrell didn't respond.

"Are you ready to deal with some hard truth and get clean?"

Tirrell scoffed. "I could use a shower."

"Don't bullshit me, boy."

"I'm not an addict," Tirrell defended himself.

Mr. Preston pushed his cup away and stood up.

"Where're you goin'?"

"Man, it's almost ten o'clock. Don't waste my damn time. I know an addict when I see one. You look like one and you stink like one."

"Don't leave, a'ight?"

"Gimme a reason to stay."

Tirrell's hands shook. "If I told you I killed a man today, what would you do?"

Mr. Preston guardedly eased back down, clasped his hands in front of him, and said nothing.

Tirrell wiped his hand over his mouth and cleared his throat. "I got involved with this woman who was slingin' dope. I got some evidence that could put her away. She said she'd hurt my family if I told anybody.

Her crazy-ass cousin did a drive-by last night and shot my grandmother."

"How do you know that?"

"I just know, a'ight?"

Mr. Preston scratched his temple. "So, why not let the police handle it?"

"'Cause I needed to take care of him myself."

"Why? 'Cause it's some noble shit you done talked yourself into?"

"No. 'Cause I ain't no punk. I'm a man."

"And that's what men do, right?"

Tirrell cut his eyes.

"Don't get me wrong. I understand the need to protect your own. I'm just wonderin' if you're sure you know what you're doin' messin' with these kinds of people. You could be openin' yourself up to a world of hurt you ain't ready for; I'm tell'ya now."

Tirrell was agitated. "I didn't go there to kill him. I just went to make sure he knew I wasn't scared of him. I just wanted them to stay away from my family."

"So you're so sure this woman and her cousin were involved in your grandmother's shooting."

"I know they were."

"People like you stir shit up and make enemies you don't even know you have."

"What do you mean people like me?"

"Junkies—cokeheads—users. Drug deal gone bad—stealin' from somebody."

They were interrupted by the waitress coming back to refresh their coffees.

Mr. Preston blew the heat from his cup and sat back. "So, what do you want me to do, boy?"

Tirrell shrugged. "Tell me I did the right thing."

"The right thing would be to face what you did and turn yourself in."

"He shot my grandmother, man. He could've killed her."

"An eye for an eye, huh?"

"You gonna preach to me, or you gonna help me?"

"Help you do what, Tirrell?"

He shrugged again.

"Look, I'm an addict," Mr. Preston confessed. "In recovery . . . but I'm an addict. I got six years' clean, but that didn't come without wadin' neck deep in a bunch of stinkin' shit, and that included denyin' what I was. I did some time for some petty bullshit. I even stole from the people I claimed to love just to suck on that glass dick. You didn't just wake up one day and decide that you was gonna start usin'. There's some shit you felt like you didn't wanna deal with. Stuff you were runnin' away from—seems to me like you're still runnin'. And until you're willin' to get buck-naked honest with yourself and with God there ain't a whole lot I can do for you. But, sooner or later you're gonna hit a brick wall. No matter what you do, you're never gonna get the feelin' of that first high again, I'm tell'ya now. I know what I'm talkin' 'bout."

"Chasin' the rabbit," Tirrell whispered.

"Exactly. So, do you want real help, or are you just blowin' smoke up my ass?"

Tirrell chuckled.

"You think this is funny?"

"Naw, you just remind me of this sergeant I had in the army."

Mr. Preston smirked. "*You* were in the army?"

"Yeah, just long enough to know I didn't want to be."

"Did you leave on your own, or did they put you out?"

"Let's just say we reached a mutual agreement."

"Were you gettin' high while you were in?"

"Hell, naw."

Mr. Preston looked at Tirrell, finding it hard to believe.

"I maybe tried coke once. But mostly I smoked weed."

"Look at you. You wanna get high right now, don't you?"

Tirrell rubbed his fingers over his eyes. "In the worst way."

Mr. Preston applauded.

"What's that for?"

"Ownin' up to your shit is what bein' a man really is."

"So, are you gon' call the police?"

"I think I'm gonna leave that up to you." He glanced at his wristwatch. "It's gettin' late, I should be gettin' home. You got some place to stay tonight?"

Tirrell pitifully shook his head in response to the question. It was a sad state. He had nowhere to go. Scotty wasn't home, he'd alienated Tasha and Marquis, his grandmother's house was cordoned off, and he could forget about Kevin.

"I don't think my wife would be too happy with me if I brought you back to my house, but I wouldn't feel right leavin' you to sleep on the street. C'mon, I'll see if I can get you into The Mission."

"The Mission?"

"Should I book you a room at the Ritz-Carlton instead?"

"Beggars can't be choosy, huh?"

"You could choose. But, those choices haven't worked out so great for you, have they?"

"The Mission it is." Tirrell moved to stand and his leg buckled.

"What's the matter?"

"Nothin'."

Mr. Preston's face registered concern. "Is that blood?"

"I had some stitches. I think they must've busted or somethin'."

"We better get you to the hospital to get it looked at."

"I'm a'ight."

"You're sweatin' and shakin'. You're not *a'ight*. Do you want infection to set in and eat the damn thing off?"

"No."

"Then we better get you looked at."

Mr. Preston helped Tirrell in the truck and drove him to hospital emergency. The chart from his initial visit was pulled. After more than two hours of waiting he was given more antibiotics, re-stitched, re-bandaged, and released.

Beds at The Mission filled up quickly, especially when the weather turned. There were fifteen bunk beds lined against one wall and fifteen bunks lined up on the facing wall in this dormitory-styled room that reminded Tirrell a lot of Army barracks. Mr. Preston managed to commandeer for Tirrell one of the two remaining.

The room was musty like sweaty socks or rancid cheese. Tirrell slid his shoes off and climbed into his bottom bunk.

An older Caucasian man in a bunk directly across from him stared. "If I was you I'd keep an eye on those shoes if you want 'em to be there when you wake up."

Remembering that his coat walked off earlier, Tirrell got up and slipped back into his shoes. He would sleep with one eye open just in case.

25

"Ms. Solomon."

"Yes."

"You can come in now."

Draped in a black knee-length trench coat with a silk scarf tied around her head, Alex looked like some sort of undercover operative following a nurse to Bobby's room. She wasn't as prepared as she thought when she pushed open the door and saw her once robust cousin bruised, battered, and connected to life support.

Alex removed the large-frame sunglasses she wore and turned to the nurse. "Is he going to wake up?"

"The doctor has him in a medically induced coma until the swelling goes down in his brain," the nurse responded.

"If he wakes up he won't ever be the same, will he?"

"It's just too early to say for sure."

"Can I have some time alone with him?"

"Of course. I'll be right outside."

Alex reached out and gently touched Bobby's hand. She tentatively sat in a chair next to the bed and closed her eyes, searching for unfamiliar words of prayer.

"I would have been here sooner, but the police had me answering questions most of last night. I called your sister in Queens. She's making arrangements to get here. Tirrell did this to you, didn't he? They think it was some sort of robbery. One of your neighbors said she heard the shot and looked out her window and saw a man running from your apartment. You have so many people in and out of your place all the time they couldn't be sure it was Tirrell, and I couldn't tell them what I suspected, or why. Everything's unraveling, but don't worry. I'm going to make sure that you're taken care of. I'm going to wire your sister some money, but I can't stick around, you know that, right? I've got some loose ends to tie up here first and then I'm getting out of the country for a while. All hell is gonna break loose when Rivera finds out what happened. He's going to come after me, and if he can't get to me he's going after Mama. I can't let that happen, so I'm taking her with me. You understand, right?"

Alex sat quietly for several minutes before finally getting up to go to the nurse's desk.

"Excuse me. Is there a way to find out if another patient is here?"

"Sure, I could look it up for you."

"Ellis . . . Betty Ellis."

"Are you family?"

"No."

"Nobody's allowed in to see her except immediate family."

"It's okay. I know her grandson and I just want to see if she's all right."

"Looks like she's still in the ICU," the nurse responded.

Alex took the elevator to the lobby and walked to the other side of the building. She walked by the waiting room and caught a glimpse of Pat Ellis inside with several other people she didn't know. When she saw Kevin headed up the hall in the other direction she ducked into a stairwell until he passed. Several minutes went by before she concluded that she'd either missed Tirrell, or he wasn't coming. She chose to leave.

As she exited through the main entrance of the hospital she crossed paths with Tasha—they stared at one another knowingly but said nothing. Alex loitered outside thinking that Tirrell might not be far behind, but he wasn't.

Tirrell left The Mission without seeing Mr. Preston, after showering and finding something suitable to wear among the clothing donations. He knew he somehow had to get the CD implicating Alex to Kevin. She was certain to be spooked by what happened to Bobby and might try a disappearing act, unless she was too busy planning a counterattack.

The first thing he noticed when he got to Betty's house was that the yellow police tape was gone. However, the chips in the bricks and the boarded window stood as a reminder that something horrendous had taken place here. He decided it best to go in through the back door in case nosy neighbors were charged to keep an eye out for him or any other suspicious activity. Dogs ran to the edge of fences and barked warnings of an intruder.

Both the front and back doors were likely to be dead bolted. He didn't have his keys. Breaking in was his only recourse. He removed his jacket and went to the side of the house where his bedroom was. He picked up a brick, wrapped it in the jacket, and punched out a section of the glass. Turning the latch, he hoisted the window and awkwardly climbed inside, being careful not to reopen his stitches. He found a piece of discarded plywood to cover the hole he'd made and grabbed some warmer clothes and his old fatigue jacket to change into. Reaching up on the shelf in the closet he pulled down the shoebox containing the CD and a yellowish dog-eared photo long forgotten of his father and mother. Shards of broken glass crunched under the soles of his shoes as he walked into the living room to have a look around. He was alarmed by the sight of dried blood all over the recliner. He stooped down and picked up a half-eaten Moon Pie and buried his face in his hands. "Noonie, I promise you I'm gonna make this right." He proceeded to the house phone to call Kevin.

"Who is this?"

"It's me. Tirrell."

"What the hell? What are you doing in the house?"

"I had to get somethin' important."

"I'm calling the police."

"Kevin, just listen to me, a'ight?"

"I don't want to hear a damn thing you have to say."

"I know who shot . . . Hello . . . Hello. Dammit!"

Kevin hung up on him.

The sound of a siren roared by but quickly faded in the distance. It was enough to cut Tirrell's invasion short.

When he left the house he headed straight to the hospital. There was a pretty clear indication of what he'd be walking into. Anne Crawl was in the waiting room along with the pastor from the church and a few other members—Tasha was there as well.

Tirrell got her attention and motioned for her to come out.

"It's good to see you." Tirrell smiled.

Tasha shook her head. "What happened to you?"

"This is my new fall wardrobe," he joked. "Tirrell Ellis, man on the street."

"I'm serious, Tirrell. What's goin' on? Who did this?"

"Where's Kevin?"

"Him and Pat are in with Miss Betty."

"Is she—"

"No, she's alive."

Tirrell threw his head back and sighed. "Can you do me a favor?" He pulled the CD out of his pocket with a piece of paper wrapped around it. "Give this to Kevin for me."

"What is it?"

"Tasha, please. It's really, really important that he gets this."

"Why can't you give it to him yourself?"

"Because he's not gonna listen to me. Please promise me you'll give this to him."

"Okay."

"I should come back when there're not so many people around." Tirrell turned to leave and came face to face with Kevin.

Pat took hold of Kevin's arm. "Baby, don't start, please. Not here."

Tirrell braced himself. "How's Noonie?"

"The doctor's treating her for some kind of post-surgical staph infection," Pat injected.

Tirrell stepped around them.

Kevin grabbed him. "Where do you think you're going?"

Tirrell jerked away. "You can't stop me from seein' her. She's my grandmother too."

"You're the reason she's in here, fool. I'm not going to let you get anywhere near her."

Tirrell looked at Tasha and the others—his eyes pleaded for mercy; there didn't seem to be any to spare.

"I guess this is what Jesus would do, huh?" he sniped.

After Tirrell left Tasha handed the disk to Kevin.

"What's this?"

"Tirrell wanted me to make sure you got it. He said it was important."

Kevin shook his head, took the disk, and tossed it in the trash.

The sun had just set over the downtown Atlanta skyline, taking it's warmth along with it. Tirrell pulled his woolen skullcap down over his ears, blew into hands, and walked up West Peachtree toward Cypress Street. He spied rounding the corner a white Acura that had passed him twice already; the third time it stopped.

"Need a ride?"

The ties that ensnared Tirrell were as viable as the umbilical cord connecting the baby to his mother's placenta. His mind and body persuaded him that he needed the nutrients that crack cocaine provided, and he was on the brink of doing just about anything to get it.

He wasn't looking or feeling much like the charming rogue who commanded salacious gazes, but he was passable in a street-boy sort of way. He leaned into the window. The driver was nice-looking enough despite the receding hairline and his pudgy middle-aged spread.

"You got pretty eyes," the man said.

"I got a lot more than that," Tirrell responded, licking his lips suggestively. *What harm would it do, gettin' a blow job from some horny ol' bastard?* Tirrell convinced himself that the price would be worth the sacrifice. Mindful of his wounded leg he gingerly climbed in the car and the man took off.

"My name's John."

No shit. Tirrell smirked. "I'm Kevin."

"So, what're you into, Kevin?"

"Whatever you wanna pay for."

"How much is it gonna cost me?"

"Fifty to start."

Tirrell could hear his heart beating between his ears. He couldn't believe that he was actually doing something this surreal.

There are a plethora of alleys and dead-end streets snaking through downtown Atlanta where one might be party to any number of illicit propositions after dark. The man found a secluded spot behind such a place and parked.

Tirrell sat anxiously, willing his erection. He closed his eyes and tried to imagine a scenario that he may have enjoyed, and unzipped his pants.

"What are you doing?" the man asked.

"This is what you want, ain't it?"

"I'm not doin' you." The man unzipped his pants. "I want you to suck me off."

The very idea was repugnant. "Sorry, man. I don't get down like that. I ain't gay."

"Then what the hell were you doin' out there?"

Tirrell's baser instinct kicked in. He wanted to punch the man, grab his wallet, and take off, but he wasn't sure how much of a fight the man would put up, and he wanted the high even more.

The man looked around to ensure privacy. "Are we doin' this, or what?" He stroked himself and reached out to pull Tirrell's head toward him.

The muscles in Tirrell's neck tensed and he resisted. "I need to see the money first."

"Shit," the man spat and pulled out his wallet, brandishing a holstered pistol simultaneously. "Satisfied?"

"You a cop?"

"If I was you'd be locked up by now."

Tirrell inched closer. He'd never entertained the thought of having another man's penis in his mouth, railing vehemently against those who assumed he was gay or made subtle or overt passes at him because of his physicality. Yet, here he was cashing in what was left of his self-respect. He disgusted himself. *This can't be happenin'. I can't be this desperate.* "Fuck. I can't do this!"

He threw open the car door and took off up the alley. He'd fallen as far down the rabbit hole that he ever wanted to go. It was time to find his way back home.

Humiliated, Tirrell went looking for Mr. Preston, and was told that he was at a meeting. He made his way back over to the building where he knew he would find him. The group was in the middle of reciting the Serenity mantra when he walked in and took a seat in the back.

Twelve of the eighteen men in the room with cards in their seats were asked to stand and read aloud the twelve traditions (one each per card) of Narcotics Anonymous.

When they were done, Charlie Preston stepped up to the lectern. "I wanna thank everybody for comin' out tonight. I see some new faces, so I just want y'all to know that you're among family. These meetings are really important to our day-to-day success in recovery, and nobody knows that better than me. I was asked to say a few words just before we got started and I wasn't exactly sure what I was gonna say—until now. Today I was faced with a situation that really pissed me off. Mr. Decker, who runs The Mission, chewed me out for breakin' the rules." He glanced at Tirrell. "Decker didn't like that I took it upon myself to bring somebody in after curfew. Didn't matter the reason. Didn't matter the circumstances. Decker wanted to let me know that he was in charge and he had to answer for what went on. He kept tellin' me how what I did amounted to insubordination and that my actions could jeopardize his job and mine. Now, to me, that was some bullshit, but I had to respect the man's position and accept and understand that it wasn't my call. I broke the rules and when you break the rules there are consequences. There was a time when somebody got up in my face like that I would have gotten mad and broke my foot off up in they ass. But, I had to learn to deal with conflict in a whole different way. We all have to learn to look at stuff like conflict, disappointment, anger, and pain in a whole new light. We can't shut down. We can't run to the pipe or to the needle when things ain't goin' like we want 'em to go. 'God grant me the serenity to accept the things I cannot change' is more than just a saying, it has to be our way of life."

When Mr. Preston was finished, various men stood to tell their stories of how their day or week had gone, and if or how they were able to overcome.

"Anyone else?"

Tirrell fidgeted and shifted uneasily before he too finally stood up, wiping the perspiration from his face and the moisture from his eyes.

"M . . . My name's Tirrell . . . and . . . and I'm an addict."

When the meeting ended the men milled about the room, talking and drinking coffee. Tirrell found Mr. Preston surrounded by a couple of guys and waited patiently to get to him. He flipped the small white chip in his hand (given for attending an initial meeting) and rolled it between his thumb and forefinger as he thought of its significance. It really did symbolize that he had "come in out of the rain," and now the hard part lay ahead of him.

Tirrell sheepishly sidled up to Mr. Preston. "I uh . . . I never thanked you for helpin' me last night. I didn't mean to cut out on you, or get you in trouble or nothin'. You're the first person to show me any kindness since my grandmother. I wasn't tryin' to piss on that. So, thank you." Tirrell turned to leave.

"Is your grandmother all right?"

"I don't know. Nobody will let me see her. My brother blames me for what happened, they all do. I blame myself. I tried to make it right. I took the information that I had on the woman I told you about and gave it to him. He, uh . . . he works for the DA's office."

"DA? Ellis?" Mr. Preston smiled. "I don't know why I didn't put it together before. Is your brother named Kevin?"

"Yeah, you know him?"

"When he worked for the public defenders office he caught a couple of my cases. He was green as grass back then. I hope he's a better prosecutor."

Tirrell smirked. "He's good at prosecutin' me, that's for damn sure."

"Would it make you feel any better to know that the man you thought you killed is still alive?"

"What?"

"You don't watch the news, do you?"

"I haven't exactly had the time. I ran into that brick wall you were talkin' about."

"Well, you made a good call tonight. You got a long road ahead of you, but you'll get through it."

"If it doesn't kill me first."

26

"Mama, it's me."

"Alexandra, how are you?"

"I'm good. Are you okay?"

"I'm fine. But, you don't sound right. What's wrong?"

"Nothing's wrong, Mama."

"Alexandra?"

"How would you like to take a trip?"

"A trip to where?"

"Nigeria."

"Nigeria? When?"

"As soon as possible."

"Alexandra Solomon, what is going on with you?"

"Mama, please. I don't have time to get into it now. I promise I'll fill you in later."

"Oh, I don't like the sound of this at all."

"Do you have your passport?"

"Yes, it's around here somewhere."

"You need to find it. I've booked a flight for you to meet me in Abuja."

"Meet you? Alexandra, you know I don't like to fly since 9/11. That's just way too far to travel alone like that."

"Okay, then I'll come to New York. I can meet you at JFK and we'll fly out together. How does that sound?"

"It sounds like trouble."

"Mama, please. I don't want to leave you in New York."

"Leave me? Why not? What's happened?"

"Can you just not ask a lot of questions right now? I need you to trust me."

"Come now, *Omolola,* you can do better than that. Does this have anything to do with . . . you know."

Alex sighed. "Yes. Some people could be after me."

"What people?"

"I can't talk about that right now."

"Is Bobby coming with you?"

"No. I'm coming alone."

"Oh, Alexandra."

"Look, Mama, I just need to get out of Atlanta for a while. Please don't make this harder than it already is. Will you go with me?"

"How long do I have?"

"A few hours."

"A few hours? How am I supposed to pack and secure the house and meet you at the airport in a few hours?"

"Can't you get Mr. Howard to watch the house for you?"

"I suppose I could."

"Then just pack enough for a few days. Whatever you don't have we'll buy when we get where we're going. Please, Mama. I wouldn't ask you if it wasn't important."

"All right, daughter. Tell me the flight that you'll be coming in on and I'll meet you."

"I need to call airlines and I'll call you back with the details."

"Daughter, you be careful."

"I will."

Alex called and changed her itinerary to include a layover in New York. After she hung up, she hurried about her apartment, packing and mentally going over anything else she needed to do before leaving Atlanta.

She'd already spoken with Travis and knew that he was more than capable, if not overly eager, to take over her legitimate business affairs. She was on edge with Bobby in the hospital, especially knowing who put him there. When she was questioned about the contents of the safe the police found in his apartment she feigned ignorance. There was little comfort in the fact that it had been over a day and the police had not returned with a warrant or any credible evidence that would link her to him in any way other than relational. The drugs they found gave them reason enough to believe he'd been attacked by a disgruntled customer. She rationalized that if Tirrell had done anything with the information he had on her she would have been arrested already.

Alex picked up her .380 from the bed and thought about slipping it into her makeup bag, but there would be no way to get it through airport security. While she thought about what to do, her telephone rang—she nearly jumped out of her skin. It was Xavier Rivera. She debated whether to answer, but ultimately decided it best to talk to him so as not to arouse undue suspicion.

"*Hola*, Xavier. *¿Cómo estás?*"

"*Muy bien*, Alex. *¿Qué tal?*"

"*Bien*. What can I do for you?"

"I hear that your cousin is in the hospital. Care to fill me in on the details?"

"He was shot. The police believe that he was a victim of a robbery."

"Was anything stolen?"

"No. Everything was locked in his safe, but the police have the contents now."

"I see. How unfortunate. What about *Señor* Ellis? Is he out of commission as well?"

Alex inhaled and threw her head back. Rivera sounded as if he knew something. She didn't dare try to explain to him what Tirrell was up to. She needed to buy more time.

"Tirrell is fine. But, I don't think he's quite ready to make a run on his own."

"Then perhaps you should come with him."

"Xavier, I think that we should probably lay low for a while, especially with Bobby's accident."

"What aren't you telling me?"

"There's nothing for you to be concerned about."

"My dear Alexandra. I have need to be concerned about every detail of this operation. If anything goes wrong your beautiful neck will be on the chopping block as well as mine. ¿Entiendas?"

"Yes. I promise you there's nothing going on that can't be handled. We just need a couple of weeks."

"Very well then. I will leave you to take care of things—for now. I'll be expecting a progress report soon."

Alex breathed a sigh of relief when the call ended. If Rivera was baiting her she wouldn't be able to get out of the country fast enough. She dialed Tirrell and got the recording that the line was still disconnected. "Dammit, Tirrell. Where are you?"

The phone rang again. The caller ID registered a restricted number. Alex vacillated before answering, thinking it may be the airlines or some such business she needed to attend to in order to finalize her departure.

"Hello . . . Hello."

The line went dead.

Tirrell hung up the payphone and scratched his head. He was sure if Kevin had seen what was on that disk—if he'd read the letter attached to it—Alex would be in jail by now. *Somethin' must have gone wrong. Maybe Kevin bein' Kevin never even looked at the CD.* He leaned against the wall in the hall outside the bay in The Mission where he slept, and racked his brain trying to remember his sister-in-law's number. "Is it 3581 or 5381?" He tried the first permutation—it was wrong. "Dammit." He tried the second—it was wrong. "Shit."

"Yo, man. You through with the phone?"

Tirrell moved away to allow the next two people in line the use of the payphone. He paced around the lobby saying aloud numbers of varying combinations until one made sense. "I got it!"

He dashed back to the phone and found one of the guys lingering on his call. Tirrell grunted and cleared his throat and huffed and puffed, but the man paid him no attention.

"Man, please. I gotta use the phone, it's a matter of life and death."

"Forget you. I'm talkin' to my girl."

Tirrell snatched the phone from the smaller-built man's hand. "He's gonna have to call you back." He slammed down the receiver.

"Man, that was foul."

"I know. I know. You can kick my ass later, a'ight? I really need to make this call."

He nearly jumped for joy when Pat answered.

"It's me, Tirrell. Don't hang up. This is really important. Please you have to listen to me. Please."

He could hear Pat sigh into the receiver.

"All right, Tirrell. I'm listening."

"First tell me that Noonie's okay."

"There's been no change."

"What about Micah?"

"Tirrell, what do you want?"

"Okay . . . okay . . . I'll get to the point. I gave Tasha a CD to give to Kevin yesterday. Please tell me he got it."

"He got it, but he threw it away."

"Dammit. Listen to me, Pat. The information on that CD was the reason Noonie got shot. There's stuff on there that can get us all in a lot of shit."

"What are you talkin' about? What did you do?"

"Do you remember that woman who came to church a few weeks ago?"

"Yes."

"She's a drug dealer."

"Are you kidding me?"

"I took a file off her computer that had a lot of names of other dealers on it and she sent her cousin after me. He shot Noonie, tryin' to get to me."

"Oh my God."

"She may be tryin' to get out of town. I have to talk to Kevin and he's not answering."

"He went to work for a few hours."

"Does he have e-mail? Can I send the file to him at work?"

"Yeah, let me give you his address."

"Mr. P, you gotta let me get on a computer."

"For what?"

"I gotta send that file to my brother and I gotta do it right now."

"The file you took from that woman's computer?"

"Yes."

Mr. Preston pushed away from his small desk and Tirrell sat down to log into his e-mail account.

Pat called ahead to tell Kevin about the file Tirrell was sending. Kevin couldn't believe the extent of the danger Tirrell had exposed them all to. He sat at his computer and waited for the e-mail to come through. While he waited there was plenty of time for him to reflect on the voice mail Tirrell left him the night Betty was shot. He thought about how shabbily he'd treated him and he considered his grandmother's words about giving Tirrell a chance to prove himself.

He clicked the e-mail open the second it popped into his mailbox. "Solomon's Temple." Kevin read the names of six alleged dealers who had been under investigation for some time. He did a computer search on Xavier Rivera and several hits came up, including ones detailing his being detained by police on several occasions in Florida and in South America on suspicion of murder, money laundering, and racketeering. Most of the entries on Alex were of events she'd planned for him and an infamous guest list. Kevin scrolled through dozens of pictures of her and an impressive array of celebrities and local officials. But, the story that piqued his interest the most was that of her marriage to a small-time hood out of New York by the name of Ray Williams, who had been associated with Rivera. He shuffled through some papers on his desk and found one with the name Bobby Williams, and the pieces all started coming together.

Kevin took all the data he had to his boss and they got a judge to expedite a warrant to bring Alex in.

"Can I help you?" Travis asked a pair of detectives entering Alex's Buckhead office.

"We're looking for Alexandra Solomon."

"Can I ask what this is about?"

"Is she here or not?"

"Ms. Solomon is out today."

"Do you know when she'll be in?"

"What did she do?"

"That's a police matter, sir."

Travis smirked. "She called in this morning. From what she told me I don't expect her back in the office anytime soon."

"What exactly did she tell you?"

"Not much, just that she needed to take a trip, and she asked me to look after things at the office and in her apartment while she was gone."

"Did she tell you where she was going?"

"No, and believe me, I asked."

While the two officers were occupied with Travis, another unit was sent to Alex's apartment—by the time they arrived she was gone.

"Ladies and gentlemen, last call for Delta flight 667 with nonstop service from Atlanta to New York's JFK airport. Boarding all rows all sections at gate B-12."

Running through the concourse, frenetically pulling her bag behind her, Alex rushed toward the gate with her ticket in hand. The gate agent smiled and assured her that she'd made it just in time; not a moment too soon as far as Alex was concerned.

She hurried up the jet-way to her first-class seat, where an attractive man seated in the aisle gallantly assisted her in storing her bag. "Thank you," she sighed breathlessly, looking over her shoulder. She eased into her window seat and peered out toward the terminal to see if she'd somehow been followed.

"Business or pleasure?"

"Excuse me?"

The stranger next to her smiled. "This trip, business or pleasure?"

"Business."

"Well, we'll just have to make the best of the flight then, won't we?"

"Listen, I don't mean to be rude, but I've got a lot on my mind and I'd really like to be left alone."

The man clearly took offense and readjusted in his seat. "Okay, not a problem."

When the plane began to taxi toward takeoff Alex laid her head back and exhaled.

Highway patrol was given a description and the plate number for the Yukon. Rental car outlets, as well as the bus station, had been put on alert, and there was no flight manifest out of Atlanta listing the name Alex or Alexandra Solomon or Williams. The police had only to assume that she was using another alias. When they discovered that her mother lived in New York they had a tangible lead that put them on her trail. The only question was, would she be flying into JFK or LaGuardia?

All the diverse cultures and ethnicities converging on JFK brought hectic energy to it, much like any other massive airport in the country. Upon checking inbound and outbound flights, there was still no indication that Alex was headed there. However, the discovery of a Jamilah Solomon, booked on an international flight to Nigeria, raised a red flag.

Armed with her photo, when the flight landed in New York, the police were waiting. Two plainclothes detectives spied an older woman in the crowd who resembled Alex, and rightly assumed that it must be her mother. They watched vigilantly as the passengers deplaned. When Alex walked past the gate and embraced the woman they pounced.

"Alexandra Solomon?"

Alex looked around as if to suggest they couldn't possibly be addressing her. "I'm sorry. I think you have the wrong person."

"No, ma'am," one of the detectives replied, flashing her photo. "We have exactly who we're looking for."

"Please put your hands behind your back, ma'am."

"You're making a mistake."

One of the detectives, a female, reached out to grab her.

Alex jerked away. "Get your hands off me."

She reached for Alex again. "Ma'am, don't make this harder on yourself."

"She didn't do anything," her mother defended her, clutching her chest and wheezing.

"We got a call from the Fulton County Police Department in Atlanta, Georgia to detain her."

"For what?"

"Attempted murder."

Jamilah Solomon gasped.

Alex continued to struggle. "Get your damn hands off me."

The more formidable male detective manhandled her and twisted her arm behind her back.

"You're hurting her," Jamilah Solomon screamed, and pounded the man in the back.

After cuffing Alex he passed her off to his partner and took hold of the elder Solomon. "Lady, are you trying to get arrested?"

"Let my daughter go!"

"Mama, I'm all right."

"I'm not going to stand here and let them do this to you." Jamilah Solomon kicked the officer.

"That's it. Let's go."

She collapsed into the man's arms.

"You don't need to be so rough with her, you jackass. She has asthma," Alex screamed. "Mama, where's your inhaler?"

The officer grudgingly eased Jamilah into a chair. Alex looked on helplessly as she fumbled through her purse for her medication.

Once her breathing returned to normal, Jamilah regained her composure. Passersby stopped, pointed, and gawked as both she and her belligerent mother were escorted away from the concourse.

27

Tirrell tossed and turned on the uncomfortable cot in The Mission, but he couldn't sleep. The pain in his muscles was excruciating. His back was drenched with sweat and he was nauseous. Feeling as if he were about to vomit, he sat up and glanced across the dark room, sickened by the sight of a mob of crusty, hard-ankled men just like him. He felt queasy, bolted to the bathroom, and emptied the contents of his stomach. He threw cold water on his face and stared at his drawn image in the mirror. "How the fuck did I get here?" He slid down the wall and sat on the floor, twitching and scratching at invisible insects he felt crawling on his skin.

Several minutes passed before he left the bathroom, fished some change from his pocket, and stole away to the payphone in the corridor. It was after midnight and he knew the phone was off-limits at that hour, but he felt a virulent pull for a fix. He knew that if he walked out the front door of The Mission this time, he wasn't coming back.

"Mr. P . . . I'm sorry I'm callin' so late. I didn't know what else to do."

"Damn, Tirrell. What happened?"

"Nothin' yet. But, my stomach is burnin', and my hands won't stop shakin'. I'm sweatin'. I just need . . ."

"C'mon, Tirrell. You gotta fight it, man. You promised me—thirty days and thirty meetings, right? You can do this. You have to."

"I can't."

"Don't tell me you can't. I know it's hard, but you gotta do it."

"Can you come and get me? Maybe we can go get some coffee or somethin'?"

"You know I can't do that. There are rules and I broke 'em before to get you in there. I can't do it again."

"Dude, I'm not gon' make it."

"Have you used at all today?"

"No."

"All right, then. A day clean is a day won. One step at a time, Tirrell. Before you know it you'll be lookin' back and you'll be amazed at how far you've come. And I'll be there to cheer you on, but only if you don't punk out and give up."

Tirrell tried to quell his anger. "I don't need speeches! I need help."

"What do you think I been tryin' to give you?"

Tirrell slammed down the receiver without so much as a good-bye. He brushed the dryness of his lips and vacillated between leaving and staying. With tears in his eyes he crept back into the bay of bunks, climbed into his bed, curled up, and rocked like a baby. "I can do this. I can do this. I can do this."

Tirrell woke up the next morning, cleaned up, and reported to the kitchen to help with breakfast. He was listless and fatigued, but he'd made it through the night.

"Withdrawal's a bitch, ain't it?"

He looked up across the counter and saw a gangling, stringy, redheaded, freckle-faced man who couldn't have been much older than he was.

"It hurts like a son-of-a-bitch," Tirrell responded.

"It gets better. Doesn't feel like it, but it does. At least that's the drill," the man said.

"Sounds like you've had a li'l bit of experience."

"I've been in and out—and in and out—now I'm back in. Third time's the charm, right?"

Tirrell smirked. "What you're sayin' is the program doesn't work."

"It works if you work it—sucks if you don't."

"So, why'd you come back?"

"I like the food."

They both laughed.

"My name's Sean."

"Tirrell."

"Well, with any luck, Tirrell, maybe we can both make it through to the other side."

"From your mouth to God's ears, Sean."

After breakfast all the men went about their various chores until it was time for a required counseling session. They were asked to participate in a trust lesson. Trust being a foreign concept for Tirrell, he chose just to sit and listen.

Sean started. "I used to shoot heroin and I was dumb enough to share a needle. Classic, right? I told myself what we all tell ourselves. 'I can stop anytime I want. I can handle it—just this one last time and no more.' But there was always another time, and another reason to use because all I wanted was the feeling that it gave me. The feeling I couldn't live without. I traded my addiction for my fiancée and a good job makin' a pretty decent salary; none of that mattered then. Now, I have AIDS and I'm an outcast to my family and so-called friends . . . Suddenly everything matters."

Tirrell squirmed and then got up and left the room. Mr. Preston was passing in the hall outside with some local volunteers who were dropping off clothing and food donations.

"You all right, Tirrell?"

He shook his head.

"Stay right there. I'll be right back."

Mr. Preston saw the volunteers to the door and came back to find Tirrell sitting on the floor. His arms were extended outward with his elbows resting on his knees. He stared blankly forward. Mr. Preston sat down next to him.

"There's this guy in there named Sean. Did you know he had AIDS?"

"Would it surprise you to know that he's not the only one? A lot of addicts wind up sick or dead."

Tirrell turned to face him.

"Does that freak you out?" Mr. Preston asked.

"Not really. I've done some shit that I never thought I would find myself doin'."

"Is that why you left the session, because you didn't wanna talk about it?"

"Yeah. Plus I was thinkin' about today bein' my birthday and I'm stuck in this place. It's not as if I got anything to celebrate anyway."

"You're alive, aren't you?"

Tirrell laughed. "Is that what this is?"

"What are you now? Thirty? Thirty-one?"

Tirrell turned to face Mr. Preston. "Damn, do I look that old?"

"I was just askin'."

"I'm twenty-three. Birthdays ain't never meant that much to me before, but I miss my family. Ain't that a trip?"

"Not at all."

"When I was growin' up, Noonie—that's what we call my grandmother—she would go out of her way to try to make my birthday special. She would bake me a German chocolate cake, from scratch, and cook all my favorite food for dinner. She'd invite Kevin and Jacqui, that's my half sister. Kevin wouldn't come. Jacqui came sometimes, and my boy Marquis—never really had that many friends my grandmother would let in her house. I took her for granted. I took a lot of shit for granted. You know I only went into the Army because she wanted me to. 'Your grandfather served his country. It made a man out of him,' she said. So, I signed up. I thought it was the least I could do considerin' all she did for me. I hated it, though. I guess in a way I hated . . ."

"You hated what?"

"Nothin'."

"You hated her for makin' you feel like you had to go? It was your choice to go. You can't be pissed off at your grandmother."

Tears filled Tirrell's eyes. "Man, I don't hate my grandmother. Why would you say some fucked-up shit like that? She's the only good thing in my life. The Army just wasn't gonna do it for me, that's all. I was never gonna get all the commendations and shit like my granddaddy got, and I didn't want to be in no damn war I didn't believe in. I saw too many of my boys get deployed and I know what that shit did to them. I didn't want the same thing happenin' to me."

"So you let them kick you out."

"It was either that, or get locked up for tryin'a kill this dude. They gave me a choice. I took a dishonorable."

"If that's all they did to you, you're lucky. Somebody must've been lookin' out for you."

"I guess."

"I did a turn in the Army too. It wasn't my thing either. But if I'd done what you did, I know my country ass would still be kickin' rocks somewhere in a government hellhole."

Tirrell scoffed. "It don't matter. Whatever I do I'll still be a screw-up."

"So you get high and that's s'pposed to change things?"

"I get high for the same reason everybody else does. So I don't have to deal with not livin' up to bein' what everybody thinks I should be, and just bein' what they expect me to be."

"How about you stop bein' so concerned about how other people see you, and change the way you see yourself? That's the only way this is gonna work."

"Wow! Why didn't I think of that before," Tirrell sneered.

"After you turned in that file incriminatin' those dealers, you had to know what might go down. What did you think they would do, welcome you into the fold? Did you really think this one thing was gonna somehow magically wipe away all the other shit you did?"

"I don't wanna talk about this no more."

"You feel guilty, don't you? 'Cause instead of makin' things better, you made 'em worse and got your grandmother shot in the process."

Tirrell got up off the floor and brushed himself off. "To hell with you, man."

"Uncoverin' truth and peelin' that onion is hard, ain't it?"

"Truth is bullshit. Just like this program. Just like you." Tirrell ran up the hall and out the door.

Mr. Preston let him go.

Tirrell stood out in front of a MARTA station like a disenfranchised beggar asking for spare change. The inhumanity was more callous because he was on the receiving end now. An hour went by—then two—before he finally had enough money for a couple of tokens to ride the train. He rode to the Kensington station, hoping to find Tasha home from the salon. He figured if she cared enough to show up at the hospital there was maybe a small part of her that had some compassion left for him.

He spied her car parked out in front of her building and it excited him. He was even more so when he noted that Darnell's wasn't there.

He was unkempt and in desperate need of a shave and haircut. In an attempt to make his appearance more suitable, he tucked in his shirt and smoothed down his hair with the palms of his hands before he knocked.

"Who is it?"

"It's Tirrell."

There was no immediate response. He didn't know whether to leave or knock again. The door finally opened.

"Can I come in? I promise not to do anything stupid."

Tasha moved back and allowed him inside.

Tirrell started to sit, but opted to stand. He walked over to the large patio doors and peered out. "Where's Darnell?"

"Out of town."

"Did I catch you at a bad time? You're not expectin' company, are you?"

"I wasn't expectin' you. But, if you're referring to Rickey, we're not seein' each other anymore."

He resisted the urge to gloat.

"Why are you here, Tirrell?"

"I'm glad you're home. I really wanted to see you."

"I heard that Miss Betty was breathin' on her own now."

"Is she? I wouldn't know."

"Kevin still won't let you see her?"

"To tell you the truth I haven't tried since the last time."

"Why not?"

Tirrell turned to face her. "Look at me. I hardly recognize myself. I know she won't."

"What have you been doin' to yourself? Where have you been stayin'?"

"It's a long story."

"You look hungry. You want somethin' to eat?"

Tirrell chuckled. "It's not gonna be a salad is it?"

Tasha laughed. "I think I could come up with somethin' better than that. Tell you what, why don't I go get my clippers and give you a trim, and you can take a shower while I fix you some food."

"Sounds good."

Tirrell took off his shirt and followed Tasha into her bedroom. She sat him down in a chair, removed a nylon cape from her bag, and snapped it around his neck. He closed his eyes and lost himself in her touch. There was nothing sexual about it, just her closeness, and her closeness made him yearn for her. She followed the haircut by trimming the stubble on his face. He reached out and caressed her hand.

"Stop," she chided. "You're gonna make me mess up."

Tasha vacuumed the loose hair on the rug when she finished. Tirrell stripped and climbed in the shower.

He called out from the bathroom. "You wanna join me?"

"I'll pass."

Tirrell removed the bandage from his leg and luxuriated in the hot water. There was no one pounding at the door waiting to be next. It was the best shower he'd had in a long time.

He cleared the steam from the mirror after he toweled off and took stock of his weight loss. In spite of everything that had gone down between them, he was overwhelmed by Tasha's kindness. He found a pair of Darnell's old blue jeans and a shirt and sweater laid out for him on her bed. As he dressed he spied her open purse on the nightstand. His nerve endings tingled, visualizing the celebratory high he could have. *If I only take ten or twenty dollars she won't miss it,* he reasoned. Just as he reached in, his conscience got the better of him and he withdrew quickly and left her room.

"I hope you don't mind, I threw the clothes you had on in the trash. Sorry, I didn't think you'd wanna put on any of Darnell's underwear."

"No." Tirrell smiled. "I think I can handle not wearin' any at all, if you can."

He sat down to a hot plate of leftover spaghetti and meatballs, garlic bread, and a salad—the salad made him laugh. She laughed too.

"I was thinkin' about goin' to see Miss Betty if you wanna come."

"You really want me to go with you?"

"I asked, didn't I?"

"That's what's up."

Tirrell ate his fill and pushed back from the table.

"You want some more?"

"No, I'm full. Thanks. I couldn't eat anything else."

"Nothing? Not even this?" Tasha turned around with a cupcake on a plate and a single candle on top. She set it in front of him. "Happy Birthday."

"I can't believe you remembered."

"We were together for almost three years. How could I forget?"

His emotions crashed like ferocious waves on the seashore.

"You should probably make a wish and blow out the candle, unless you like wax with your chocolate."

Tirrell took Tasha's hand and kissed it.

She pulled it away. "I need to finish the dishes. We should get goin' soon if we're gonna make it to the hospital before visitin' hours are over."

Tasha let Tirrell have time alone with Betty while she waited outside to warn him if Kevin was coming.

The room was overrun with flowers and cards from the hotel where Betty worked and from the church and her neighbors on Eastland Avenue. Tirrell sat at the side of her bed and caressed her forehead. He took her hand and gently squeezed, willing her to open her eyes—grateful that she was still alive. He hadn't felt that God was in the prayer-answering mode of late; still, he knew that Betty believed. He quoted the 23 Psalm. Other than "Jesus wept," it was the only passage he'd ever memorized. "'Yea, though I walk through the valley of the shadow of death, I will fear no evil, for the Lord is with me.'"

When he got up to leave he took the chip he'd been given from the NA meeting, put it in her hand, and leaned in to kiss her cheek. "I love you, Noonie."

The temperature had dropped nearly ten degrees by the time Tasha and Tirrell left the hospital. While walking through the parking garage to her car, Tasha noticed that Tirrell had broken out into a sweat. He sat shivering in the passenger seat.

She cranked up the heat. "Are you okay?" she asked.

"I will be."

"Are you comin' down with somethin'?"

"No. Nothin' like that, but it's nice to know you still care, Tasha."

"You're not yourself, that's all I was sayin'."

"Who am I then?"

"What I meant was, the way you looked when you came over. The clothes you had on. That's not the Tirrell I remember."

"A lot's changed."

"Are you still seeing that woman you were with at that party?"

Tirrell turned and glared out the window.

"Sorry, it's none of my business." She placed her hand on the gear shift to put the car in drive. He put his hand on top of hers.

"Tirrell, your hands are freezing."

He cupped them to his mouth and blew into them. "They'll warm up in a minute."

They sat silently, not even listening to the radio, as Tasha navigated away from the hospital.

Tirrell finally looked at her and then looked away. "Do you ever wonder what could have happened between us if we'd stayed together? I mean, if I could have loved you like you deserved to be loved?"

"Tirrell, don't."

"I think about it a lot, especially lately. I think about when we first met. I think about the baby we could've had together. But you were right, I would've been a fucked-up father. I was selfish and arrogant as hell. If I was in your shoes I would have probably had an abortion too. You did the world a favor."

Tirrell's thoughts tapered off. Moments passed before he spoke again. "Man, what I wouldn't give for some . . ."

"For some what?"

"Never mind. Forget it." He turned, reached up, and stroked the side of her face. "Despite all my shit we were good together for the most part."

She pulled his hand away and held on to it. "When we weren't in bed together we were toxic. I was insecure and I was doin' a lousy job tryin' not to show it, and you were eatin' it up. I guess I did change some after I lost the weight. I finally got it. I didn't need you or any man to make me feel good about who I was. I should thank you for not bein' able to give me what I thought I wanted, otherwise, I may never have found it myself."

Tirrell directed her to drive him to the train station so that she wouldn't have to see where he was headed.

"One day I hope you find whatever it is that's gonna make you happy, Tirrell."

"You don't know how much it means to me what you did today." He took her hand again and ran it over his face. She didn't pull back. "I still love the smell of that lotion you wear. You think some day you'll forgive me and we can be friends?"

"Tirrell, we can't go back down that road again."

"Yeah, I don't know what I was thinkin'. Forget I said anything."

He softly touched his fingers to her lips, trembling, hesitant, and kissed her.

Tirrell arrived back at The Mission with minutes to spare before curfew. Mr. Preston was standing out front having a cigarette when he walked up.

"You missed a meeting, and you're real close to bein' locked out for the night."

"I wasn't somewhere usin' if that's what you're thinkin'."

"Did I say anything about that?"

"You were waitin' on me, weren't you?"

"You're awfully full of yourself, you know that?"

"So I've been told."

"I didn't think I would see you back here at all after the way you stormed out of here this afternoon."

"Yeah, well I thought about it. After I spent some time with an old friend I decided that I needed to."

"A girl?"

Tirrell laughed. "Yeah. She took me to the hospital to see my grandmother."

Mr. Preston offered Tirrell a cigarette. "Looks like it did you some good. Got your hair cut. Got a shave."

"Yeah. I think it helped more than I thought it would."

"You came back, so that must mean that you don't think me or the program is bullshit anymore."

"Yeah, sorry about that. I didn't mean . . ."

"No big deal. It comes with the territory."

Tirrell squashed the remainder of the cigarette. "I guess I better get inside."

"Tirrell."

"Yeah."

"Happy birthday, man."

Tirrell flashed a crooked smile. "See you in the mornin'."

"I'll be here."

28

Alex was justifiably uneasy as she sat in a Fulton County jail cell. Every time a guard walked by, or she heard a loud noise, she wondered if it was someone coming for her who was sent by Xavier Rivera. If he didn't know before, there would be no way he couldn't know now.

"You got a visitor," a female officer said, sliding open the iron bars.

"Is it my lawyer?"

"No. It's some federal agent with ADA Ellis."

The mannish guard cuffed Alex and led her to a holding room. She felt exposed without the visage of makeup and the designer duds she'd been accustomed to. The orange jumpsuit, harsh lighting, and yellowing walls were telling and did little for her. She was determined not to show her angst.

"Ms. Solomon, I'm Detective Cobb. This is Special Agent Oliver from the FBI, and I assume you already know ADA Ellis."

"What can I do for you gentlemen?"

"Maybe the better question is what can we do for you?" Detective Cobb responded.

"For starters you could let me out of here."

"Why would we do that?"

"Because you don't have anything to hold me on."

"I wouldn't say that," Agent Oliver said. He pushed some papers across the table toward her. "These look familiar?"

Alex glanced down then looked back up. "Should they?"

"This is a spreadsheet we printed from a file obtained by Tirrell Ellis. There are some interesting names on this list: major players, dates, financial transactions."

Alex remained aloof.

"Take a look at the name at the top of the page. Why don't you save yourself a lot of trouble and fill in the blanks for us?"

"Since you're so smart, Agent Oliver, why don't you fill them in yourself?"

"How long have you been on Rivera's payroll?"

"I'm not on anyone's payroll, or in anybody's pocket."

"Any of Xavier Rivera's drug money finding its way into your event planning venture?"

"I have no idea what you're talking about, Detective."

"Are you and Rivera lovers?"

"Don't be ridiculous. The only reason I'm acquainted with Xavier Rivera is because he hired me to plan several parties for him."

"And the 'product' mentioned in the file, I suppose, was party favors?"

Alex lifted her hands to inspect her nails, and the chains hanging off the cuffs rattled.

"You're looking at a long list of state and federal charges that could have you doing time until you're eligible to collect Social Security, assuming that the program is still around when you get out."

Alex cut her eyes at the weasel-faced FBI agent.

"The police found over fifty thousand dollars worth of cocaine in the safe in Bobby Williams's apartment when they finally got it open."

"What does that have to do with me? I don't keep tabs on Bobby."

"You were married to Ray Williams, right?" Detective Cobb inquired.

"So?"

"So, we know that he was connected to Xavier Rivera. He dies. You pick up where he left off."

Alex smirked. "That's a nice story, Detective. You should write crime novels as a side job. I hear they're all the rage."

Kevin impatiently jumped in. "Tirrell says when he took that file you threatened my family. My grandmother's lying in the hospital. Are you responsible for that?"

"My cousin's in the hospital in a coma. Is your brother responsible for that?"

"Does the name Nathanial Allen mean anything to you?"

"Should it?"

"We know about the house on Hardy Avenue."

"I don't know anything about a house on Hardy Avenue."

"What about Rivera's compound in Miami?"

"Of course I've been there. I've already told you I planned parties for the man."

"Tirrell Ellis has been there too, and not as an event planner," injected the agent. "So, if you didn't take over your husband's business with Rivera, and you're not guilty of the attempt on Betty Ellis's life, why did you run?"

"I didn't run. I was going to New York to visit my mother. Last time I checked there was no law against that."

"You were travelling under the name Angela Sissoko. You had a fake driver's license and a fake passport, that's a federal crime. We also know that you were planning to take a connecting flight to Nigeria, where you . . . or should I say Angela Sissoko has an account at the Bank of Abuja," Kevin noted.

The FBI agent spoke again. "Those forged documents alone could get you twenty years. We could work a deal if you agree to cooperate and testify against Rivera."

Alex's brow arched and she squirmed. It was dizzying being volleyed questions from all three men. "I'm not saying anything else until my lawyer gets here."

"If this scares you, it should. I don't see a man like Xavier Rivera sitting on the clock, waiting to see how all of this plays out," the agent sneered. "Give us something we can nail him on, Ms. Solomon, and we could put you in protective custody until we get Rivera out of the picture, otherwise, there's no telling what he might do. All it would take is one call to the attorney general to get the ball rolling."

Alex leaned into the table and met the agent's gaze. "You're wasting your time. I don't have anything else to say."

Kevin went back to his office and stared intently at Alex's list, pondering just how deeply Tirrell would be implicated and how much hell he'd unleashed on his family. He'd e-mailed him back, not knowing where he was, but they needed to find him and bring him in before anything happened to him.

An office assistant knocked on his door. "Hey, Kevin, there's some guy named Preston here to see you."

"Preston?"

"He says it's about your brother."

"Tell him to come in."

Mr. Preston walked in and Kevin recognized him instantly. "What are you doing here?"

"Nice to see you again too, Mr. Ellis."

"You know something about Tirrell?"

"He's stayin' down at The Mission."

Kevin fell back in his chair. He'd had dealings with several of the residents there on any number of occasions who had run-ins with the law. He knew what it meant for someone to be there.

"You didn't know?" Preston asked.

"No, I didn't."

"Do you care?"

Kevin ignored the question. "What can I do for you, Preston?"

"Nothin' for me, but maybe you could do somethin' for your brother. I was with him when he sent you that e-mail the other day. He told me about the Solomon woman."

"So?"

"He's reachin' out to you, man. Look, I get that you and him got issues, but he needs his family if he's gonna get through this program."

"Who the hell are you to waltz up in here and tell me what Tirrell needs? Why do you care?"

"Somebody has to. Too many of us get wrote off. A lot of guys don't ever get their lives back on track, most of 'em don't have family, but Tirrell may still have a chance."

Kevin folded his hands, perched them under his chin, and leaned on the desk. "So, what do you get out of all of this?"

"I get to help. Six years ago I hit the wall and somebody reached out and gave me a hand when I needed it most. If they hadn't, I could be in prison right now, or I could still be strung out, or dead. Is that what you want for Tirrell? Would it make it easier on you if he was dead?"

Kevin sighed heavily. "Are you finished?"

"Yeah, I guess I am."

"All right, you said what you came to say. You can leave now."

The hydraulics of the steel prison doors grated, clanked, and squealed open.

"Solomon, you got another visitor."

"Who is it?"

"He says he's your attorney."

"He? Did he look Hispanic?"

"No, he looked white." The guard laughed. "Why, you want a date?"

Alex's eyes shifted nervously.

"You wanna see him or not?"

She stood and absently put her hands up. The guard cuffed her and escorted her back to the holding room. When she walked in, an innocuous-looking man in an expensive suit with a pasty face and thinning gray hair stood to greet her. She'd seen him before. He was one of Rivera's attorneys.

"Ms. Solomon, please have a seat."

The man looked at the guard. "May I have a few minutes, please?"

The woman moved to the other side of a door with a glass window between them so that she could keep her eye on them both.

"Where's my lawyer?"

"I had a lovely little chat with Ms. DeLucca. We came to the conclusion that it would be in your best interest for me to see you first."

"Xavier sent you?"

"He's very unhappy with the recent turn of events. That wasn't very smart of you to have kept files on him."

"I didn't say anything to anyone."

"Perhaps not yet. I'm here to ensure that you don't."

"What are you going to do?"

"That depends on you."

Alex bit her bottom lip and clutched her hands together. "I'm not going to say anything."

"The Feds can be very persuasive."

"Look, I only had the file to keep business contacts in order."

"Are you sure you weren't keeping it as an umbrella for a rainy day?"

"I didn't give the FBI the information—it was stolen."

"Yes, that was very careless of you, too. How did it happen that you ended up in bed with an ADA's brother?"

"It's not what you think."

The man leered. "Enlighten me, please."

"When I first met Tirrell I didn't know who he was. Bobby convinced me that we could use him to our advantage."

"I was sent here to bail you out; however, that's going to prove a bit of a challenge now that the federal authorities are involved."

"So, what now?"

"As you know, my client doesn't like loose ends." The man leaned in closer. "You introduced Mr. Ellis into Mr. Rivera's life, so it may be time that we *un*-introduce him."

Alex's throat tightened. "What's going to happen to me?"

The man stood and walked to the door. "Whatever's going to happen next may already be out of all of our control. Oh, and I am sorry to hear about your cousin. It was such a loss. He was a good man."

"What do you mean *was?*"

"I understand he didn't make it."

Alex gasped.

"You didn't know. Collateral damage, you under-stand. Unfortunate accidents happen all the time."

The threat was implicit. Alex knew she was next. After the man left, the guard came back in to take her back to her cell.

Alex pulled away. "I can't go back there."

The guard snatched her arm. "You don't have a choice."

"Yes, I do. I need to talk to Agent Oliver right away."

"Oh, I'm sorry," the guard replied. "The request line is closed."

"You don't understand. I've got information that they need."

"Then you'll have to wait to give it to them."

"It can't wait," Alex yelled. "I have to talk to him now!" She softened her tone. "Please. This is impor-tant."

The guard sighed. "I can have someone call the DA's office. I can't promise anything. In the meantime you got to go back to your cell."

Ladies and gentlemen, if I could direct your atten-tion high above the center ring. The Amazing Alexan-dra will now attempt a death-defying walk across a tightrope over a pit of voracious lions.

Alex tried to laugh through her tears, but there was nothing amusing about her circumstance. She was feel-ing squeezed literally between the proverbial rock and hard place. Bobby was dead. And if Xavier Rivera was gunning for her, no steel bars or concrete walls would keep him from it.

An hour passed before the guard came back.

"Well, did you get in touch with him? Is he coming?" Alex queried.

"Mr. Ellis is gone for the night. But, I got good news for you; that FBI agent is still here."

Agent Oliver walked up and the guard opened Alex's cell and let him inside.

"I was hoping you would come to your senses," Agent Oliver said.

"Why didn't you tell me what happened to Bobby?"

"I only just found out myself."

"You said you could put me in protective custody? Witness protection?"

"That all depends on the validity of the information you have. And since you were just a party planner I doubt very much we could make a case with anything you have to say."

Alex scoffed. "You know damn well I was more that. That's why you're still here, isn't it? If I give you Rivera I need your word that you will protect me and my mother."

"Look, we've been after Rivera for a very long time. You give us everything we need to put him away and I'll do everything I can possibly do for you and your mother."

"I want full immunity and I want it in writing."

"Give me something to work with, Ms. Solomon."

Alex grabbed hold of the bars, closed her eyes, and took a deep breath. "I know something about the undercover agent who washed up in the Everglades last year."

"What specifically do you know that hasn't already been reported?"

"You want Rivera. I want a deal."

"All right, I'll make a call."

"And I want to be moved out of this cell—tonight. I don't feel safe here."

"Fine."

Within the hour Alex was transported from the jail and moved to a windowless underground federal facility in downtown Atlanta, where she was joined by her mother. Despite the guarded security of the location she still feared for her safety. Xavier Rivera's influence was much too wily. There would be no rest until he was brought to justice.

29

Pat was finishing up the dishes when Kevin walked in. He slid his arms around her waist and rested his head on the back of hers.

"I'm so tired I could just sleep right here," he said. "Where's Micah?"

"I put him to bed a little bit ago. He tried to stay up as long as he could and wait on you. He wanted to make sure you got home okay. He keeps asking if the same thing that happened to Miss Betty is gonna happen to you."

"Damn." Kevin went to the refrigerator for a beer.

Pat grabbed a towel to dry her hands. "I convinced him that nothing was going to happen to you and that everything was going to be all right. Everything is going to be all right, isn't it? Kevin?"

"I went by the hospital on my way home." He showed Pat the chip in his hand.

"What is this?"

"It's something you get from Narcotics Anonymous. I found it in Noonie's bed. I think Tirrell left it there."

"Narcotics Anonymous?"

"I had a visit from this guy today who works at The Mission downtown. He told me Tirrell was staying there."

"Tirrell's on drugs?"

Kevin slumped down in a chair at the kitchen table. "It would explain a lot."

"What about the file he sent you? How does that woman fit into all of this?"

"Tirrell's mixed up with some bad people, baby."

"What kind of danger is he in?"

"The less you know the better." The telephone rang. Kevin got up and answered. "Hello . . . Hey, Mama. I'm good. You? No, Noonie hasn't come around yet. Micah's fine. To tell you truth there's been so much going on, Thanksgiving is the last thing on my mind. No, I don't think coming out to California right now would be a good idea. I want to be here just in case . . . No, I don't think she's going to die. Why would you say something like that? I'm sorry; it's been a long day. Look, I just got home and I'm beat. I'll call you later, all right?" Kevin hung up the phone, rubbed his eyes, and sighed.

"Are you gonna tell Gloria what's happening?"

"Absolutely not. I don't want her to know any more than she already does. In fact, I don't want you and Micah to be here if anything else should go down."

"What are you talkin' about?"

"I think you should take Micah and go to New Orleans and stay with your sister for a couple of weeks until this all blows over."

"No. I'm not leaving you here."

"It's not up for discussion. If Noonie was shot because of Tirrell, there's no telling who else might be in the line of fire, and I can't lose you, or Micah."

"I don't want to lose you either."

"I can take care of myself. But, I can't do my job if I'm worried about the two of you."

"Kevin."

He took her face in his hands and kissed her. "I don't want to argue about this, baby. You have to go."

"What about my job?"

"Take tomorrow off. In fact, take some vacation time. Tell them you have a family emergency and you need to go out of town for a few weeks. Do this for me, all right?"

She knew he wasn't backing down. "All right, I'll go."

He kissed her again.

She responded in kind. "I thought you were tired." She smiled.

"I just need to be close to you right now, is that all right?"

Kevin took Pat by the hand and led her out of the kitchen and up the stairs. He kicked off his shoes, loosened his tie, and slowly unbuttoned his shirt. He took her in his arms from behind and pulled her blouse over her head. His fingers tugged at the fasteners and undid her bra. Her breasts fell free as he slipped the straps over her shoulders and ran his hands slowly down her body.

She tossed her head back and he kissed and nibbled her neck. His beard tickled and aroused as did the hair on his chest brushing against her back. She moaned when he unzipped her skirt and pushed it away from her hips. He turned her around, palmed her thighs, hoisted her up to his waist, and laid her on the bed. Shucking his pants and underwear, he gently climbed on top of her.

"I love you so much," he whispered, removing her panties. "I don't know what I would do if anything ever happened to you."

"Nothing will."

Her back arched upward and she gasped as he entered, slowly, purposefully. Their bodies found a familiar rhythm. The strength of his love for her made its own music.

***

Kevin woke early the next morning, sat up on the side of the bed, and watched Pat sleep. He'd done this before when he was worried about a case, or there was something weighing heavy on his mind. Thoughts of his grandmother's recovery and Tirrell's problems made it hard for him to rest. The peaceful look on his wife's face and the soft purring noise she made reminded him that no matter how bad things got, she would be there to support him.

Pat's eyes fluttered and she woke up. "What are you doin'?"

"Watching you."

"I can see that. What time is it?"

"Time for you and Micah to get on the road."

Pat pulled herself up. "Kevin, I don't think we should go."

"I told you it's not up for discussion. You already agreed."

"I changed my mind."

"C'mon, Pat. Don't give me a hard time about this, please. You'll just be gone long enough for all of this to blow over."

"But you don't know when that's going to be."

Kevin shook his head. "No, I don't. But I want you safe." He started to the door.

"Where are you goin'?"

"I'm going to get Micah up and packed. You should do the same."

Pat rolled out of bed and scurried around the room, picking up clothes that had been thrown about the previous night, and then she went to the bathroom to get ready.

The telephone rang as they ate breakfast together. It was the hospital calling to report that Betty was conscious. It would be one less thing for them to fret about.

After seeing Pat and Micah off safely, Kevin headed to the hospital.

He entered the room with a huge arrangement of multicolored tulips and Betty's face lit up. He kissed her and then found a space to set them among the other flowers, cards, and get-well wishes.

Betty cleared the hoarseness in her throat. "Lord, it looks like somebody died in here. I guess I almost did, didn't I?"

"Don't even joke like that. You had us all scared that we were going to lose you."

"I'm a tough old bird. God ain't quite ready for me yet."

Kevin frowned. "How're you feeling?"

"Like I've been asleep for a hundred years. I know my hair must look a sight."

"You look fine."

"I know better than that." She pursed her lips. "Where's the rest of the family?"

"Pat and Micah went to visit her sister in New Orleans. Mama called. She and Jacqui wanted to come, but I told her it would be best for her to stay in California for now, considering there wasn't anything they could do here. Miss Anne and Pastor Eason have been out here almost every day."

"Micah's all right?"

"Yes, he's fine."

"What about Tirrell? Is he all right?"

"Noonie, do you remember anything about how you got here?"

"The doctor told me I was shot in the stomach. Last thing I remember was watchin' TV and the next thing I know I'm wakin' up in here. Who would do such a thing?"

Kevin looked down at his hands. He wanted to tell her everything, but he wasn't sure she was strong enough to handle it, or that she would believe it happened because of Tirrell. Fortunately, a nurse came in to check Betty's vitals and granted him a reprieve. He used the opportunity to step out and call Pat.

"Where are you?"

"We just got into Alabama. Is everything okay? How's Miss Betty?"

"She looks good. She's going to be all right."

"Thank God. Did you tell her anything about Tirrell?"

"No."

"Are you still going to see him?"

"I think I have to."

"Kevin, be careful."

"I will. I'll call you later. I love you."

"I love you too."

The nurse came out and informed Kevin that he could go back inside. In order to keep Betty from getting overly excited he knew he had to tell her something.

"I want to call Tirrell," she said. "I need to check on him."

"You can't," Kevin followed. "His cell phone is disconnected."

"How much does he owe?"

"Noonie, that's nothing for you to be concerned about right now. Tirrell is fine. In fact, he's been here to see you."

"Where is he now?"

"He's staying with friends."

"Is it Marquis?"

"No."

"Then who? Lord, it's not that woman, is it?"

"No. Not her—someone else."

"I want to see him. Would you please go by wherever he's stayin' and bring him here?"

"Yeah, I can do that."

"And, Kevin, promise me—no more fighting. Not now."

"I promise, Noonie."

Balancing slightly to the left of full disclosure wasn't going to do her as much harm as knowing what her beloved Tirrell had gotten himself into.

Kevin headed to The Mission as he promised, where he found Tirrell sweeping the floor.

"Wow, look who's here," Tirrell sneered. "How'd you find me?"

"Charlie Preston came to see me."

Tirrell looked around and saw Mr. Preston talking to a couple of the guys in the adjoining room. Mr. Preston glanced up and acknowledged him.

"I need to talk to you, Tirrell."

"I don't know, Kev. My calendar's pretty full, sweepin' and moppin' and shit. Maybe I can fit you in next Tuesday."

"Cut the crap, Tirrell."

"Why do you wanna talk to me all of a sudden?"

"It's about Alex Solomon."

"You got the e-mail I sent you, right? You locked her ass up, right?"

"Look, Tirrell, we need to go somewhere private."

"Yeah, a'ight." Tirrell laid his broom against the wall. "Yo, Mr. P, I need to go have a talk with my brother. I'll be back in a few, a'ight?"

Mr. Preston nodded and Tirrell grabbed a jacket from the front closet and followed Kevin out. He chuckled when he got into the Explorer.

"What's so funny?"

"I was just thinkin' about the last time I was in here. You're not gonna hit me again, are you?"

"Don't tempt me."

They drove off.

"So, how'd you end up in this place, Tirrell?"

"'Cause I didn't have the money to get a room at the Marriott. How do you think?"

"Still sarcastic as hell, I see."

"And you're still a pain in the ass."

They pulled into a drive-thru, ordered two coffees, and found a parking space off Spring Street.

"How'd you get your hands on that file you sent me?"

"I saw Alex workin' on somethin' on her computer. She told me it was somethin' about some event. I knew her cousin Bobby was into some shady shit, so I figured it was about more than she told me. I found this jump drive she hid and the first chance I got I forwarded it to my e-mail. If you hadn't been such a dick and tossed that CD I left for you, you would've had the info a lot sooner. What did you think it was anyway, love songs?"

Kevin sighed and pressed on. "You know Xavier Rivera."

"Yeah, I met him."

"You've been to his place in Miami?"

"Yeah, and I know about this place over on Hardy Avenue. I went there with Bobby more than a few times."

"You know he's dead right?"

Tirrell's jaws tightened. "What happened?"

"We think one of Rivera's people got to him. I want you to come down to the police station with me and give a full statement."

"I gave you the file."

"That's not enough. We need every detail you can remember. Anything you saw or heard that could help put your girlfriend and Rivera away."

"And me. I get arrested too, right?"

"What are you talking about?"

"I was with Bobby Williams when he transported cocaine over state lines."

"Do you want the same thing that happened to Noonie to happen to the rest of us?"

"None of y'all ain't never gave a damn about me except Noonie."

"What about your nephew, huh? Don't you care about what happens to him?"

"You know I do. I never meant for any of this to happen."

"But it did, Tirrell. If you really want to fix it, you have to go all the way, even if it means doing time."

"That would be just what you want, right? Get me out of the way once and for all."

"Isn't one of the steps of NA to make amends, and to right the wreckage that you caused in people's lives?"

"I ain't got that far yet. I'm barely out of step one."

"You want to be a man, go all the way."

Tirrell grabbed the door handle. "I'm outta here."

"Wait."

"For what?"

"I need your help."

"That promotion not comin' as easy as you thought?"

"This is not about my damn job, Tirrell."

"Really?"

"I'm sorry for givin' you shit. But, you've got to admit, trouble seems to follow you everywhere you go. Now you've got a chance to do something good. Do this for Noonie. You at least owe her that much."

"Oh, no, the hell you didn't. You wanna throw Noonie up in my face."

"That's not what I'm doing."

"You could have fooled me."

"She's awake, Tirrell. She's asking for you."

"I wanna see her."

"Later. Right now you've got to give your statement so we can put Rivera out of business before he slips out of the country like Alex Solomon tried to do."

"What do you mean tried?"

"The day you sent that e-mail she was on a plane to New York. She was going from there to Nigeria with her mother. She had an alias set up and everything. You said Alex did this to Noonie. Do you think Rivera's going to stop coming after our family if she gets away?"

Kevin removed the NA coin from his jacket pocket and tossed it to Tirrell. "I found this in Noonie's hospital bed."

"Why'd you take it?"

"You can give it back to her when you see her."

Tirrell got back in the Explorer and closed the door. "Fine. I'll do whatever I have to do."

When they got to the police station, Kevin saw Alex in one of the interrogation rooms with Agent Oliver and a US Marshal.

Alex glanced up at Tirrell with a smug look on her face and turned away.

"Give me a minute," Kevin said.

He parked Tirrell in another room guarded by an officer, and went in to see what was going on. He didn't know whether to be relieved or stunned that she'd made a deal.

"You should be happy, Mr. Ellis," Agent Oliver said. "Ms. Solomon is cooperating and has agreed to give us everything we need to nail Rivera's ass to the wall. I've got a team raiding his Miami compound as we speak. We've not only got him on drug charges; we'll have him for the murder of a federal agent, too."

"What?"

"It seems Ms. Solomon was clever enough to get a video recording on her cell phone."

"What about Tirrell?"

"Get his statement. Right now I would think he needs to be concerned about what the locals are going to do to him. We'll know where to find him if we need him."

Kevin was infuriated that Alex Solomon would never have to answer for what he assumed she'd done to his family. His contempt for the process fell on deaf ears.

Tirrell was questioned about Bobby Williams, but denied seeing him the day he was shot and confessed that he was somewhere getting high. With no witnesses and no physical evidence linking him to the shooting he was released into Kevin's custody.

Tirrell smoldered as Kevin drove him back to The Mission. "I can't believe this shit."

"What?"

"What? Did you just get dropped off on the planet?"

Kevin scoffed and cut his eyes.

"Alex just gets a pass? A new name? A different location? She doesn't have to pay for any of this?"

"Look, I'm as upset about all of this as you are, but there's nothing I can do."

"Oh, you're *upset*. Well, that makes me feel so much better."

"All the Feds wanted was Rivera."

"Fuck Rivera. I thought this was supposed to be about what happened to Noonie, too."

"We didn't find the Mustang you and Marquis said you saw. And there was nothing to tie her to the shooting since you never saw who was in the car."

"Yeah, well she wouldn't have bothered to get blood under her manicured nails," Tirrell shot back. "It was Bobby. I know it just as well as I know my own name."

"We can't prove that, Tirrell. And since he's dead it's not like we can ask him about it."

"Then I'm glad I did what I did."

"What are you talking about?"

"Nothin'."

"What did you do, Tirrell?"

Since he'd already denied his involvement Tirrell had second thoughts about incriminating himself. If Kevin had questions about what really happened to Bobby Williams he didn't ask.

"Shit," Kevin spat.

"What is it?"

"It's that van again."

"What van?"

"I'm not trying to be paranoid, but I think we're being followed."

"How do you know?"

"I thought I saw this van at The Mission and then when we stopped for coffee, and now he's behind us again."

Tirrell turned around. "You sure?"

"There's only one way to find out." Kevin switched lanes on the interstate to make certain they weren't being tailed, the van pulled directly behind him. When he slowed, the van slowed. He gripped the steering wheel and accelerated and the van stayed close. With a sudden jerk, Kevin swerved in between two other cars, nearly colliding with a small truck moving into the lane from the other direction—horns blared in disapproval. The van sped away.

"What the hell?" Tirrell sighed.

"I don't know." Kevin signaled and exited the interstate.

"Where're we goin'?"

"I need to stop and get a pack of cigarettes."

"Since when do you smoke?"

"Since when is it your business?"

They pulled up to a convenience store. Kevin went inside and Tirrell went to the side of the building to take a leak. He finished up and headed back just as Kevin started out of the store. The van that had followed them on the interstate squealed onto the parking lot and Tirrell spotted a gun barrel pointing out of the passenger side window. He flashed on the Mustang and the night Betty was shot, but this time Kevin was the target.

Tirrell bolted toward him. "Kevin, look out!"

It was too late. The first round ripped into Kevin's left shoulder and smashed the glass door behind him. Tirrell leapt in front of him, knocking him to the ground, and took the second blast to his back. An Asian woman inside the store screamed hysterically and dropped behind the counter. When he was certain that it was all clear, the male store owner ran out to see what happened. Kevin grabbed his arm and struggled to pull himself from under the weight of Tirrell's body.

"Oh shit," he cried. He trembled as he cupped Tirrell's face. "Oh shit."

"Is he dead?" the rattled store owner queried.

"Call an ambulance!"

The man turned to his wife inside and yelled in Korean for her to call, as onlookers swarmed from every direction. Tirrell's body slumped over Kevin's leg and blood spilled out like water and pooled around them. Kevin leaned against the wall of the building and wept.

By the time the DEA and the FBI executed the raid on Xavier Rivera's Miami compound he'd already fled and they found nothing. Alex was quick to remind Agent

Oliver of her immunity, and it was her cooperation that gave them the ammunition to round up two of the six dealers listed in her files who operated out of other states. It would be solely up to them to track down and prosecute Rivera when and if they found him.

After hearing about the blatant attack on Tirrell and Kevin Ellis, Alex feared more for her safety, and with good reason. As a condition of her deal, she was still pegged as the government's key witness. Regardless of their safeguards, if Rivera was in a country that didn't have extradition to the United States (and it was a sure bet that he would be) she knew not to rest too comfortably. The only thing she had left to barter with was her life, and if a hit had already been arranged, that life wasn't going to be worth a whole lot.

30

Given all that had transpired, neither Thanksgiving nor Christmas were the joyous occasions they had been in years past. While most people feasted on turkey and dressing and all the other trappings of the season of abundance, Tirrell, who barely escaped death, lay in a hospital bed attached to a catheter, intravenous drips of various fluids, and a machine that pumped morphine into his system.

"Dammit," Tirrell spat. "I need somethin' else for this pain. This fuckin' pump ain't workin'!"

"That's because you just pushed it. You know it's locked and you gotta wait ten minutes for the next dose," the burly male nurse retorted as he maneuvered him for a dressing change.

Tirrell's eyes filled with tears. He gritted his teeth and scowled. "I'm tellin' you this shit ain't workin'. Why can't you give me what you gave me the other day?"

"Just let me get done here and I'll call your doctor to see if he can order anything else for you, okay?"

After the nurse finished redressing Tirrell's wound, another nurse came in to draw blood. This routine had become the norm over the days following the surgery to remove the bullet from his back. Tirrell had been examined, monitored, poked, prodded, and, in his estimation, damn near bled dry. He was bombarded with redundant questions about how he was feeling, or sleeping, or his pain level and appetite. His legs were covered and massaged by long sausage casing–like sleeves that helped to prevent blood clots, as he lay for days on end wondering if he would ever walk again.

The morphine was finally kicking in. Just when he thought he had a few minutes to close his eyes and get some sleep before someone else burst in to cart him off for another X-ray or therapy, Mr. Preston tapped on the door and stuck his head inside the room.

"Care to see a friendly face?"

"Yeah, come on in," Tirrell responded groggily.

He tentatively entered and approached the side of the bed. "I won't stay long. I just wanted to stop by and see how you were."

Tirrell smiled. Since the day Mr. Preston first reached out to him, he'd become more of a father figure than any man in his life. He was happier to see him than his pride was willing to reveal.

Mr. Preston pulled up a chair and sat down. "After gettin' all these narcotics in your system you gon' have to start the program all over again, you know that, right?"

"Yeah, I know."

"And you thought it was rough before." Mr. Preston chuckled. "You're gon' need some serious rehab now."

"Yeah, but right now I just wanna enjoy this, a'ight?"

Mr. Preston shrugged. "So, how does it feel to be a hero?"

"Hero?"

"It was all over the news there for a while, you takin' a bullet for your brother."

"Yeah, that was pretty stupid, huh? It was more than he would have done for me."

"It wasn't stupid at all," Mr. Preston countered. "You showed how much of a man you really are, deep down—where it counts."

"Yeah, and look where it got me. I'm so fuckin' ec-static I could dance. Oh wait, I forgot, my legs don't work no more."

"Man, you don't know how lucky you are. That bul-let could've taken you outta here. I hear you could be walkin' again as soon as the swellin' goes down around your spine, you just have to be patient."

"I'll just be happy to pee standing up."

"I don't think you need to be feelin' sorry for your-self. I'm tell'ya now, things could be worse."

"It don't matter no way. It ain't like Kevin gives a damn. It's been like six weeks and he hasn't been to see me one time. I mean he could have at least sent a damn thank-you card or somethin'."

"Doesn't change the fact that you did a courageous thing."

"Doesn't make it any easier either," Tirrell shot back. "Nothin' I do will ever be good enough for any of 'em."

"You know if I want to hear a baby cry I could go down to the maternity ward."

Tirrell shook his head and turned away.

"I know it's hard, but you got a lot more fight left in you, otherwise, you would have checked out already. You gon' be all right. Here, I got somethin' for you." Mr. Preston pulled a plastic bag from the inside of his jacket and handed it to him.

Tirrell's eyes lit up. "It's an iPod."

"I didn't know if you had one already. I figured if you didn't it would help you pass the time."

"Thanks, man."

"Well, look here. I'm gon' head out and let you get some rest."

"I appreciate you, Mr. P. Thanks for comin'."

They bumped fists.

"I'm proud of you, son. I'm gon' be right here to help you if you want it. "

Tirrell's eyes misted as he watched his mentor leave. He sniffled, wiped his hand over his nose and mouth, and cleared his throat, resisting the urge to cry. He lay back on his pillow and closed his eyes. As he drifted off to sleep he whispered, "God, grant me the serenity to accept the things I cannot change; courage to change the things I can; and wisdom to know the difference."

When he woke up Betty was sitting by his side.

"Hi, baby. How're you feelin'?"

He yawned. "Noonie, what are you doin' here again?"

"What are you talkin' about? Where else would I be?"

"You didn't drive, did you? You're barely out of the hospital yourself. You know you shouldn't be drivin'."

"Boy, I was takin' care of myself long before you were born. I suspect I can continue doin' just that."

"That's not what I meant."

"I know."

"You were just here yesterday."

"And I'm gonna be here tomorrow and the next day, until you come home. I got the place all ready for you. Marquis even built a wheelchair ramp up to the porch."

"That should come in handy. I ain't got no insurance. They'll be kickin' me out of here soon."

"You don't have to worry about payin' no hospital bill. Your brother is takin' care of all of that."

"Are you serious?"

Betty nodded.

"Well, I'll be damned," Tirrell responded. He glanced at his grandmother, realizing what he'd said. "Sorry."

Betty continued as if his comment didn't register. "I still can't believe all this happened because of that—

that woman. I could have lost both you and Kevin. I knew she was no good when I first set eyes on her."

"It's not all on her, Noonie. I made some bad choices and got myself into a lot of this shi . . . I mean stuff on my own."

"She still caused you a lot of pain, and if there's any justice at all one of these days she's gonna get exactly what she deserves."

"So, where is my generous big brother?"

"I'm right here." Kevin pushed open the door, carrying a box of food that Betty had prepared. "I had trouble finding a place to park."

"What's all this?"

Betty stood and started pulling covered bowls from the box and setting them on the adjustable rolling table in front of Tirrell.

"I know firsthand that the food in here don't taste like much, and I wanted to make sure you got some good home cookin'. I checked and they told me it would be okay for you to have."

"Thanks, Noonie." Tirrell rubbed his hands together with anticipation, pulled a plastic lid from one of the bowls, and inhaled the mouthwatering aroma of baked macaroni and cheese.

"Micah threw a fit," Kevin injected. "He really wanted to come see you. We told him he should probably wait a couple more days."

"That boy really loves his uncle," Betty affirmed.

"Unlike his father," Tirrell sniped.

Kevin massaged his left shoulder where he'd been shot. "I uh . . . I know I should've come before now. I was just having a harder time than I thought."

"Sorry to disappoint you, bruh. I'm still here."

"Tirrell, don't talk like that," Betty chided.

A respiratory therapist pushed into the room and dispelled the tension. "Well, Mr. Ellis, I was going to ask if you already had lunch, but I can see that you got that covered. Is that macaroni and cheese I smell?"

"It sure is," Betty responded, easing back into her chair. "Would you like some? There's plenty."

"No, thank you. I just wanted to see to it that Mr. Ellis was using his spirometer. You don't want pneumonia setting into those lungs, do you?"

Tirrell held up the device and waved it in the air. "I got it right here."

The woman nodded and excused herself from the room.

Tirrell absently checked the other containers in the box. "So, Kev, Noonie said you were takin' care of all the hospital stuff."

"It's the least I could do. I figured I owed you."

Betty patted Tirrell's hand and nodded. "Baby, you better eat up before the food gets cold," Betty injected. She pulled a napkin and plastic utensils from the box and handed them to Tirrell. Without hesitation he started in on the macaroni.

"Noonie, I need to head back to the office," Kevin injected.

"So soon? We just got here," Betty responded.

"Sorry. I've got some paperwork I need to finish."

"Any word on Alex?" Tirrell asked.

Kevin shook his head. "As far as the world is concerned Alexandra Solomon no longer exists."

"That bitch," Tirrell whispered under his breath.

Kevin cleared his throat.

"Okay, baby. We need to go now. But I'll be back tomorrow."

"Noonie, you don't have to do that."

"What did I say?"

Tirrell smiled.

"Don't worry. I won't be driving. I'll see if Anne Crawl or Marquis can bring me."

Noonie stood, leaned in, and kissed Tirrell's forehead. "I just thank God that both my boys are all right." She gathered her purse and turned to leave. "I love you, baby."

"I love you too, Noonie. Oh and uh, Kev . . . thanks."

Kevin nodded and exited behind Betty.

A week later Tirrell was released from the hospital. He barely had time to settle in before he was saddled with an aggressive rehabilitation regimen, and a physical therapist who quite often pushed him beyond the limits of where he thought he could go.

"Man, I can't do it!"

"Yes, you can. You've come this far. Now, give me two more."

"I can't, you asshole."

"Do you want to walk again, or do you want to spend the rest of your life on wheels?"

Tirrell clenched his teeth and held his breath. Perspiration trickled down his forehead and pooled in his ears as his therapist assisted him in pulling his leg up and bending it at the knee toward his chest.

"Fourteen. C'mon . . . c'mon. You got this. One more."

By the end of a grueling set of leg lifts and knee bends Tirrell felt as if he'd run a marathon, and cursed his therapist for making him work so hard.

"You'll thank me later." The man chuckled as he lifted Tirrell back into bed.

"I uh . . . I could really use somethin' a little stronger than they gave me for this pain," Tirrell groaned.

"How bad is it?"

"It's bad. Real bad."

"I'll call your doctor and let him know."

"C'mon, don't you have somethin' you can give me?"

"You took your allotment of Tramadol already."

Tirrell picked up a bedpan at his side and threw it at the man. "You can't expect me to get through this shit if I'm in this much pain!"

"And you can't expect me to be your dope dealer either. You may as well man up, take what the doctor prescribed you, and deal with it. Do you want pain relief or you wanna get high?"

Tirrell turned away in disgust.

Betty knocked at the bedroom door as the therapist collected his gear and prepared to leave. "How's everything goin' in here?"

"We're all done for the day," the man said as he headed out. "The poor baby can't take any more."

"To hell with you, Alan," Tirrell spat, flinging his towel at the man.

Betty's brow furrowed. "Tirrell."

"It's all right, Ms. Ellis," the man assured her. "I'm used to it. I'll show myself out."

Betty handed Tirrell a bottle of water. "Are you up for some company?"

Before he could answer Micah jetted past his great grandmother and bolted into the room. "Uncle Tirrell!"

"Hey, li'l man."

Micah stopped just shy of jumping onto the bed. "What's wrong?"

"Daddy said I should be careful because you can't walk."

"It's just temporary. See?" Tirrell strained to lift his leg—it barely moved. "I'll be back to normal in no time. Now c'mere and give me a hug."

Micah reticently embraced him. "I missed you."

"I missed you too."

Kevin entered the room with Pat in tow.

"Micah, get down."

"It's okay, Kev. He's fine."

"You look good, Tirrell," Pat said.

"I'm gettin' better."

Betty smiled. "It's so good to have my family all safe under one roof."

"Well, I guess now is as good a time as any to make an announcement." Kevin beamed. "The family might be getting bigger real soon."

"What do you mean?" Betty asked.

Pat smiled. "We're having a baby."

Betty was moved to tears. She clasped her hands to both sides of her daughter-in-law's face. "I am so happy for the both of you."

As the attention shifted to Pat and Kevin's good news Tirrell grunted, attempting to raise his leg again.

Betty turned to him. "Tirrell, are you all right?"

"Yeah, I'm fine. Just tired."

"We should clear out of here and let you rest," Kevin suggested.

"Kevin, isn't there something you needed to say to Tirrell?"

Kevin cleared his throat and stepped over to the side of the bed. He teared up as he reached into his pocket and pulled out a medal his grandfather had been awarded, and pinned it to Tirrell's T-shirt.

"What's this?" Tirrell asked.

"It's the medal Granddaddy was given for bravery when he was in Vietnam," Kevin responded. "I meant to bring this to you sooner, but I had a hard time finding it. You saved my life and I couldn't think of a better way to let you know how grateful I am, except to give you this. You earned it. You earned my respect, too, man."

Tears streamed down Betty's face watching the two. Kevin reached out and shook Tirrell's hand.

"What? No hug? No kiss?" Tirrell smirked.

"I'm never gonna forget what you did for me," Kevin continued.

"Don't worry," Tirrell said soberly. "I'm not ever gonna let you."

"We're family, right?" Kevin allowed. "Brothers."

"Brothers," Tirrell repeated.

Kevin's acknowledgement was bittersweet and more rewarding than anything Tirrell could have ever asked for. In that moment he didn't feel like an outsider looking in. For the first time in his life he had the family he'd always wanted. The family he'd almost given his life to deserve.

Epilogue

It had been some months since Alexandra Solomon had completed the evaluations and counseling sessions mandated by the witness protection program, and another spring had settled in. Her new identity notwithstanding, she longed for the life she'd abandoned: her important clients, the expensive clothes, the extravagant parties. Try as she might she couldn't reconcile the fact that it was a life she could never go back to. She turned and studied her reflection in the mirror mounted on the bedroom wall. Her appearance was much changed. Her hair had grown out and was no longer the pixie coif she'd been identified with. The figure that commanded the attention of men whenever she entered a room had been stretched beyond the point of recognition. She thought about Tirrell. Sitting down on the side of the bed she picked up the phone for what seemed the hundredth time in as many days and dialed his number. She hung up before completing the call. "What the hell am I doing?" She knew the rules and yet felt compelled to reach out to him. She held her breath, picked up the phone, and dialed again.

"Hello."

Hearing his voice caused her heart to skip. She swallowed back the dryness of her tongue and exhaled slowly through her nose.

"Hello."

Her mouth opened to form the words and she slammed down the receiver. She stood, moved to the window, and stared out over the quiet California community where she and her mother had been stashed. Rubbing her hands over her protruding baby bump she resolved that he would never know. She was prepared to take that secret to her grave.

The End

Sneak Peek . . .

Avenging Alex

At the sound of a crackling rumble of thunder, Alex threw back the comforter and sprang out of bed. She cautiously pulled the curtain back to see that the wind was blowing a tree branch against the house. A streak of lightening flashed across the sky and illuminated what she thought to be a man watching her from the other side of the street. Was it the same man she'd seen the day before?

A muffled scream clung to the back of her throat as she jerked away from the window and darted to the nightstand next to her bed to retrieve her .380 semiautomatic. It was against the program's policy for her to have a gun in her possession, but she was not about to leave her life completely to chance or in anyone's hands but her own. Whatever she'd seen was gone when she moved back to the window to get another look. The telephone rang and startled her. She hesitated to answer, but decided she was being silly and needed to before the noise woke her mother.

"Hello."

"Hey, it's me. I just got your message. Is everything all right?"

Alex peered back toward the window. "Yes . . . uh . . . I mean, no. I think I just saw someone outside."

"You think?"

"I can't be sure, but it looked like someone was watching the house."

"The same man you told me about?"

"I don't know. Maybe."

"Are all the doors and windows locked?"

"Yes."

"Is the alarm set?"

"Yes, it's armed."

"I'm on my way. I'll be there in fifteen minutes. Don't open the door to anyone but me. Understand?"

"John, you don't have to—"

"Yes, I do. I'm on my way."

Alex hung up the telephone and held the gun close to her breast. Damsel in distress was not a role she fit comfortably into, but she had to admit she was glad to have a man like John Chase to watch out for her.

Without turning on the light she picked up her terry-cloth bathrobe from the foot of the bed, slid into it, and crept slowly across the carpeted floor. She opened the bedroom door and looked up the dark hallway, first one way and then the other, just to satisfy herself that no danger was lurking. She tiptoed from her room to a room directly across the hall. The glow of the nightlight illuminated the pastel clouds and chubby-cheeked angels plastered on the walls surrounding her baby's crib, as if somehow the notion of the inanimate wallpaper was protection enough.

Alex inched closer. She breathed a sigh of relief as she watched her baby sleeping. She leaned in and readjusted the soft white blanket covering her and caressed the girl's face.

"Alexandra."

Alex jumped nervously and spun around, aiming the gun in her hand at her mother, Jamilah.

The woman shrieked. "Oh, for the love of God."

"Don't sneak up on me like that."

The woman caught her breath. "You know I can't stand those things. Please, put it away."

Alex relaxed and lowered the gun. "I'm sorry. It was raining so hard. I thought I heard something. I just wanted to check on the baby."

"With a gun?"

"I needed to be sure."

"Did you call John?"

"He called me. He's on his way over."

Jamilah sidled up beside the crib and peered inside. "This precious angel can sleep through just about anything. She reminds me so much of you when you were a baby."

"I'm not a baby anymore, and I'm definitely not sleeping so well at all these days."

Alex kissed her daughter's forehead and turned to leave the room—her mother followed. The girl made a cooing noise and wriggled a bit but didn't wake. Alex put the gun back in its hiding place and proceeded into the kitchen. She pulled a bottle of Grey Goose vodka from the freezer, and filled a glass with ice.

"Would you like a drink?"

The woman waved her hand and shook her head.

"What woke you besides the storm, *Omolola?*"

"Don't you mean *Adriane?*"

Her mother's expression soured and she grimaced. "I don't care what name the government gives you, you will always be my *Omolola.*" Jamilah brushed her hand over her lush, peppery mane and took a seat at the kitchen table.

"I want this nightmare to be over," Alex continued. "I want to stop seeing Xavier Rivera in every shadow."

Harkening back to her previous life, she supposed this existence was justifiable recompense for how she and her former associates made others feel when threatened: anxious, scared, and constantly on edge.

"You think vodka will help you sleep?" Jamilah asked.

"It sure as hell couldn't hurt."

"*Omolola,* I'm worried about you."

"You don't need to. I'm fine, Mama. Go back to bed."

"Now, how are you going to tell me not to worry? You're not eating. You're not sleeping. I'm going to worry about you as much as you worry about your own child. I just wish I could make this better for you somehow."

"Mama, you've done everything you could possibly do. You gave up your entire life because of me. It's my fault you had to sacrifice so much."

Jamilah stood and went to Alex. She put her arms around her and gave her a big squeeze. "Don't take this all on yourself. It was my decision to come with you. And they're going to find that man, you'll see. We're going to be all right, Alexandra. We have John here to look after us."

"Yes, but for how long? He's got his own life. He's got other cases."

"He's going to be here for as long as we need him. Besides, I have a feeling that man likes you."

"Mama." Alex pulled away, nearly blushing. "What would make you say something like that?"

"I see the way he's been looking at you. It may have been awhile, but I can still tell when a man feels something for a woman."

Alex pondered her mother's words as she savored the alcohol in her glass. "He's just doing a job, and that job does not include having a relationship with the woman he's supposed to be protecting."

"Uh huh." Jamilah smirked. "I think I will have that nightcap after all." She pulled a glass from the cupboard. "John Chase is a man, and that's all I need to know."

Alex grabbed the bottle and sat down at the table. "Romance is the last thing I need to be thinking about right now; especially with someone like him. I don't

have the best track record when it comes to relation-
ships."

Her mother joined her. "Tirrell Ellis is nothing like
John Chase, in case you hadn't noticed. Neither was
Raymond for that matter."

The doorbell rang and both women gasped and froze
in mid-thought. Jamilah clutched the top of her blue
satin robe close around her neck and started to get up.
Alex reached out her hand to stop her and went ahead
of her. She leaned into to the peephole, but it was too
obscured to make anything out.

"Adriane," the mellow baritone called out. "It's John."

Alex disarmed the alarm and threw open the door as
fast as she could unlock it. The presence of the solid,
good-looking, 220-pound, six-foot-two-inch inspector
was reassuring. His confidence was one of the things
she found most appealing about him. She'd consistent-
ly been drawn to that attribute in a man. Her husband
was like that; so was Tirrell, at least, in the beginning.

"What have I told you about opening the door without first making sure you know who it is?" the man
chided.

"You don't think I recognize your voice after all this
time?" Alex repressed the urge to smile.

Despite himself, John smiled. He looked over her
shoulder and nodded to Jamilah. "Is everybody all
right in here?"

"We're fine," Jamilah assured him.

"I checked around the grounds," John continued. "I
didn't find anything out of the ordinary."

Alex moved away from the door and allowed him to
enter. He stomped his wet shoes on the mat outside
before stepping in. Jamilah hurried to the counter and
grabbed a handful of paper towels to give to him.

"Thank you." John took the towels and wiped his brow and clean-shaven head.

"Inspector, can I fix you a drink?" Jamilah offered.

"No, I'm fine." He turned his attention to Alex. "Could you make out anything about the man you saw outside?"

"I'm not even sure there was a man," Alex admitted. "It may have been just my imagination playing tricks on me."

"Alexandra," Jamilah injected, "you didn't tell me you saw someone outside."

"Because I'm not even sure I saw anything at all."

"Whatever it was it scared you enough to call John over here."

Alex rubbed her eyes and moved to the kitchen table for her glass. "John, it really wasn't necessary for you to come over here in the middle of the night like this. I'm sorry I dragged you out of bed or whatever."

"You didn't drag me anywhere. I wasn't asleep. You, your mother, and your little girl are my prime concern right now. Until we get Rivera we don't know who's out there who could be after you, so we need to be vigilant. And that includes you all getting used to calling each other by your new names, even when you think you're alone and no one can hear you."

"I know," Alex agreed.

"I just hate being called Janette," Jamilah complained.

"You're gonna have to," John insisted. "If I'm gonna do my job effectively, you have to play your parts in all of this. Otherwise, we may as well lead you right to the slaughter. Xavier Rivera is going to do everything in his power to find you and keep you from testifying. I've gotta do everything I can to keep you safe."

Jamilah interpreted the look that passed between her daughter and the stalwart inspector and smiled as she poured more vodka into her glass and pretended to yawn. "Well, if you two will excuse me, I believe *Miss Janette* is finally ready to get back to bed."

"Good night, ma'am."

Alex left the kitchen and returned with a bigger, more suitable bath towel from the linen closet in the hall. "Here. Give me your jacket and you take this."

John peeled off the wet rain slicker, exchanged it for the dry towel, and sat down.

Alex took the raincoat, hung it on a doorknob, and watched him as he rubbed and patted the moisture from his face, arms, and neck. "Are you sure I can't fix you something to drink?"

"I'll take a cup of coffee if it's not too much trouble."

Alex pulled a filter from the cupboard and filled the coffee pot with water. She felt his eyes watching her from behind and shook her head.

"What's wrong?" he asked.

"Do you think it's going to be like this forever?"

"What do you mean?"

She turned around, pulling the tie on her robe tighter, and walked over to the table to sit down. She picked up her glass and swirled the remnants of ice with her index finger. "I'm not used to being the one who's afraid all the time. I'm used to having a certain amount of control over my life. I hate that I've allowed myself to be put in a situation for it to be taken away. I can't get over the fact that even when they catch Xavier, I still may not be able to go back to the way things were."

John leaned forward, resting his elbows on his thighs with the towel draped around his neck, rubbing his hands together. "Look, I know you're scared. It's all right. We've taken every precaution to protect you."

"Do those precautions include you sticking around after he's caught?"

They looked into each other's eyes. The concentration in his gaze caused her to blink and look away. She tossed back the watered-down remains in her glass and went to the counter.

"I think the coffee is ready. Cream and two sugars, right?"

John cleared his throat and sat back in the chair. "Right."

Alex poured two cups of coffee and returned to the table. Their eyes darted nervously as they gingerly sipped the hot brew. Neither seemed to want to be caught looking at the other.

"I didn't mean to imply anything by what I said," Alex confessed. "Blame the vodka."

"I think I've heard that song before," John quipped.

Their mutual laughter masked the growing tension.

"I guess this is my lame attempt at getting to know a little more about you after all these months. I mean you've got this huge file with every sordid detail of my life since the day I lost my first tooth."

John put his cup down on the table. "There's not a whole lot you need to know about me."

"Why not? You're not married, are you?"

He averted his gaze.

Alex's eyes widened with surprise, given all this time she never thought that he might be. "Oh, wow. You are, aren't you? Damn, I must really be slipping. I used to be able to smell a married man from across the room— even if he didn't wear a ring." She looked at his hand as he absently rubbed the finger where a wedding band had been.

"For the record I'm separated."

"Separated as in different living arrangements, or separated as in 'we've got our problems but we still sleep together'?"

"It's complicated."

"Isn't it always?" Alex stood up and walked into the adjoining living room. "I can't believe I . . . You know what, it's late. You should probably go home. We'll be okay."

John followed. "I wasn't trying to upset you. I just didn't think my personal life was relevant."

"You're right," Alex snapped. "It's not. I just feel really stupid right now."

"Well, you shouldn't."

"I should have realized from the moment I—"

"From the moment you what?"

"I've depended on you more than I should have, that's all."

"Your safety is my job."

"You've made that more than clear."

John sighed, exasperated. "Are you pissed off at me now?"

"More so at myself." Alex walked over to the door where John's damp jacket hung, picked it up, and held it out to him. "As usual, Inspector, you've done an excellent job of looking out for us, but like I said, it's late."

"Alex . . ."

"For the record the name is Adriane. Remember?"

John lingered for a few seconds longer before leaving the house, and waited in his car until Alex shut the door.

After locking it, she went around rechecking the windows and doors before returning to the bottle of vodka she'd left on the kitchen table. Curling up at the end of the sofa, she poured another drink, and turned on the television. Her eyelids were heavy with exhaustion.

She scanned the channels, fighting the sleep she desperately needed, berating herself for feelings she had no right to have. She waited for the demons that would inevitably invade her dreams.

ORDER FORM
URBAN BOOKS, LLC
78 E. Industry Ct
Deer Park, NY 11729

Name: (please print): _____

Address: _____

City/State: _____

Zip: _____

QTY	TITLES	PRICE

Shipping and handling-add $3.50 for 1st book, then $1.75 for each additional book.

Please send a check payable to:

Urban Books, LLC

Please allow 4-6 weeks for delivery

ORDER FORM
URBAN BOOKS, LLC
78 E. Industry Ct
Deer Park, NY 11729

Name: (please print):_____

Address: _____

City/State: _____

Zip: _____

QTY	TITLES	PRICE
	16 On The Block	$14.95
	A Girl From Flint	$14.95
	A Pimp's Life	$14.95
	Baltimore Chronicles	$14.95
	Baltimore Chronicles 2	$14.95
	Betrayal	$14.95
	Black Diamond	$14.95
	Black Diamond 2	$14.95
	Black Friday	$14.95
	Both Sides Of The Fence	$14.95
	Both Sides Of The Fence 2	$14.95
	California Connection	$14.95

Shipping and handling-add $3.50 for 1st book, then $1.75 for each additional book.
Please send a check payable to:
Urban Books, LLC
Please allow 4-6 weeks for delivery

ORDER FORM
URBAN BOOKS, LLC
78 E. Industry Ct
Deer Park, NY 11729

Name: (please print): _____

Address: _____

City/State: _____

Zip: _____

QTY	TITLES	PRICE
	California Connection 2	$14.95
	Cheesecake And Teardrops	$14.95
	Congratulations	$14.95
	Crazy In Love	$14.95
	Cyber Case	$14.95
	Denim Diaries	$14.95
	Diary Of A Mad First Lady	$14.95
	Diary Of A Stalker	$14.95
	Diary Of A Street Diva	$14.95
	Diary Of A Young Girl	$14.95
	Dirty Money	$14.95
	Dirty To The Grave	$14.95

Shipping and handling-add $3.50 for 1st book, then $1.75 for each additional book.

Please send a check payable to:

Urban Books, LLC

Please allow 4-6 weeks for delivery

ORDER FORM
URBAN BOOKS, LLC
78 E. Industry Ct
Deer Park, NY 11729

Name:(please print):_____

Address: _____

City/State: _____

Zip: _____

QTY	TITLES	PRICE
	Gunz And Roses	$14.95
	Happily Ever Now	$14.95
	Hell Has No Fury	$14.95
	Hush	$14.95
	If It Isn't love	$14.95
	Kiss Kiss Bang Bang	$14.95
	Last Breath	$14.95
	Little Black Girl Lost	$14.95
	Little Black Girl Lost 2	$14.95
	Little Black Girl Lost 3	$14.95
	Little Black Girl Lost 4	$14.95
	Little Black Girl Lost 5	$14.95

Shipping and handling-add $3.50 for 1st book, then $1.75 for each additional book.
Please send a check payable to:
Urban Books, LLC
Please allow 4-6 weeks for delivery

ORDER FORM
URBAN BOOKS, LLC
78 E. Industry Ct
Deer Park, NY 11729

Name: (please print): _____

Address: _____

City/State: _____

Zip: _____

QTY	TITLES	PRICE
	Loving Dasia	$14.95
	Material Girl	$14.95
	Moth To A Flame	$14.95
	Mr. High Maintenance	$14.95
	My Little Secret	$14.95
	Naughty	$14.95
	Naughty 2	$14.95
	Naughty 3	$14.95
	Queen Bee	$14.95
	Say It Ain't So	$14.95
	Snapped	$14.95
	Snow White	$14.95

Shipping and handling-add $3.50 for 1st book, then $1.75 for each additional book.

Please send a check payable to:

Urban Books, LLC

Please allow 4-6 weeks for delivery

ORDER FORM
URBAN BOOKS, LLC
78 E. Industry Ct
Deer Park, NY 11729

Name: (please print):_____

Address: _____

City/State: _____

Zip: _____

QTY	TITLES	PRICE
	Spoil Rotten	$14.95
	Supreme Clientele	$14.95
	The Cartel	$14.95
	The Cartel 2	$14.95
	The Cartel 3	$14.95
	The Dopefiend	$14.95
	The Dopeman Wife	$14.95
	The Prada Plan	$14.95
	The Prada Plan 2	$14.95
	Where There Is Smoke	$14.95
	Where There Is Smoke 2	$14.95

Shipping and handling-add $3.50 for 1st book, then $1.75 for each additional book.
Please send a check payable to:
    Urban Books, LLC
Please allow 4-6 weeks for delivery